Guest From Hell

Second Edition

Guest From Hell

Hell

Second Edition

Mike Faricy

Library of Congress Control Number: 2023915098
paperback ISBN: 978-1-962080-29-3
e-Book ISBN: 978-1-962080-30-9

MJF Publishing books may be purchased for education, Business, or promotional use. For information on bulk purchases, please contact the author directly at mikefaricyauthor@gmail.com

Published by

MJF Publishing
https://www.mikefaricybooks.com

Acknowledgments

I would like to thank the following people for their help and support:
Special thanks to my editors, Kitty, Donna and Rhonda for their hard work, cheerful patience and positive feedback.

I would like to thank Ann and Julie for their creative talent and not slitting their wrists or jumping off the high bridge when dealing with my Neanderthal computer capabilities.

Special thanks to Ann for her patience.

Last, I would like to thank family and friends for their encouragement and unqualified support. Special thanks to Maggie, Jed, Schatz, Pat, Av, Emily and Pat for not rolling their eyes, at least when I was there, and most of all, to my wife Teresa whose belief, support and inspiration has from day one, never waned.

Prologue

It wasn't quite dusk on the humid night they suddenly appeared at the side of the cabin and headed for the dock. Cabin was a colloquial term. Yes, it was on a lake, all three stories, but it had central air, internet, a designer kitchen, a theatre room, six bedrooms all en suite, and almost a million dollars' worth of oil paintings hanging on the walls. Sheldon Smeet was out on his dock sipping bourbon and admiring the cigar boat he'd purchased last spring. It was a gorgeous thing that, unfortunately, had been tied to the dock since the day it arrived three months ago.

Thankfully his visitor had left. As wonderful as the sex was after her vodkas and his promise to correct the eviction papers, he was glad to see her head down the road in her red Audi. He sipped the expensive bourbon and admired the cut crystal glass, almost two hundred years old with an Irish harp cut in the center. He was enjoying the peace and quiet, unaware anyone else was around until he heard the heavy footsteps on the metal dock. There were four of them. Of course, by then it was too late, nowhere to run, and he couldn't swim. He caught his breath and took a sip from the crystal glass to steady himself.

"Sheldon. Thought we might find you down here. Wondered if you'd come to a decision on our offer. I think we've been more than patient. It's been two weeks, and we told you we needed an answer right away."

"With everything that's been going on, I've turned that over to my major investor. His team is examining the offer and—"

"Sheldon, Sheldon, Sheldon. We've had this conversation before. The way you've set things up, you have the final say. I think it would be nice if you gave the go-ahead, now."

"It's being examined, and we're in the process of weighing options. It shouldn't be too long," he said and drained his glass.

"I see, I see. Okay, fair enough. Now, is this yours?" He nodded toward the cigar boat. "It looks fast."

"Yes, I um, actually haven't had the opportunity to use it. But it's supposed to be very fast."

"Haven't used it? Why not?"

"Actually, I don't know how. I'll need someone to chauffeur me around. I know, it sounds crazy, but that's the case."

"Don't know how to drive it. That can't be much fun. Tell you what, Liam here, he grew up on a large island. I'll bet he knows how to drive this thing. Liam, you think you could start this baby up?"

"No problem, boss."

"Oh, listen, thanks fellows, but really, you don't need to—"

"Nonsense, Liam, fire this puppy up."

"No really," Sheldon said as Liam hopped over the side and settled into the captain's chair. A moment later, the engine started, and the water began churning at the rear of the boat.

"See? There you go, Sheldon. All set. You sure you don't want to sign that paperwork right now? I brought a copy. We can get your signature right here." He snapped his fingers at one of the men behind him, and he was handed a pen. "What do you say, Sheldon. You ready to sign?"

"Hey, come on now. I told you my partners are going over the paperwork. I'll have an answer for you in the next day or two, and then we—"

"I don't think you're listening, Sheldon. I don't want to wait a day or two. You get the woman out of the place. We do the deal, and everything works out for the best."

"I told you I can't. I have to wait for my partners to review—"

"Yeah, I guess you did tell me that. Let me ask you something, Sheldon. You left or right-handed?"

"What? Um, left-handed. What does that have to do with anything?"

"One more chance, Sheldon. Will you sign the documents? I'm even adding a please. Please sign the documents."

"All right, I've heard just about enough. I want you out of here and off my property immediately. Do you hear me? Immediately or I'm calling the police."

The man shook his head and said, "Bad move, Sheldon. Tell you what. Let me hold that glass, it looks expensive."

"Looks expensive? Now, I want all of you out of here immediately."

The large man nodded, half-turned, and suddenly stomped on Sheldon's foot. As Sheldon screamed and bent forward, the man grabbed the crystal glass. "Damn it, Sheldon. I warned you, but you wouldn't listen. Okay fellas, get on with it."

The two men suddenly grabbed Sheldon and forced him to his knees. The larger of the two pushed him down, placing his knee in the small of Sheldon's back while the other man took hold of Sheldon's right arm and pulled it toward the prop on the large outboard engine.

"No, no, no," Sheldon shouted and then screamed.

One

Heidi had been treating me like a king ever since she picked me up. "No, Dev. You're always doing such nice things for me. You are not buying dinner. I'm paying. Was there anything else you wanted? Another drink? More dessert?"

I was enjoying myself. Heidi had been treating me like a king ever since she picked me up. She'd made reservations at the Saint Paul Grill, a top-notch place that I loved. She didn't say a thing when she picked me up. Usually, I heard something like, 'That's what you're wearing?' But not tonight. I ordered a rare steak and no vegetable, she just smiled, leaned over, and gave me a kiss. She smiled when I ordered dessert, apple crisp with cinnamon ice cream. On any other night, she'd skip dessert then eat two-thirds of mine. Tonight, she only took one little spoonful when it was set in front of me. To be honest, she was acting so nice I wondered what was up.

When we stepped out of the restaurant, she said, "You feel like going anywhere? Or, if you want, we could just head back to your place. I'm dying to give you a back rub."

"Heidi, what's going on? You've been so nice to-night. I don't think I've ever seen you like this before."

She laughed. "Oh Dev, sometimes . . . What, I can't try to please the one man I adore? I know, why don't we head over to The Spot. We can grab a drink, get you in the frame of mind for some late-night romance. You can think about all the different things you might like to do later on."

"That part certainly sounds fun. But, The Spot? Didn't you tell me to never, ever mention the place in your presence? You make me take a shower after I've been there, so you don't contract any germs."

"Mmm-mmm, you're such a sweetie," she said, pinching my cheek almost too hard. I was just about ready to scream when she let go and gave me a kiss. "I don't know. I may not be able to wait. Maybe we should just climb into the back seat of my car. Want to?" she said and flashed her eyes.

"But just a minute ago you wanted to go to The Spot?"

"Are you kidding? The opportunity to go to The Spot with my stud-muffin? Let's do it. I can show you off and lay claim to you in front of all those wenches who are always hitting on you."

"You're talking about The Spot, right? The bar just across from my office?"

"Yeah, where else? Let's go there, but we're only staying for one. I want to get back to your place and have you all to myself. I've got plans for you tonight, mister. I hope you've rested up."

"Yeah. Let's go for one."

Heidi climbed in behind the wheel, leaned over, and gave me a big kiss then headed toward The Spot. She softly rubbed my inner thigh the entire way there. I got another big kiss once she pulled alongside the place.

"Mmm-mmm, let's not take too long, Dev. You've got me all worked up. God, I'm ready to eat you alive. Grrr-Grrr," she said then laughed and climbed out of the car. We headed in the side door. The place was maybe half-full, but then it was barely nine. Heads turned when we walked in. Heidi had been in before, but she hadn't darkened the doorway in at least three or four years. The last time she was here, a guy was standing naked at the corner of the bar, drinking a beer. I mentioned it to Jimmy the bartender that night. 'Well, yeah, it's his birthday' he'd said, suggesting it was okay because the guy was in his birthday suit. Heidi had waited for me out in the car and vowed she'd never, ever set foot in there again.

So now, here she was, prancing through The Spot, walking as if she was on a fashion runway. She placed one foot directly in front of the other, shaking her attributes. As she strutted past, every male in the place focused on her. Her short, very tight skirt displayed the hint of an extremely small thong on her rear. I knew one of the guys, and just as I said, "Hi Timmy," his wife hit him on the shoulder to get his attention back.

Heidi pranced up to the bar as two ne'er-do-wells smiled and made room for her between them.

Mike was bartending tonight. "If you don't mind me saying, you look like the sort of woman who could do a lot better than Dev Haskell."

Heidi gave a little laugh and said, "You kidding? He's way more than I can handle."

Shocked looks fell across every face within hearing distance.

"What'll it be, ma'am?"

"I think just a glass of wine for me."

"Red or white?"

She didn't blink. "The red would be perfect."

"The usual, Dev?"

"Yeah, thanks, Mike."

I started to take my wallet out as Mike placed a glass beneath the Summit IPA tap. Heidi placed her hand on my arm. "No, darling. I'm getting this."

"But you bought dinner."

"And now I'm buying you an after-dinner drink. You sure you wouldn't like a bourbon or an Irish whiskey?"

"No, thanks, the beer is just fine."

Mike placed an empty wine glass and an airline bottle of red wine on the bar. "Eight dollars, even," he said.

Heidi slid a ten across the bar, smiled, and said, "Keep the change."

"I don't know, Dev. Such a nice woman and she ends up with you. Thank you, ma'am. Just a warning,

you've got a lot of work to do," he said and nodded at
me.

TWO

Morton met us at the front door. He was a big fan of Heidi's. He'd already chewed up at least a dozen of her thongs. As she stepped into the front entry, she gave him a healthy rub behind his ears and said, "Oh Morton. How are you? Have you been a good boy? Have you? Oh, good boy, Morton. Good boy."

Morton's tail was wagging back and forth, slamming against the open door and then the wall.

"Give me just a minute while I let him out back," I said. "Come on, Morton. Come on."

He'd just shoved his nose between Heidi's thighs and didn't appear to be interested in going anywhere at the moment.

"Morton. Come on, outside. Morton. Outside. Come on. Let's go."

"Apparently, he's not listening to you, Dev."

"Who can blame him?"

"Come on, Morton. Outside. Treat, Morton. Come on. You want a treat? Come on, Morton."

His tail continued to slap against the wall.

Heidi gave him another rub behind the ears and then said, "Come on, Morton. Let's go outside. You've been stuck in the house for a couple of hours. Come on, Morton. Let's go." Heidi pushed his nose away from her thighs and headed for the back door. Morton followed in hot pursuit, ignoring me completely. Heidi opened the back door and stepped out onto the porch. There was a worn green tennis ball in the middle of the porch, and she kicked it into the backyard. Morton bounded off the porch after the ball. They were back inside after a couple of minutes.

"Can I pour you a whiskey or something before we go upstairs?" she asked, raising her eyebrows.

"Yeah, a little whiskey might be good. I'm pouring, so don't even suggest. You've done way more than your fair share tonight. I've been nothing but a complete load the entire evening. Now it's my turn to wait on you."

"Dev darling, I just want to show you how special you are."

"Heidi, by and large, you've always been good to me. And I hope you view me in the same light. But tonight was over the top. I got the feeling you would have brushed my teeth for me if I asked you."

"Dev, can't I be nice to you and you just accept it? You don't have to question it. I love being kind, and grateful, and loving, and compassionate, and—"

"Not to worry, Heidi. You're all those things and more. Really you are, but tonight, I mean, wow."

"Maybe you should get used to it. I tell you what. Since you want to do something for me, why don't you pour me a glass of wine and I'm just going to slip into something a little more comfortable. Okay?"

"Okay. I'll be up in a couple of minutes."

She headed for the stairs with Morton following close behind.

"Morton, treat," I called and rattled the lid to the cookie jar where I kept the dog biscuits. He stopped and looked then glanced at Heidi climbing up the staircase. He seemed to ponder the alternatives for a long moment then hurried back into the kitchen, tail wagging, for the sure thing.

Three

I took my time filling Heidi's wine glass and my glass of whiskey. When I brought them up to the bedroom, Heidi was in bed leaning up against the headboard. The overhead light was off and just the lamp on the end table next to her was on. She was wearing a very small, black lace affair that didn't even begin to cover. I'd seen church veils that were larger. It was gorgeous.

I stood in the doorway, staring.

"Oh, you like?"

"It's gorgeous. I don't think I've ever seen it before."

"I know you haven't. I thought you might like it. I got it especially for tonight."

"Oh man, that is one sexy little number." I hurried around to the far side of the bed and set her wine glass on the table next to the lamp. I ran back around the bed, set my whiskey glass down, and quickly kicked off my shoes. I pulled my trousers off and tossed them on the floor.

"Oh Dev, you are getting me so hot. Get in here. Hurry up, I really need you."

I started to unbutton my shirt. The second button seemed to be stuck somehow, and I pulled on the shirt, four buttons flew off and bounced against the wall. Not that I cared. I let the shirt drop onto the floor and climbed into the bed.

"Oh, much better," Heidi said and tossed her little lace affair onto my head.

"Heidi, this has been the most wonderful night we've had in a long time, maybe even ever."

She pushed me down onto the pillow then hopped on top of me. "And it's not over yet. You just never realized how absolutely infatuated I am with you, Dev. It's all I can do to keep my hands off of you."

"Well, don't worry about that now. Please, help yourself."

"Oh, I intend to," she said, She ducked beneath the sheet and began to slide down my chest. She had just finished kissing my navel, and I was thinking, *'Oh this is going to be so good.'* When suddenly, she popped her head up and said, "Hey, I don't know if I should even ask you this, but, well, I have a friend who could maybe use some help. I was just wondering if you'd consider talking to her and seeing what you might be able to do for her."

"A, a friend?" It suddenly wasn't making sense at the moment. "Maybe we could discuss this a little later. You were just about to—"

"Oh, yeah, sure. But see, well, she's out of time." She suddenly climbed off me and leaned back against the headboard. She took a deep breath and exhaled as if she'd just run some gauntlet and made it safely to the other side. She grabbed her glass of wine, took a sip, and then held it in front of her as if it were some force shield that would keep me at bay.

"So here's the deal. I've known Roxanne LaRue, I call her Roxy, I've known her since kindergarten. It's where we met."

"Maybe we could get back to the matters at hand, Heidi, and discuss this over breakfast."

"Relax, this'll just take a minute. So, like I was saying, we met in kindergarten and became fast friends on the first day. We always picked one another for our teams. We jumped rope, played Barbies, went to the same high school. Both of us went to the U, but she dropped out after a couple of years and started her career as a professional dancer."

"Professional dancer?"

"Yeah, that's right. Anyway, things didn't work out. To make a long story short, she bought a house on the night before the 2008 recession hit. Of course, the property value dropped by fifty percent. The bank called the loan. She borrowed from another firm and has kind of been dodging ever since."

"Dodging," I said and took a sip of my whiskey.

"Yeah, like I said, it hasn't worked out the best for her. Anyway, now she's going to be evicted. Some rough guys served her notice, threatened her, and she's supposed to be out of her place by next week."

"Next week? How long has this been going on? Usually, she'd have to be in arrears for some time, maybe six months or so."

"Well, that might have been the case. I'm not exactly sure. But these really rough guys, two of them, served her with the notice and told her she only had a week to get all her stuff out of there."

"A week? And she was just served?"

"Yeah," she said and took a sip of wine. "If you could maybe talk to her because the way she was served doesn't seem to make any sense to me."

"Yeah, I suppose I could. But you're the financial wizard. Have you checked this out?"

"You mean her being in arrears? Yeah, that part is legit, although the interest rate she was paying is ten point five. That's more than double the national average. Right now, it's about four point two."

"Double the national average? What bank did she go through?"

"Third National."

"Third National? Aren't they the ones having all sorts of problems? They're under some sort of investigation right now, aren't they?"

"As a matter of fact, they're under a number of investigations, and Roxy's been involved in some of that."

"Involved?"

"Yeah, she um, maybe had a bit of a personal relationship that facilitated getting the mortgage, and well, the feds are in the process of checking that out. Now the bank wants to get her off the books as fast as possible."

"She isn't one of the women supposedly associated with the bank president, what's his name, is she?"

"His name is Sheldon Smeet, a real jerk. And to answer your questions, yes. She more or less earned the mortgage, if that translates."

"Meaning she probably wasn't qualified to begin with."

"Certainly not for the amount she was given. I mean, if the house had been available for say two hundred thousand, yeah she maybe would have been qualified, if she could have held onto her job."

"So, what happened? She got fired or quit and couldn't make the payments?"

"That's part of it. The other part is that she was in way over her head. The property was appraised at nine-seventy-five and—"

"Nine-seventy-five as in nine hundred and seventy-five thousand dollars?"

"Yeah, and she actually ended up paying a million two."

"What?"

"Yeah, she's got a bit of a problem."

"But they financed her?"

"Well, between her relationship with Sheldon Smeet and his basically bypassing all the standard loan provisions and signing off on her loan, yeah, they financed her. Financed her at ten point five percent."

"Heidi, what am I supposed to do?"

"Well, you know certain people. Certain types of people, and I was just thinking if you could maybe get these scary guys to back off. You know."

"Actually, no, I don't know."

"Could you at least talk to her and maybe hear her side of the story?"

"Her side? Does she even know it?"

"Well, yeah, there is that. But maybe if you talked with her, you know."

"Okay, yeah sure, Heidi. I'll talk to her. Thanks for thinking of me. Since she's a friend of yours, I'll see what I can do. Now, where were we before you brought up your friend Roxy?"

"Oh, thank you, Dev. Thanks so much. If you just talk to her, I know it may be mission impossible, but if you could at least take a look. It's just that I've known her since we were little girls, and everything that's gone wrong has been due to her own bad decisions. I know all that. But she's still my oldest friend."

"Okay, for you, I'll do it."

"Oh, thanks," she said and drained her glass of wine. "I've been agonizing over this ever since I learned the news. God, I feel like a giant weight has been lifted off my shoulders. Honest to God, I mean, I feel exhausted. You mind if we just go to sleep?"

Four

Louie shook his head. "So what? You're going to go over the paperwork on the loan?" Louie said. Louie Laufen, attorney. Also known as **the** attorney to represent you in the Ramsey County court system when you've been charged with a DUI, Driving While Intoxicated. He's also my officemate. When he asked if I was going to go over the paperwork, he said it in a tone that suggested, *'What idiot thought this up.?* Since numbers and paperwork are not exactly my strong suit.

"No, that's not what I plan to do. Apparently, there are a couple of rough guys who want her out of the house within the week. That sounds a little rushed to me, and then theoretically, she would still be liable for whatever the loan is. By the way, the loan is at ten point two percent."

"Ten point two? That's nuts."

"You think? Just the little I've learned checking out this Sheldon Smeet guy on Google, he's a real piece of work."

"I'm always reminded of the words a wise man told me years ago," Louie said. "You got the Feds on your ass. They already got you. At that point, it's just a matter of time before they decide to snap the trap."

"I don't know. Maybe she can plead stupid or offer assistance to the Feds or something. Sounds like she doesn't have the money and maybe never will. But if she could hang onto and sell the place, maybe she could knock down that payment due amount."

"It all seems like a pretty tall order."

"Well, first things first. Maybe I try to get the thugs off her back. Then take it from there."

"Do you have a plan for the thugs?" Louie said.

"As a matter of fact, I do."

Five

The following morning, I was in the process of putting the first part of my plan to work. I was meeting Roxanne LaRue for lunch over at The Burger Bitches. It was a little burger joint with a couple of booths against the far wall that would be nice and private. The place sits on a corner just across the street from the old railroad station downtown. It's about fifteen feet wide with a 50s vintage luncheon counter and is run by a woman I know named Siobhan. She was a former professional dancer, think stripper, who did five years in Minnesota's only state prison for women, located in the town of Shakopee. The railroad station had been turned into condos a few years back and gave Siobhan an almost built-in clientele. Not that she needed it. She does up a mean burger, has won all sorts of awards, and there's a line out the door every day for two hours over the noon hour. The staff is all female. It's one of those places where guys in suits and motorcycle colors mingle, and there are never any problems. I got there early just to be sure I could score one of the booths on the far wall.

"I don't believe it, Dev Haskell? Long time no see, baby."

"Hey Siobhan, yeah, long time no see. How's it go-ing?"

"Working my ass off."

Quite an accomplishment. She'd put on about sixty pounds since the last time I saw her. Apparently, she still had a lot more to work off.

"You getting something to go, or do you intend to grace us with your presence today?" she said.

"Actually, meeting someone down here. Friend of a friend. Would it be okay if I grabbed one of the booths? We might be there awhile."

"You're good but better grab it now, they fill up quick. What can I get you?"

"Maybe just a glass of water while I wait."

"Bad idea, Dev. Everyone'll be giving you the evil eye wondering when you're gonna get your ass out of there. Connie," she yelled, "do up a strawberry malt and bring it to this degenerate looking guy in the St. Paul Saints jersey. He'll be wasting his time and taking up space in the back booth."

"Thanks, Siobhan."

"You don't know what I'm gonna charge you, sweetheart."

"Just be nice."

Forty-five minutes later, I was just about finished with the strawberry malt and was checking my cellphone for the umpteenth time when a sexy voice said, "You must be Dev Haskell. Heidi's told me all about you."

I looked up as Roxy leaned down and gave me a kiss on the forehead. She was wearing a too-small t-shirt that was stretched to the limit and cutoff jeans that were so short the pockets hung down an inch or two below the jeans.

"No, my name's Bill but sit down anyway."

She didn't look at all flustered. Instead, she said, "Oh, sorry, I'd love to join you, but I have to meet a guy. Maybe we could get together some other time?"

"Just kidding, you must be Roxy."

"Oh. Yeah, Heidi was right. You're a piece of work," she said, sliding in across from me. "Nice to meet you, Dev."

"Likewise. Heidi said you two go back quite a ways."

"Yeah, little kids on the first day of school and we quickly became best of friends. She was always the studious one. I'm still the party animal. What's that you're drinking?"

"Strawberry malt. I highly recommend it."

The noon rush was in full swing, and the crowd was two deep all along the lunch counter. Everyone was waving cash as they waited for their orders to be filled. The place smelled of cheeseburgers, fries, and onion rings.

"They have a bar?" she said, looking around.

"A bar? No, they don't. The place is run by a friend of mine. She did some time, got out, and started this place. With her record, she was never going to get a liquor license. Plus, she hires other women just out on parole trying to work their way back into society, so strawberry malts are about as good as it's gonna get."

"I guess I could try one."

I saw Siobhan staring at us through the crowd, studying Roxy. I pointed at my nearly empty malt and pointed at Roxy. Siobhan nodded and gave me the thumbs-up.

"So Heidi didn't tell me much, other than you've been dealing with some mortgage problems and I guess you got served with an eviction notice."

She shrugged and said, "Yeah, a couple of jerks. They're going to be back tomorrow at eleven. Said I have to be out or they're gonna throw me out."

"Do you have the funds to bring your loan current?"

"Hello. If I had the money, we wouldn't be sitting here. Hell, if I had the money, I wouldn't have done that worthless dip shit, Sheldon Smeet. Talk about a lousy screw, and now he's come back and is really screwing me."

I was quickly arriving at the conclusion that, other than buying lunch for Roxy, there was nothing I could do to help her. "I understand you've been interviewed by the Feds. Did they ask you about the loan procedure?"

"The loan procedure?" she scoffed. "You kidding? Sheldon and I had a three-day meeting in a hotel room in Las Vegas where I drank martinis, wore a smile, and pretended Sheldon was the best thing since sliced bread. After that, I signed a couple pieces of paper, and he handed me the keys on the plane ride home."

"And you got a loan for a million two?"

"Yeah, I guess. At least on paper. But he never said anything about a loan. It's not like I ever saw any money. I mean he had this cool place, and I got to move in. He would stop by a couple of times a week, always called to make sure no one else was there before he showed up. I mean, it was all working great as far as I was concerned. Then all of a sudden these two big, hairy guys show up, tell me I have to be out of there in less than a week and oh, by the way, I owe Sheldon's bank over a million bucks. A million bucks? I could be dancing from now till doomsday, and I'd never see a million bucks."

Siobhan suddenly appeared with a strawberry malt and set it down in front of Roxy. "Here you go. Say, don't I know you from somewhere?" she said, studying Roxy.

Roxy looked up and said, "Cherry?"

"That was a few years back, honey. And you were, no wait, don't tell me. You're, yeah, you're Kitten. Right?"

Roxy laughed and said, "Yeah, that was the name I used then. Now I just go by my real name, Roxy."

"You still dancing?"

"Not exactly. I'm more into the ah, private client thingy. You know, hanging on some rich guy's arm, making him look successful."

"That working out for you?"

"Sometimes," Roxy said. She took a long pull on the straw standing in the strawberry malt, suggesting the conversation was over.

"Well, you ever need a part-time gig, let me know. We open at eleven and close at three."

"Thanks, but I'm doing just fine."

"Yeah, I'm sure you are. I'll leave you to it. Nice seeing you, Kitten," Siobhan said. She gave me a nod and stepped away. The crowd automatically made a wide path for her as she headed back behind the lunch counter.

We talked for another twenty minutes, not that I really learned anything. Roxy took a final sip of her malt. It was barely half-empty. "You interested in seeing the place?"

"I guess I could take a look. You got the time?"

"Nothing scheduled. I'm parked around the corner. I'm in a red Audi. Why don't you follow me?"

I left a ten-dollar bill on the table and headed out the door. I gave Siobhan a wave as I left, and she pointed her index finger and thumb at me in the shape of a gun and fired then shook her head back and forth as if suggesting I'd never learn.

Six

Roxy's house was in a trendy suburb called North Oaks. It was more like a small forest with winding roads and houses that were hidden from one another by trees, so you'd never have to deal with your neighbors. The right rear of her Audi was dented, and the taillights were broken. The bumper hung at about a thirty-degree angle and had a length of yellow rope wrapped around it that went into the trunk. I followed Roxy along a winding road and through two stop signs where she barely slowed. She finally pulled into a gravel area in front of a contemporary redwood structure. She parked over a large oil slick that I presumed was caused by some leak in her engine. I pulled in alongside her.

"Did you have an oil leak in your car?" I asked as we climbed out of our respective vehicles.

"What?"

"I saw the oil stain on the gravel, right where you parked. Wondered if you had a leak or maybe had to replace a seal or something in the engine."

"Oh, I don't know. That red light is on so often I just ignore it now."

"You might want to get it checked. Something like that can get really expensive if you let it go for too long."

"Yeah, whatever. So anyway, this is it. Like I said, we partied in Vegas for three nights, and Sheldon gave me the keys. Said as long as I took care of him, well, take a look for yourself."

I'm not that big a fan of contemporary structures, and this place wasn't going to change my opinion. As a matter of fact, it appeared rather small, maybe just twenty feet wide.

"Come on inside and take a look," Roxy said as she slipped a key into the lock. The door, and in fact the entire front of the structure, was stained redwood. I guessed it was maybe fifteen years old. All the redwood appeared overdue for another coat of stain by at least five years. The door was a large beveled glass panel surrounded by a four-inch redwood frame. When she opened the door, she bent down and picked up three or four envelopes from the floor, mail. At least two of the envelopes were bordered in red, suggesting late payment notices. She stepped inside and tossed the mail onto a foot-high stack of unopened envelopes. Red appeared to be the color of choice on the envelopes.

The entry looked out over a large room with two fireplaces ten feet below us. We had to descend on one of two curving staircases that brought us down to the main floor. The house extended behind either fireplace so essentially, just the front entry was visible from the road.

A little white dog suddenly appeared, barked twice, and ran to Roxy. She picked up the dog, kissed it a couple of times and said, "This is Madame."

"Nice to meet you," I said and reached out to pet Madame. She barked twice and did not look happy.

"Oh, no, no. He's just a friend. Now you be nice. So this is the living room," Roxy said, ignoring Madame. Empty glasses, wine and champagne bottles, and over-flowing ashtrays were scattered around the room.

There was a large painting of the same man above either fireplace. He was grey-haired, bald with a reddish nose and blue eyes. In one painting, he was seated behind a desk, and in the other, he was standing next to a chair, holding a roll of documents in his right hand. They looked like the kind of paintings you might see in a courthouse or a state capitol.

"Who's that guy in the paintings?"

Roxy half-groaned and said, "That's Sheldon Smeet. As if it isn't bad enough he's screwing me. Just to make things worse, I have to look at him first thing every morning. It makes me put something on before I leave the bedroom. He's not getting a free peek. You want something to drink?" she asked, holding a wine bottle up toward the double doors leading out to a wooden deck. I presumed checking to see if there was any wine left in the bottle.

"No thanks, I'm good, but help yourself."

"Don't mind if I do," she said then poured what was left from the bottle into a glass sitting on the coffee table.

The glass already had lipstick along one side. Hopefully, it was her lipstick.

She gave me a twenty-minute tour of the rest of the place. It certainly could have used a good cleaning, but it would have taken a crew of four or five a full day. Bottles, cigarettes, clothes, dirty dishes, a pile of sheets and towels in one of the hallways, she'd turned the place into a disaster. There were three bedrooms. You'd probably want to burn the bed linens rather than waste the time attempting to clean them. At the end of the tour, one thing was apparent, Roxy was an absolute slob.

Seven

I stopped at home to pick up Morton. He met me at the front door then ran to the backdoor and barked, anxious to get outside. No sooner had I let him out the backdoor than the doorbell rang at the front. A proper looking lady was standing on my front porch. She was wearing a sundress, had a large black purse hanging from her arm, and she gave me a broad smile as I opened the door. I pegged her age at maybe mid-forties, and I was not in the mood to sign up for a political action committee or donate twenty-five dollars to someone's campaign.

"Yeah," I said, not sounding all that friendly.

"Good afternoon. Mr. Haskell?" she said as a slight hint of very nice perfume drifted in through the front door.

"Yes," I said, amazed she knew my name, but then again both political parties rented out the voter registration records, so she probably had a list of everyone on the block.

"Mr. Haskell, my name is Amanda Williams. I live on the next street over. I've seen you walking your dog," she said.

"Morton, yeah, he's a handful."

"Exactly why I'm here this morning."

"Hunh? What's he done?" If he got out again and dug up someone's flowers . . .

"Your dog, Morton, lovely name by the way. Not to worry, he hasn't done anything, at least that I'm aware of. However, based on my casual observation, it would appear he could do with a little training. I hope you don't think I'm out of line. You see, I serve on the board of the St. Paul Kennel Association. We're dedicated to improving the lives of our canine friends and, much like children, one of the best ways is to teach them boundaries. That can be accomplished in a positive way that, first and foremost, increases your dog's personal pride while, at the same time, makes him just that much more enjoyable to be around."

"So what you're saying is you would like me to train my dog?"

She smiled. "Not exactly. What I'm suggesting is, with the close proximity of our locations, perhaps you would consider a daily tutoring session for Morton."

It was my turn to smile. "I've attended two, no wait, three dog training classes over the past couple of years. We've never finished one."

"Never finished? Well, see, therein lies part of the problem. Once we find the comfort zone for your four-legged friend, the task of education and training becomes that much simpler."

"That sounds wonderful, really it does. Here's the problem. In two cases, it was strongly suggested we try some other venue and, in the third instance, the vote was unanimous from all the other attendees that Morton and I should not return. It seems he was much more interested in mating with some of his fellow students, and that seemed to cause a bit of a problem for all the other attendees."

She smiled at my explanation. "I wonder if you wouldn't consider leaving him with me, oh say two or three mornings a week. If, after two weeks, you haven't noticed any improvement, by all means, stop. On the other hand, if you note an improvement, perhaps we could work out some form of remuneration."

"Are you saying you'll take him for three mornings a week and work on training him, and if I don't see any improvement, I don't have to pay you?"

She seemed to think about that for a moment and then nodded. "Yes, that about sums it up."

"When can we start?"

"Would tomorrow morning be too soon?"

"No, not at all. As a matter of fact, I think it might work perfectly. What's your address?"

She reached into her purse and handed me a business card.

"Four-fifty-six," I said, reading the house number from her card. So you're almost straight through, just a house or two up on the next block."

"Exactly."

"Okay, We'll be over around nine tomorrow morning. See you then and thank you for stopping, Addison."

"It's actually Amanda, and the pleasure was all mine. Nice to finally meet you in person, Mr. Haskell."

"Please, call me Dev."

"Until tomorrow," she said. She turned, walked off the porch, down to the sidewalk and waved. I watched as she strutted down the street and around the corner. She was not hard on the eyes.

Eight

Louie came awake just as Morton hopped in when I opened the office door. He bolted upright in his desk chair and rested his elbows on the picnic table that served as his desk. It took him a moment to get his bearings. As I sat down behind my desk, he said, "You guys sleep in today?"

"I wish I had. It would have been a better use of my time." It was almost three in the afternoon, and I was only now getting to the office after meeting with Roxy and then talking with Amanda.

"Client meeting?"

"Not really. I met with Roxy LaRue. The woman who's Heidi's friend."

"The woman with the million two mortgage and the eviction notice? How'd that go?"

"Not well. And upon careful analyzation, not a surprise. Her act is definitely not together. The woman's a space cadet."

"How so?"

"Oh man, where to begin? The place is a mess, dishes all over, piles of laundry, a dog that doesn't like me. She's got a stack of unopened past due envelopes.

You know, the ones with red on them that say open immediately. I mean the stack was a foot high, I'm not kidding, and she just tossed four more onto the pile like she didn't even care."

"Maybe she was going to open them once you left."

"I don't think so. Her place is up in North Oaks."

"That can be some pretty pricey real estate up there. You were actually in the place?"

"Yeah, she gave me the twenty-five-cent tour."

"And?"

"And it's nice, of a type, or could be, if you like a contemporary style, lots of redwood, and large paintings of Sheldon Smeet hanging over both your fireplaces."

"Hmm-mmm, I'd ditch the artwork. What do you think about the valuation of the place?"

"You know, given the location and the size, yeah, a million two could be accurate, maybe. But she told me how she got the property, and there is no way the deal was legit. Get this. Sleaze ball Smeet takes her to Vegas for three nights. They party out there for seventy-two hours. She provides her services and can barely remember her own name. Then, on the flight home, he hands her the keys to the place. He has her sign some documents, which she didn't bother to read. Why would you? Now, lo and behold, she's on the hook for a million two at ten-and-a-half percent."

"That's not going to stand up in court. Just for starters is anything notarized? This sounds like Smeet created a flagrant—"

"Smeet isn't the problem. There has to be someone behind this with some muscle. I know the guys who served her the eviction notice threatened her, threatened her big time. As a matter of fact, they're supposed to be back tomorrow morning. Look, bottom line, she's going to have to get out of there. I think a conversation with the federal authorities investigating Smeet would probably confirm she isn't liable based on the bogus paperwork. Basically, what I think it boils down to is Smeet put her up there to partake in her charms, and gorgeous thing that she is, she's not worth a million two. I'm thinking Smeet is on the hook to someone for that dough, and he passed it off to Roxy just to buy some time. Anyone with any brains will take one look at her and know she could never qualify for that loan or maybe any legitimate loan."

"So what are you going to do?"

"I honestly don't know. I guess the first thing to do is to get whoever is threatening her to stop. Then somehow move the property back onto Smeet's lap, and he can deal with the mess."

My cellphone rang. It was Heidi.

"I better take this, Heidi calling for an update."

"Haskell Investigations."

"Hi, Dev. It's Heidi. How'd it go with Roxy today?"

I took a deep breath, wondering exactly what to tell her.

"Dev? You there?"

"Yeah, Heidi. Sorry, just finishing something up here. How'd it go? Well, I have a little better understanding of the situation. Have you ever been out to her place?"

"No, all I know is it's up in North Oaks."

"Yeah. It's a contemporary place. Could be nice with some work. Here's the bottom line. She's been set up, basically. I know she's a friend, so no offense, but I'm not sure she even understands that."

"Did you tell her?"

"Yeah, about a half-dozen times."

"What did she say?"

"She's of the opinion that she owns the place. She doesn't. Sheldon Smeet had her sign some bogus paperwork, but there is no way in hell she can be held accountable. I would guess he may have borrowed some money from not the nicest bunch of guys, and he's trying to pawn the payback onto Roxy. She's basically in the place because she was servicing Smeet."

"What do mean service— Oh."

"Yeah, exactly. The place has two large paintings of Smeet hanging over the fireplaces. When I saw them, I was thinking giant dartboards. Is the place worth a million two? Maybe, given the location and if it was cleaned up. On the right day, yeah, it could be worth that much. But there is no way in hell there can be any legal paperwork tying her to that place. She's being used, so that's one thing. Now, the other issue is these guys threatening her. I think I might have a way to deal with that."

"What are you planning on doing?"

"Dealing with the problem, that's all you need to know. Look, Heidi, I know you two are long-time friends and all, but this Roxy is not exactly squared away."

"She's always been a little crazy, Dev. It's one of the many things I like about her."

"I get that, I guess. So this is what's going to happen. I'm going to head out there tomorrow morning. I'd like to meet with these guys who want to evict her and see if we can't arrive at some sort of agreement. In the meantime, do you have any connections with the Federal Investigators looking into the Third National Bank?"

"You're thinking of going after Sheldon Smeet?"

"Let's just say I want to make sure they're aware of this situation and what transpired. But first things first, those two eviction guys are due back tomorrow, and I'd like to discuss things with them."

Nine

The following morning, I walked Morton around the block to Amanda Williams' house. I'd been past the place a million times but never inside. It was a three-story red brick home with cream-colored trim, probably built around 1900. The front porch covered the first two floors. Morton strained on the leash the entire way, and I kept repeating the name Amanda, so I wouldn't screw it up again. By the time I rang her doorbell, it felt like my arm was going to be pulled out of the socket. She appeared at the door almost immediately and waved at me through the beveled glass panel before opening the door.

"Hi, sorry we're a little early," I said as she opened the door. She wore navy blue shorts, a white top, and sandals.

"Not a problem, please come in."

We stepped into the entry, and she closed the door behind us. Morton immediately thrust his nose between her legs. Fortunately, Amanda didn't even blink. She held her hand out for the leash and then walked Morton back and forth down a hallway that led to the back of the house. No fool he, and by the third time, he was no longer straining on the leash and appeared to be walking alongside her naturally.

"That didn't take long. What did you do that got him to comply so quickly? Usually, he's straining with me all the way around the block. By the time we get back to the house, I have to ice down my shoulder."

She laughed and shook her head in a way that suggested 'Idiot.' "It's really more a case of using proper posture and assuming the alpha position. It's not that hard once you know what's required."

"You'll have to teach me."

"I'd love to. Let me have him for a couple of hours. You fed him this morning?"

"Yeah. He's eaten and done his business."

"Good, then we can get started. I have a course set up in the back, and I'll introduce him to that in just a moment. If you can swing by any time after twelve noon, that should work out just fine. When you come to pick him up, I'll show you what we worked on and a couple of the things you can do to encourage him."

"I'll see you then, Amanda, and thank you."

"The pleasure is all mine. Enjoy your morning," she said and closed the front door behind me.

Ten

I was parked outside of a four-story red brick building down on Payne Avenue. The building sat between Slattery's Saloon on one corner and PayDay Loans on the opposite corner. It wasn't quite nine, and there were four people standing out in front of PayDay waiting for them to open. I was waiting for my friend Luscious Dixon.

Luscious played in the NFL at one time. He was not what you would call small, even lined up against other NFL guys, he stood out. Add about five years out of the league and another fifty to seventy-five pounds and you're talking some real size. He still worked out every day and remained in very intimidating shape. He'd done pretty well in the NFL, although he had a bit of a problem with his anger management issues. I thought he might be the perfect backup for the discussion I hoped to have with the two gentlemen this morning.

Luscious was ten minutes late when he finally appeared, coming around the corner of Slattery's. I hoped he hadn't been drinking. I took the McDonald's bag he carried as a positive sign. He almost walked past my Jeep

Cherokee. I lowered the passenger window and called to him.

"Luscious, you forget about me?"

"Oh, Mr. Dev, I was wondering where you was. This a new car you got?" He examined the car, probably trying to read the graffiti someone had sprayed along the passenger side a few weeks back. I'd decided ten bucks' worth of spray paint was a lot less expensive than the twenty-two-hundred dollar estimate I was given for a new paint job.

"You forget about our appointment?"

"No, just needed a little something to tide me over for this morning," he said and raised the McDonald's bag by way of explanation. "Mind if I just sit in the back?"

"Not at all. Hop in. It's good to see you, Luscious. It's been too long." I held my hand over the driver's seat as Luscious wiggled into the back. The car rocked from side to side as he worked his way into place. Once he was settled in, the car leaned decidedly to the right. He stuffed a muffin with bacon and a fried egg into his mouth, licked his fingertips, and grabbed my hand. I attempted to squeeze his hand, but it was like trying to squeeze a brick, no give whatsoever.

He said something indecipherable through a mouthful of biscuit, bacon, and fried egg, and we started on our way. I brought him up to speed with the little bit of information I had. Luscious, along with being large, was fairly smart, and he asked a number of questions in between cramming another bacon and egg biscuit into his mouth. I had counted a total of five biscuits by the time I turned off the road and parked next to Roxy's Audi.

We climbed out of the Jeep. Luscious stood there rolling his shoulders, moving his head from side to side, and cracking his neck back and forth a couple of times, all the while glancing at the trees surrounding the place.

"Oaks, maples and unfortunately ash. Too bad, those ash trees get infested with ash-bore, and they're gone in no time. Once they're infested, all you can do is remove them."

I was about to ask how a guy who lived on a street without trees knew all that but decided against it. "Come on. You need to meet Roxy. She's a piece of work. I'll let her tell you about her meeting a few days ago with these guys. They're supposed to be back here around eleven this morning."

I pressed the doorbell, and we could hear bells chiming inside.

"Westminster Chimes," Luscious said. "I always liked those. My grandmother had them in her home." Good thing he liked them, I had to press the doorbell two more times before Roxy finally answered.

"Oh, hi Dev. Sorry about that. I was just in the middle of my utthita parsvakonasana pose. I try to hold it for two minutes," she said and stared wide-eyed at Luscious towering behind me.

"What?" I had no idea what she was talking about.

"An extended side-angle pose, a standing asana," Luscious said.

"Yes, that's exactly what it is," Roxy said with a surprised look on her face.

"Roxy, this is my friend, Luscious Dixon. Luscious, meet Roxy. We're hoping we can talk to the gentlemen when they stop by later this morning. We'll see if they won't maybe back off for a bit while we try to figure out exactly what's going on."

"Yeah, well, please come in. Come in. Luscious? That's a wonderful name," Roxy said. She was wearing tight red stretch shorts. Very tight, almost but not quite a thong. They left nothing to the imagination. Her matching red stretch top appeared to be maybe two sizes too small and barely covered her chest. Her midriff was exposed and featured a flower tattoo surrounding her navel with a blue jewel of some sort piercing her navel. Luscious almost had to duck coming in the door. I glanced to the side, and the pile of unopened mail was still there.

"Come on downstairs," Roxy said and then stepped back so I could go first. She slid in between Luscious and me and let me get five or six steps ahead. "So, Luscious, you're into yoga?"

"Not so much. I work out daily, weights mostly. I use yoga before and after my workouts to stretch. Before I begin, I take five minutes to focus my concentration, and when I'm finished, I take ten minutes to relax."

"Oh, wow. You'll have to show me what you do."

"I'd be happy to."

There was the sound of waves breaking on a shore playing on a laptop computer on the coffee table. Roxy had moved a number of empty wine bottles to the far side of the coffee table to make room for the laptop. A blue yoga mat was spread out on the floor.

"Can I get you guys something? I picked up some pastries at the store, and I've got some decaf on."

"Decaf?" I said, not hiding my disappointment.

"That sounds very nice," Luscious said.

Eleven

In very short order, it became painfully obvious I was the third wheel while Roxy and Luscious went over yoga moves. They were stretching and angling on the same yoga mat. Luscious was at least three times larger than Roxy, and based on the sheer size of the man, he was taking up most of the mat. For her part, Roxy didn't seem to mind and, in fact, had moved to about a quarter of an inch away from Luscious, facing him as she stretched.

I did the only sensible thing I could think of. I grabbed two chocolate doughnuts from the bag in the kitchen and joined Madame sitting out on the deck. The deck ran along the entire length of the house and overlooked a small pond with what appeared to be a beaver hut at the far end. A pair of Mallard ducks and a half-dozen little ones were swimming across the pond. There were three different bird feeders mounted along the railing of the deck. All empty, by the way. Different kinds of birds were chirping and flying about, cardinals, finches, robins, blue jays, and a few I was unable to identify.

I sat down at a picnic table, ate the two doughnuts, watched the birds, checked my cell for messages, and pretended I was on vacation. At a quarter to eleven, I stepped back into the living room.

Roxy and Luscious were now seated on the yoga mat facing one another. Roxy's legs were draped over Luscious's massive thighs. She was close enough that her knees were almost resting against his hips. He was so much larger than she was that she had to lean back, and she had placed two pillows behind her for support. Their eyes were closed, their palms rested on each other's thighs, and they were in the process of taking very deep breaths and slowly exhaling.

I wasn't sure I should interrupt. So, instead, I said, "I'll just step outside in case they get here a little early. Come on up when you're finished, Luscious."

Neither one acknowledged me, and I headed up the steps. I let off a little groan as I climbed the steps and watched out of the corner of my eye. Neither one so much as moved. When I opened the door, I called down-stairs, "I'm stepping outside now," and closed the door behind me. I took up a position leaning against the back of my Jeep Cherokee. I stood there, enjoying the peace and quiet for another fifteen minutes. Not so much as a kid on a bicycle rode past. Just birds chirping, a couple of squirrels chasing one another around an oak tree. I heard a cricket chirping near the corner of the entrance.

A black Cadillac Escalade, the preferred thug vehicle, suddenly sped around the bend. I could feel the vibrations from the bass player thumping inside the Escalade as it approached, and once again, I reminded myself to invest in a hearing aid company. As the driver slammed on the brakes, the Escalade skidded across the gravel, raising a cloud of dust and stopping at an angle next to the Jeep. Once the dust settled, I noticed the bumper sticker, MILF Hunter, in red letters on a white background. The vibrations from the bass player suddenly stopped just as both front doors opened simultaneously. Two guys with full beards, dark eyes, and ponytails stepped out. A dinging noise sounded, indicating the keys were still in the ignition. The dinging stopped once they slammed the doors closed.

They looked like they could be brothers. Faded black t-shirts, black jeans, ponytails, and beards covering up acne scars. The driver wore black cowboy boots with a silver metal cover over the toe and around the back of the heel. The other guy had on a pair of work boots. I guessed probably steel-toed. They took their time strutting toward me, and I got the impression they'd practiced the routine. Luscious could show up any time now, and it would be all right with me. The guy in the work boots spit off to the side, and I took him to be a tobacco lover.

Twelve

The driver with the cowboy boots said, "So who the hell are you?" He had just a few flecks of grey in his beard around his chin. I guessed he might be the older of the two.

"I'm a friend of Roxy's. I'm thinking you two are the guys who served her the eviction notice a couple of days ago."

"You got that right. You here to hand over the keys?" They both laughed, but it wasn't a funny laugh. The guy in the work boots took a step to the side.

"Actually, no. I'm here to tell you we have some folks looking over the paperwork and there seems to be a couple of problems."

They gave one another a quick glance. "Problems? What kind of problems?"

"Well, first of all, the timing sucks. I mean a week to move out and that's the first thing she's heard from you? Come on. The law states six months, and you guys—"

"The law?" the guy in the work boots said and spit dark brown tobacco juice on the ground in front of me.

"Six months? Who you trying to kid? Here's the deal, pal. If that little bitch doesn't already have her perfect ass out of here, we're gonna drag it out in the next five minutes. And there ain't nothing you can do that's gonna stop us. Might be best if you got your ass out of our way too, before you get hurt."

I was really hoping Luscious would make an appearance right about now. "Hey, fellas, I was hoping we might talk this over. No point in anyone getting upset. But I'm afraid you're liable to be going about this the wrong way."

The guy in the work boots nodded, spit once more, and said, "You know, Tony, he may have a point. Maybe we have been going about this the wrong way. How about this?" he said and swung a mean left hook at me. I blocked it, jumped in close, and gave him a solid head butt on the bridge of his nose. The head butt knocked him backward. His eyes seemed to cross just as I was grabbed from behind.

I waited for the guy's next move behind me, but all I heard was, "Ouch, ouch, ouch," and he suddenly released me.

I spun around ready to swing, and there was Luscious with a handful of ponytail, lifting the guy halfway off his feet as he said, "Let go of my friend, dipshit."

Luscious half-spun him around and swung. I heard an audible crack as he landed a solid punch on the guy's chin, while knocking his feet out from underneath him. Luscious continued to hold him up by the ponytail, and the guy's mouth seemed to have moved sideways. His jaw hung at an angle never intended, and his eyes glazed over.

The idiot I'd head-butted had blood flowing down his chin. He uncrossed his eyes, reached behind his back, and began to pull out a pistol. I gave him a solid right-handed fist into his Adam's apple. The pistol dropped to the ground, and he grabbed his throat with both hands. I took a step back and kicked a field goal up between his legs. He dropped onto all fours and curled into the fetal position. I pushed the pistol away with my foot and picked it up. Luscious had already taken the pistol from the idiot he'd knocked out.

"Check the glove compartment, Luscious, while I find out who these clowns are."

As Luscious walked over to the passenger side of the Escalade, I ripped open the back pocket of the guy in the fetal position and took his wallet. He groaned and muttered, "No, please, please."

"You guys think you're tough? Coming over here and threatening a woman. You better up your game, pal." I opened the wallet, three twenties, sixty bucks. I grabbed the cash and stuffed it in my pocket. I looked at his driver's license, James Massinni. I pulled it out of the wallet along with his credit cards and knelt down beside him. He was breathing deeply now, slowly starting to re-cover. I held the credit cards and the license in front of him.

"Okay, Jimmy, you listen and listen good. I know who you are, and now I know where you live. If so much as a bird shits on this girl's car, I'm going to blame you, and we're going to come get you. Not just the two of us, but the whole gang. So word to the wise, find a better way to spend your time. Understand? I said, do you understand?" I pinched his broken nose to make my point. He moaned and nodded.

"Good. Now we're going to put this other idiot into your back seat, and if you know what's good for you, you'll drive him to the emergency room. Along the way, you better think about how lucky you are."

I pulled the wallet out of the other guy's back pocket. His jaw remained at a strange angle as he slowly regained consciousness. The driver's license identified him as Anthony Massinni. He was probably called Tony by everyone but his mother. "Hey, Tony, if you can hear me, we're going to put your ass in the back seat, and your dumb shit brother, Jimmy, is going to take you to the ER. I don't want to see you around here ever again. If you're stupid enough to come back here, next time we won't be so nice."

He had a fifty-dollar bill and some ones in his wallet. I took them along with the license and the credit cards.

"Luscious, you find anything in the glove compartment?"

Luscious shook his head and held up a small box of nine-millimeter ammunition. "Just this, nothing else but some road maps."

"Hang onto the ammo and help me put this clown in the back seat."

As Luscious came around the back of the Escalade, I opened the rear door. Before I could turn around to help, he had Tony Massinni on his feet and was moving him toward the car. Tony was still pretty much out of it and moved one of his feet about every third step. Luscious lifted him into the seat and fastened the seat belt around him.

Jimmy Massinni had risen up on all fours and was still taking deep breaths. Luscious helped him to his feet, meaning he somewhat gently yanked him up and walked him to the driver's door. He lifted him up and helped him slide behind the wheel. The dinging sounded, signaling the keys in the ignition.

"Jimmy, I'd like to say it was nice to meet you, but it wasn't. Now get your dumb ass out of here and get your brother to the ER. I'm not kidding. You guys even think about pulling any more shit around this house or anywhere near Roxy, and you won't have to worry about driving to the hospital. Now get your ass out of here and don't ever come back."

He turned to look at me, but it wasn't a threatening look. The blood continued to flow from his nose, drip off his beard, and soak into his t-shirt. He nodded and turned the key in the ignition. His brother Tony groaned from the back seat.

I closed the door and said, "Watch out, Luscious. He's just stupid enough to try and run us over." Fortunately, he just backed up and slowly drove away.

Thirteen

As the Escalade disappeared around the bend, heading back the way it had come I said, "Thank you, Luscious. Your timing could not have been better."

"You think they'll be back?" he asked as he handed me the box of nine-millimeter ammunition.

"I think those two idiots will think twice about it, at least for a while. But they were just delivering a message. They didn't expect to find you and me here. I guess we'll just have to see what happens next, but if they were working for Sheldon Smeet, he seems stupid enough to try something else."

"So we're going to hang around for a while?" He sounded hopeful.

"Actually, I don't know what else we could do. It could be days before someone comes around, and even that might never happen. I'm thinking I can drop you off back in town, and then I'm going to try and figure out what the hell is up with this Sheldon Smeet character. I might be wrong, but I don't peg him as the kind of guy who would have a connection with two knuckleheads like those guys. I'm worried there might be someone else besides Sheldon involved here."

"But what's going to happen if they decide to come back and Roxy is all alone?"

"Yeah, I get what you're saying, but short of us camping out here, I don't see what else we could do. Like I said, it could be days before someone shows up, or they may never come."

"I think maybe I might ask Roxy if she wants me to stay. Just to play it safe if they decide to come back or she needs something. You okay with that?"

Yeah, right. After the yoga preview I witnessed, I figured Roxy needing something would have absolutely nothing to do with me hanging around. "If you want to stay here and maybe provide security or something, it's fine with me. In fact, I have a feeling she just might appreciate the offer."

"I think I'll mention it to her, make sure she's safe."

"While I'm thinking of it, here's a couple of bucks just to cover your time for the last hour or so." I pulled the fifty and the three twenty-dollar bills from my pocket and handed them to Luscious. I kept the ones and hung on to the credit cards.

"Oh, you don't have to do that, Dev," Luscious said as he quickly pocketed the money.

"Not a problem, Luscious. You just call me if you need anything like a lift back into town."

Luscious nodded and said, "Not to worry. I just want to keep an eye on things around here."

We headed back inside. The yoga mat was positioned in front of one of the fireplaces, only now there were two fluffy pillows lying at one end. The half-dozen empty wine bottles and the ashtrays had been cleared off the coffee table. In their place sat two bowls filled with salad and a plate of tasteless looking crackers, no doubt gluten-free. Roxy stepped out from behind one of the fireplaces carrying two bottles of sparkling water. She had a paisley cloth wrapped around her. The cloth barely hung down below her hips and was almost, but not quite, see-through. It appeared she had nothing on underneath the cloth.

"Oh, I thought you were going to wait outside and talk to those guys when they showed up," she said, sounding completely oblivious.

"They've already come and gone," I said.

"They have? What did you say to them?"

"Luscious just told them we weren't interested." I set the two pistols and the box of ammunition on an end table next to one of the couches. Roxy looked at the pistols for a long moment before she shook her head, probably in an attempt to clear her mind. I'm sure it didn't work.

"Dev, do you want to join us for lunch?" she said. Just to get her message across, she added, "I'm all out of salad makings, but you could have some of those crackers."

"Gee, thanks for the offer, Roxy. But I want to go back to my office and do some research on Sheldon

Smeet. If it's okay with you, Luscious is going to stay here just to make sure you're safe."

Roxy gave a quick wave over her shoulder without looking. "Okay, Dev. Thanks, see ya. Come on, Luscious. You look like you could use a back rub to help you relax. We can have lunch whenever we're finished." Roxy took his hand and headed over to the yoga mat.

I let myself out, double checking the door to make sure it locked behind me.

Fourteen

On the way back into town, I took the Maryland Street exit off of 35E. A few blocks later, I took a left and headed down Rice Street. It was two in the afternoon on a weekday, essentially the middle of a workday. Not that you'd know that based on the pedestrian traffic. A number of working-age people wandered around aimlessly, with nowhere to go and all day to get there.

I pulled to the curb in front of Born's bar. There's no nice way to put it. It's a shit hole. The city requires everyone stupid enough to go in the place to be patted down, have their ID's checked, and then have a metal detector security wand waved over them. The bar was currently closed for seventy-two hours, yet again, for failing to follow the city's requirements two months ago when there was another shooting in the place.

Does the place create trouble? Yes, obviously. But on the other hand, when it's open, the cops know where a good number of the troublemakers are, so maybe that's an incentive not to close it down completely. Anyway, it was closed for seventy-two hours, and that struck me as the perfect place to leave the Massinni boys' credit cards. My own attempt to help those less fortunate.

I got out of the car, took the half-dozen credit cards out of my pocket, and left them on the windowsill. Two women stopped and gathered them up before I was even back behind the wheel of my car. They didn't even look at me. They just picked up the credit cards, stuffed them in the back pocket of their sprayed-on stretch pants, and hurried down the street toward the liquor store.

I pulled in front of Amanda's house and climbed out of the car. I was halfway to her front door when I heard a female voice call from behind me. "Dev. Hi Dev, we're over here."

I turned and saw Morton and Amanda just rounding the corner of the block. Morton immediately lunged and strained at the leash, but Amanda quickly said something, and whatever it was, he pulled back alongside her and continued at her pace. His tail was wagging from left to right, but he remained next to her right leg.

"Just stand there and don't say anything. I want to see how he reacts when we get next to you," she said.

As they approached, I thought for sure Morton would jump or at the very least strain against the leash, but he never did. Amanda walked past me then turned and walked around me in a circle three times. Morton glanced at me, but he didn't jump, lunge or bark. When Amanda stopped, he immediately sat and looked at me.

"Unbelievable. What did you do? I've never seen him so well-behaved."

"It's really quite simple. You simply have to assume the alpha position. Once you do that, everything more or less falls into place."

"My new favorite position. You'll have to show me."

She smiled and said, "It's not simply a stance or even a voice. It's the overall sense you emulate that automatically exudes the alpha confidence, sending the message that you're the boss."

"Do you position your feet a certain way? Hold the leash just so? Have a pocket full of treats you give him to encourage that thought?"

"No, not exactly." She glanced at her watch. "Oh, dear. I have another appointment coming in about five minutes. I'm going to hand you back his leash, and remember that means you're now in charge. Okay."

"Well, let's give it a try."

Amanda handed me the leash and said, "Now, don't worry. It's going to take some time for him to get used to you as the alpha character in your relationship. Expect some pushback or, in Morton's case, some pullback."

Morton remained perfectly calm for maybe four or five seconds. Once Amanda began to walk away, he strained on the leash and began to bark. I grabbed onto the leash with both hands and pulled him back. "Morton, sit. Sit, Morton." He ignored me.

"I'll see you two the day after tomorrow," Amanda said and climbed the steps to her front porch. I pulled

Morton over to the car and opened the rear door. He hopped right in and laid down on the back seat.

We drove down to the office. God only knew where Louie was this afternoon. Morton had been asleep in his bed next to the file cabinet for at least an hour. I had Googled Sheldon Smeet and was working my way through about a hundred newspaper articles and news reports. No surprise, the bottom line was, Sheldon Smeet was a slimeball. I couldn't find anything that specifically mentioned the North Oaks property where Roxy had been staying, although there were a number of articles regarding Smeet's 'real estate holdings' and some awfully shady practices. Five separate individuals, all women, relayed similar experiences to what Roxy was experiencing. Although it seemed, in each of those cases, they complied with the eviction order, only to have it labeled fraudulent later. The five were currently in a class action suit suing Smeet for the funds they had paid, along with million-dollar sums for mental anguish.

It seemed clear that, sooner or later, Sheldon Smeet was going to find himself behind bars. The thing that amazed me was that he had been allowed to continue in this manner for so many years. Folks like me can't let the license plate on our car expire for twenty-four hours without getting pulled over. But that upper one percent seems to be able to get away with everything.

In the office, my back and shoulders were killing me after being hunched over for a couple of hours reading on my laptop. I stood, extended my arms, and turned left to right at my waist. My back cracked a couple of times and immediately felt one hundred percent better. I rolled my shoulders and casually glanced out the window as a black Cadillac Escalade pulled up across the street and parked behind my Jeep Cherokee.

My first thought was shit, the Massinni brothers. But then the driver's door opened, and a rather fat figure oozed out from behind the wheel. Fortunately, he didn't have a beard, so it wasn't one of the Massinni's. Unfortunately, it was none other than Fat Freddy Zimmerman, enforcer for local St. Paul crime lord, Tubby Gustafson. Fat Freddy opened the rear door, and I could see Tubby sitting in the back seat, yelling into his cellphone. Even from across the street and one story up, Tubby's face appeared flushed. Fat Freddy just stood next to the open door, smiling and waiting patiently. After a couple of minutes, Tubby put the phone down, shouted something, and then gradually slid out of the seat. As they waddled across the street, the odds were slim to none that they had an appointment at the hairdresser across the hall from my office. I debated running down the hall and hiding in the ladies' room, but that would leave Morton here alone. I took a deep breath and waited for the staircase to begin creaking.

Fifteen

A number of groans accompanied the sound of creaking stairs. The door to the office swung open and in stumbled a red-faced Fat Freddy Zimmerman with Tubby Gustafson bringing up the rear. Morton looked up from his bed, recognized both of them, placed his paws over his eyes, and went back to sleep. Tubby waddled toward my client chairs and waited for Freddy to pull one out for him. Once he was seated, he removed the silk cloth from the upper pocket of his wrinkled suit coat and proceeded to wipe the perspiration from his face. Fat Freddy sat there with his eyes closed, taking deep breaths.

"You need to get an office in a building with an elevator, Haskell, you nitwit. How in God's name do you expect to service elderly clients?"

"Would you be willing to cut me a deal on the office rent in one of your buildings, Mr. Gustafson?"

"Don't be stupid, Haskell. First of all, N. O. spells no. Secondly, I'm trying to think of a quicker way to empty out all the tenants on a floor, and I can't seem to come up with one. Now please, don't ever bring up that ridiculous idea again. Word on the street is you've taken up the cause against the Massinni organization. Even went so far as to assault two of the younger lads while they were in the middle of an eviction process."

'*It had been a little more than three hours ago. How in the hell did Tubby already know about it?*' "Um, well, you see, sir, I can explain that. We merely wanted to discuss the possibility of—"

Tubby held his hand up and half-shouted, "Silencio. I'm not the least bit interested in what your objective

was. The fact of the matter is, you created a large problem for them and a—"

"That wasn't my intent, honest, Mr. Gustafson. I
thought—"

"For God's sake. Do you ever bother to listen,
Haskell? Now shut up." Tubby looked over at Fat Freddy
and said, "The next time he interrupts me, I want you to
cut off one of his fingers and cram it down his throat."
Fat Freddy reached down by his ankle and came up with
a black something. He pressed a button, and a switchblade flashed open.

"Now, where was I?"

"A large problem, sir," I said and immediately re-
gretted opening my mouth.

"Yes. You created a large problem for them and an
even larger opportunity for me."

"Opportunity?" I said, sitting up and smiling. I
waited for congratulations, but none came.

"Rumor on the street is you sent two of them to the
hospital. How did you come to interact with them in the
first place?"

I took a deep breath and gave Tubby the short version. I left Luscious completely out of my explanation.
He was going to have enough problems just trying to survive a day with sex-crazed Roxy, let alone worry about
whatever Tubby had in mind.

"So you see, sir, all I did was take the opportunity
to explain to both gentlemen that we were having some
trouble with the wording of their mortgage contract and,

well, the fact that they were going to charge a ridiculous interest rate on the loan.”

“And what exactly is your relationship with the current holder of the mortgage, this Roxy LaRue person?”

“Roxy? Really no relationship. She’s just a friend of a friend. I only met her a couple of days ago. The way the loan agreement is written, it’s not going to stand up in any court. Yes, she signed it, but frankly, I think she could declare mental incompetence or something. This Sheldon Smeet guy, he’s the one who took her to Vegas for three nights and gave her the keys to the place on the flight home. I just read online he’s under federal indictment. I think it will only be a matter of time before he’s behind bars for a good long while.”

“That’s exactly what I wanted to hear. The real losers here, and believe me they are losers, will be the Massinni family. Now to that end, let me give you a piece of advice, Haskell. It would serve you well to be out at this North Oaks property this evening. Once the sun goes down, the Massinni family will be there in force to evict this woman.”

“How did you learn this, if you don’t mind me asking?”

“I do mind, Haskell. Knowledge of any involvement is way above your pay grade. Suffice to say, Dante Massinni, the father of those two idiots, is down in the emergency room at Regions Hospital as we speak. I suspect he’s not a happy camper right about now,” Tubby said and rubbed his hands together as he laughed.

"What if Roxy isn't home when they go back there?"

"It doesn't work like that, Haskell. If she's not there, they'll merely pile her belongings out front and set them on fire. There, problem solved, at least as far as they're concerned."

"Any idea how many of them there will be?"

"How many? No less than a half-dozen. I'll need you out there to make a stand. Frederick will be in the shadows."

I looked over at Fat Freddy, and he grinned.

"No offense, Mr. Gustafson, but don't you think it might be better if we just called the police?"

"Please, Haskell. Don't try to think. It never seems to work with you. Now, I want you out there this evening, and Frederick will be available to ensure your safety. There, problem solved. Just do as you're told, Haskell, and learn to shut the hell up. Very well. I'll count this as my good deed for the week. Remember, be out there before sunset. Any questions? No. Good. Frederick, if you would be so kind as to get the door. Our business here is finished."

There was no point in saying anything but, "Thank you, Mr. Gustafson. See you tonight, Freddy."

Tubby ignored my comment, and Fat Freddy flipped me the bird as he headed for the staircase. I watched out my office window as they exited the building and crossed the street. Freddy held the door for Tubby as he slid into the back seat. Once in, he immediately took out his cellphone and dialed a number. I wondered if he might have been reporting on our meeting.

Fat Freddy closed the rear door, looked up at me, gave me the finger again, just in case I missed it the first time, and climbed behind the wheel. I watched the Escalade head up Randolph Avenue, take a right onto 35E, and disappear from sight. I figured I'd better give Luscious a call.

I placed three calls, actually. Fifteen minutes apart, and he never answered. My first thought was the bad guys were already there. My second thought involved the image of Luscious involved in some deep, personal interaction with Roxy. Luscious returned my call a couple of hours later.

"You called, Dev," he said and then yawned.

"Yeah, is everything going all right out there, Luscious?"

"Couldn't be better."

"How's Roxy doing?"

"She was fantastic. I mean, she's fine. She's taking a little nap right now."

"Well, listen. I have it on some pretty good authority there are liable to be some visitors tonight after dark. I'm going to head out there about seven tonight, just so you're not alone. I've got some other folks lined up to help, but you probably won't see them, if you get what I'm saying," I said. I couldn't see any advantage to mentioning Fat Freddy and some other thugs would be lingering in the background.

"Actually, Dev, no, I don't get what you're saying."

"I mean they'll be hiding, Luscious. Ready for any potential trouble."

"You sure that's necessary? Roxy and I kind of had an evening planned and—"

"I'll be out there around seven, Luscious. See you then." I really didn't want to dwell on what the two of them had lined up.

Sixteen

I took Morton home, filled his food and water dish, and put some music on in the background. Then I headed up to North Oaks in rush-hour traffic. There was nothing 'rush' about it. What would normally have been a twenty-minute drive took the better part of an hour. It was stop and go all along the interstate in intervals of about ten feet. I couldn't imagine having to drive in this every day, but then if you did, I guess you'd just find a radio station you like, turn it on, and listen to the music.

I drove about fifty feet past Roxy's and pulled into what looked like a small logging trail. I drove maybe fifteen feet off the road, just far enough so my car hopefully wouldn't be spotted by anyone casing the house. Then I walked back to Roxy's.

Luscious answered the door after I rang the doorbell a couple of times. His hair was messed, his shirt was on backward, and he was wearing boxers. He had lipstick smooches on the side of his cheek and his neck. A smile seemed to be permanently plastered on his face.

"Hi Luscious, everything go all right this afternoon?"

"Couldn't have been better, Dev. Thanks for bringing me out here and telling me to stay."

"I didn't actually tell you to . . . Oh never mind. No sign of those two idiots from this morning?"

"No, nothing. You think they'll come back?"

"Those two probably won't, but like I said on the phone, I got word the group they're with, the Massinni family, are planning something for tonight once it gets dark."

"Any ideas what that might be?"

"I wish I knew, Luscious, but I can't think of anything. Maybe try to set my car on fire? I parked over in the woods; hopefully, they won't see it. I suppose they could try to spray paint something on the front of the entrance or take a chain saw and cut off the deck. I just don't have any idea. How's Roxy holding up?"

Luscious let a sheepish grin roll across his face. "She's doing pretty good. She was kind of tired, so she's grabbing a nap right now."

"You wear her out?"

"We wore each other out," he said then seemed to catch himself. "I think she's probably just tired after worrying about all this stuff. She's got a suitcase packed just in case she has to leave in a hurry."

"Hopefully, things won't get to that point. I don't suppose she has anything planned for dinner."

"She might not, but I do. There's a gas grill out on the deck, and I got a bunch of burgers thawing in the kitchen. You feel like cheeseburgers for dinner?"

"Yeah, that would be perfect. Why don't you get me her car keys? I want to move it away from the house just in case we have visitors tonight."

I hopped in Roxy's Audi. The thing reeked of perfume. Two empty coffee cups from Starbucks sat in the console. A third one was on the floor on the passenger side. Two gym bags were in the back seat along with a grocery bag full of sweaters. When I turned the car on, a red light flashed indicating low oil. I drove into the small trail and parked the Audi behind my car.

As I came down the staircase and entered the living room with the two fireplaces, I noticed the yoga mat was still on the floor in front of one of the fireplaces. Only now, the pillows clearly had been used, along with an open bottle of lubricant, a pair of pink plastic handcuffs with fluffy pink feathers, and a battery-operated appliance.

Luscious came around the corner and pretended not to notice. His hair was combed, he wore jeans, and his shirt was no longer on backward. He hustled me out onto the back deck while he went back into the kitchen to grab a couple of beers.

I sat out on the deck with him, sipping a beer and eating some Bar-B-Que potato chips from the bag. Roxy and her dog Madame were nowhere to be seen. We sat at the picnic table on the back deck and ate cheeseburgers on a plate, without a bun. I had one, and Luscious ate three. I would have killed for another couple of beers but felt, under the circumstances of possible visitors later in the evening, another beer probably wouldn't be the best idea.

Madame, with Roxy following, made her appearance a little after eight. "Oh, hi Dev. I must not have heard you come in."

"I tiptoed," I said, not sure she got the joke.

"How'd you sleep?" Luscious asked as she gave him a hug and kissed him on the top of his head.

"I was out like a light. Did you take a nap?"

"I maybe dozed off for a couple of minutes. Can I interest you in a cheeseburger?"

"No, I think I'll just make up a salad if it's all the same," she said, which was probably a pretty good idea since we'd eaten all the burgers.

Madame jumped into Luscious's lap. It appeared they were now best of friends. Roxy strolled back out of the kitchen about five minutes later with a small salad consisting of lettuce, a couple of cherry tomatoes, black olives, and sunflower seeds. The sight of the thing made me glad I had scored a cheeseburger when I did.

Dusk arrived about half-past eight, and by nine, it was dark. We had Roxy settled in the living room watching a special on the Kardashians on the sixty-inch TV. I noticed that the yoga mat and attending items were nowhere to be seen. Luscious loaded the two nine-millimeter pistols we took from the Massinni brothers that morning. He gave one to me before he headed out onto the deck and then down the steps and into the woods. I took the staircase up to the front entry and stepped outside.

The front was illuminated by a series of recessed lights. I was tempted to turn them off but decided it might look like we were just waiting for someone to show up. I took up a position beneath a large oak tree maybe twenty feet from the front entry and waited. Then I waited some more.

Not so much as a car drove along the road. With the exception of the occasional cricket, it was deathly quiet. After two hours or so, I thought I heard car doors slamming but maybe not. No car drove down the road. There was no sign of headlights in any direction. My heart was pounding, and I was afraid, if anyone was out there, they'd hear it and know where I was.

Some branches snapped in the woods behind me, and then all was quiet for a few minutes. Time seemed to be standing still. Suddenly, off to the right, a figure momentarily appeared before fading back into the woods. I waited and watched but didn't see anything else.

Maybe twenty minutes after that, I thought I heard a brief scream, but it could have been a bird, maybe a crow or something. Two figures suddenly emerged from the woods and crouched as they ran along the front entry-way. Another figure passed me off to the left, no more than five feet away. Like the other two, he crouched and ran along the front entry. All three stopped a couple of feet on either side of the front door and the glass panels. Theoretically, no one would be able to see them from inside the house.

One of them pulled a small object from his pocket, and suddenly a cellphone lit up. The screen illuminated his face. It looked like he might be sending a text message, but then the screen went dark, and I heard him whisper, "Damn it."

Another one of the three shouted, "Shut up." Clearly, they'd never been involved in any midnight raids. I wasn't sure what they planned to do, but whatever it was, it couldn't be positive. I had to decide what to do and quickly. I didn't know if they had a firebomb, dynamite, or just a can of spray paint.

I crouched down and slowly moved parallel to them. Fortunately, they were too focused on staring at the glass panels in the entryway to pay any attention to me. Colors from the sixty-inch TV Roxy was watching down in the living room swirled around on the ceiling inside.

The guy who'd yelled 'shut up' scurried up to the front door and tried the doorknob. Thank God I'd locked the thing. He moved a couple of feet back and pointed what looked like a sawed-off shotgun at the door.

"I wouldn't do that. It's a really bad idea," I said and assumed a two-handed grip on my pistol and pointed it at the back of the guy's head. "Now everyone just stay nice and still, so no one gets hurt."

Seventeen

One of the three turned to look at me.

"Don't look back here, dumb shit. Put your hands up over your head. Come on, all of you. Get 'em up while you still can. Okay, you, with the sawed-off. Carefully hang on to that by the front of the barrel and set it on the ground behind you. Slowly. Yeah, that's right. Now you, on the right, put that pistol on the ground behind you, hold it by the barrel."

He started to turn around.

"I didn't say turn around, damn it," I shouted. "Next time one of you doesn't listen I'm gonna shoot, just to get your stupid attention. Hang onto the damn barrel and carefully set that thing behind you."

As he did so, I stepped closer. "You, last guy, do the same."

He set the pistol behind him, and I stepped over, pressed the barrel against the back of his head, and kicked the pistol further back.

"If you don't mind me saying. I don't think you know who you're dealing with here, and you're making a big mistake. You want to leave, we won't follow you, and you can just live happily ever after." This from the guy who had the sawed-off shotgun.

"Maybe you don't know who you're dealing with. We warned those two fools this morning, but apparently, they didn't have a chance to spread the word. With Dante spending all afternoon in the ER, you'd think you guys would learn."

At the mention of Dante, two of them flashed a quick look at one another.

"How many of you are there tonight?" I said.

No one answered.

"They're not answering, chief. Can I shoot one of them, so they know we're not kidding?" I said, hoping they thought there were a number of us connected by radio or something. I had to say, if Fat Freddy was out here somewhere, he was doing a damn good job of hiding.

"No, let me pick him. The one who had the shotgun, he seems to be the boss," I said, hoping they were buying into the idea there were a lot of us. I took a step closer and pushed the barrel up against the back of his head. "I want to know how many of you are out here. How many?" I said and pushed his head forward with the barrel. "How many?"

"It's just the three of us," the guy to the right said. "That's all, just three of us."

"Shut the hell up," the guy with my pistol against the back of his head said.

I pushed his head forward with the barrel. "You shut up, dip shit. First of all, you're lying because we already got one of you. Second of all, I warned your ass."

"You ain't got the balls, pal."

I stepped back, pointed the pistol at the sole of his foot and fired. I missed. Four feet away and I missed.

"If that was supposed to scare me, it didn't work. Now, why don't you—"

I fired again, this time from just three feet away.

"Ahh. God. Ahh, Jesus," he screamed and rolled on the ground.

"How'd that work for you? You still a tough guy?"

"You, you shot me. You shot me, damn it."

"I told you that was what I was gonna do, but you had to be the tough guy. Okay, how's it working out? Now you," I said and jammed the barrel up against the back of the head of the guy who said they were the only ones there tonight. "I'm going to ask you one more time. If you don't tell me the truth, I'm going to shoot you, only it won't be in the foot. Nod your head if you understand."

He nodded his head. The guy with the hole in his foot had his eyes squeezed shut and his jaw clenched. He was groaning and moving from side to side. He did not look happy.

"Now, how many are here?"

"There's just four of us, honest that's all. It was my cousin in back, Gabe. Is he okay?"

"You guys should find a new line of work. This one sure as hell isn't working out for you."

I heard a branch suddenly snap off to the side of the house. I grabbed the guy who just told me there were four by the shirt collar and put the barrel up against the back of his head. "Whoever you are, you better come out nice and slow, or your buddy here is gonna get it. We called the cops, and they're on the way so get your ass out—"

"Easy, dude. It's me," Luscious said and stepped around the corner. He had someone draped over his shoulder.

"You okay, man?" I said.

"Yeah. Bit of a disagreement." He indicated the guy over his shoulder with a nod. He stepped over and laid the guy out on the oil stain from Roxy's car.

"Gabe? Gabe, you okay, man?" his cousin cried.

"Search these idiots. Make sure they're not carrying," I said and kept my pistol trained on the three. The guy in the middle had stopped rolling from side to side, but he was hanging onto his foot and working hard to stifle his groans. Luscious pulled a Ka-Bar knife from the first guy he searched. He pulled a small revolver that was strapped around the ankle of the guy I shot in the foot.

As he went to search the one who told us there were four of them, the guy said, "I got a sticky holster in the front of my belt. That's all I'm carrying. I swear. Honest."

Luscious pulled the holster from his belt. It looked like a small nine-millimeter in the holster. Luscious continued with a thorough search of him and came up empty-handed.

"Where's your car parked?" I said.

"It's back there, around that bend," he said.

"Who's got the keys?"

"I do. I'm driving."

"Take his keys and get the car," I said to Luscious.

"You're going to let 'em go? The rest of the guys might want a piece," Luscious said and grinned.

"Let's keep everyone out there in position, just in case. We're going to let you douchebags go. But last time. Two guys this morning and you four tonight. After this, no one gets away, understand?" The two still kneeling with their hands raised nodded vigorously. The guy with the hole in his foot just gritted his teeth and groaned.

Luscious grabbed the car keys and headed off down the road. He was back ten minutes later, driving a dark blue panel van. I collected wallets from the four of them, took their cash, driver's licenses, and credit cards and tossed the wallets into the van. The guy Luscious had carried was beginning to come around, but he needed help getting inside the van. The other two guys helped their wounded pal into the back. He wasn't looking so tough right now.

"Be sure to tell Dante Massinni we're not going to be so nice next time," I said as the two unharmed jerks climbed into the front seat. "Now get out of here before we change our mind."

The van headed back around the bend and disappeared from sight.

"What do you think?" Luscious said.

"I think we've been awfully lucky. I'd guess they've had their fill, at least for tonight. Let's check on Roxy and then I think I'll take off. It's been a crazy day."

Eighteen

Roxy was just fine if you didn't dwell on her being completely oblivious. She'd been involved in whatever current scam the Kardashians were running and hadn't even heard the gunshots at her front door. That didn't seem to bother Luscious, but he thought it might be a good idea if he went home and got a decent night's rest.

We checked the door locks, said good night, and beat a hasty retreat out of North Oaks. I dropped off Luscious in front of his building and told him I would give him a call in the morning. Once again, Morton met me at the front door and then ran to the back door and barked so I would let him out. I poured myself a little Jameson and went on the internet for forty-five minutes. I had an email from Heidi asking if anything was going on with Roxy.

I sent her a two-line response. *'Everything is fine. Call me tomorrow and I'll bring you up to date.'* I logged out, shut down my laptop, and hopped in the shower. I was asleep about a minute after my head hit the pillow.

It was still dark outside when Morton started barking. I looked at the digital clock. It was just a little after four in the morning. "Morton, go back to sleep and—" The doorbell suddenly rang three or four times. Morton barked again.

"Oh, God. Hang on, hang on. I slipped on my jeans and stumbled down the staircase. Morton continued to bark, but the big baby remained up on the second floor watching me through the banister in the hallway. The doorbell rang another half-dozen times. "All right already, all right. Morton, will you please shut the hell up."

I flipped on the porch light, and there was Roxy. She was wearing a t-shirt and a red thong. She held Madame in one arm and rested her other arm on the handle of a large suitcase.

"Roxy?" I said when I opened the door.

"Sorry to barge in on you like this," she said, barging in through the front door and not looking sorry.

Morton barked a couple more times then hurried down the stairs just as Roxy put Madame down on the floor.

"Everything okay? What happened?"

"Oh, I couldn't sleep so I was watching this movie where these zombies take over a town, and the few survivors all get together in this house, but the Zombies surround it and started eating the survivors and well anyway, it really weirded me out, so I grabbed my suitcase, fled the scene, and here I am."

"What?" I still wasn't awake.

"I figured I'd be safest with you, and well, I don't know where Luscious lives."

"Yeah, well, come on in, I guess." I looked at the suitcase she had wheeled in. It was too large for carry-on luggage, and if she bent down, she could have hidden behind the thing.

"Nice place," she said, looking around. "Sorry, I know it's kind of late, but I'm used to dancing until two, and then I would, um, maybe do some stuff for a couple of hours, you know."

I wasn't going to touch that last line. "Yeah, sure. Might as well come on upstairs. You can have the guest room."

Morton and Madame were busy smelling one another. Morton's tail was wagging back and forth, announcing the fact he was in favor of our early morning visitors.

Roxy bent down and picked up Madame then said, "Would you mind grabbing that suitcase and leading the way? We'll follow you."

I wheeled the suitcase over to the staircase then grabbed the handle with both hands and began to climb the stairs. God only knew what she'd packed in the thing, but it was really heavy. I had to lift with both arms and force it at the same time using my right leg to get it up to the next step. I finally made it to the top of the stairs just in time. I caught my breath then wheeled the suitcase down the hall past my room to the guest room. I stepped in and flicked on the light.

It was late summer, and the bed had three winter coats piled on top of it from last April. "Oops, sorry about that," I said and wheeled the suitcase next to the dresser. I gathered up the coats and said, "You two can camp in here. The bathroom is just across the hall. The coffee is set to begin perking at seven in the morning. If you're up before me, feel free to help yourself to anything in the kitchen. I've got an extra food and water dish, so I'll dish something up for Madame in the morning. Anything else you need?"

"Oh, this is so nice of you, Dev. I really appreciate it. No, I think we'll be just fine. Would you mind leaving the hall light on, just in case?"

I didn't want to ask, just in case of what? "No problem. Come on, Morton. Let's let them get some rest. We'll see you two in the morning," I said and partially closed the door on my way out. Morton and I headed back into our bedroom. I think I fell asleep just as my head hit the pillow.

Nineteen

When I woke, a bright sun was peeking around the corners of the window shades. My digital clock read half-past seven. I was lying on the very edge of my bed, and it felt like Morton had stretched out, and his legs were up against my back. There wasn't room to even roll over, and I had to carefully crawl off the edge of the bed to see how he was positioned and get him to move.

When I looked, Morton was curled up on the far side of the bed. Madame was curled up on the pillow sleeping just above Morton. Roxy was stretched out in the middle of the bed. As I crawled off the edge of the bed, her legs and arms automatically extended out. She remained sound asleep and seemed to levitate and take up the little remaining space I had just vacated.

I picked my clothes up off the floor, closed the bedroom door behind me, and headed for the bathroom. I showered, shaved, went downstairs, and had two cups of coffee. I left a note saying I'd be back in ten minutes and walked up to the restaurant/bakery at the end of the block and purchased two caramel rolls. Roxy, Morton, and Madame were apparently still asleep when I returned.

I went online and checked the news. There were three reported shootings last night, but fortunately, none of them were reported up in North Oaks. I checked the obituaries to make sure I wasn't listed. I read the gossip column, skipped the national news coming out of D.C., and had another cup of coffee.

About half-past eight, Morton and Madame strolled into the kitchen. I let them out, filled food and water dishes for both, and put on a fresh pot of coffee. An hour later, I heard the shower running. The shower continued for a good half hour. Just before eleven, Roxy strolled into the kitchen. She was dressed in jeans that looked to be spray-painted on, a t-shirt that left nothing to the imagination, and she was barefoot. She had gold rings on the middle toes of both her feet.

"Good morning, Roxy. How'd you sleep?"

"Oh, Dev. Your bed is so comfortable, and there's room for all of us." No mention of her leaving the guest room and crawling in. For that matter, she didn't bother to mention showing up on the front porch at four in the morning either. It was weird.

"How about some coffee?"

"Oh, I'd love some. Um, two teaspoons of sugar and a tablespoon of milk."

Really? "How 'bout I let you handle that part of it." I filled a coffee mug, making sure there was plenty of room for the milk and sugar. I handed her a set of measuring spoons, grabbed the milk out of the fridge, and slid the sugar bowl in front of her. "Hey, I picked up a couple of caramel rolls at this little bakery at the end of the block. They're just out of the oven, still warm when I bought them, so they're nice and fresh."

"Oh, thanks, but I really shouldn't."

I put the plates with the caramel rolls on the kitchen counter and slid one across to her. I took two forks and two knives out of the silverware drawer and placed them in the middle of the counter.

"I really shouldn't," she repeated.

"Not a problem," I said and cut a piece of my caramel roll. The caramel dripped a long, sticky strand from the piece I'd just cut to the plate. I placed the piece in my mouth. "Mmm, good. So you slept well?"

"Oh yeah, I almost always do," she said, like it was an everyday occurrence to climb into someone else's bed in the middle of the night. But then, maybe that wasn't too far from the truth. She pulled the caramel roll plate closer to her. "Maybe just a taste." She cut a piece barely large enough to be stabbed by the fork and put it in her mouth. An orgasmic look washed across her face. "Oh my God! You're right! These are really good."

Five minutes later, I cleared both empty plates and put them in the dishwasher. I puttered around the house for thirty minutes, arranged the kitchen, made my bed, refilled the water dishes, and straightened things up a little. Roxy was stretched out on the living room couch, sipping coffee and watching TV. Actually, she wasn't watching TV. She was flipping through channels and complaining that there was nothing good on, or she whined she'd already watched the movie that was on. Surprise, surprise.

"What are your plans for today, Roxy?"

"Plans?" she said, like it was something she'd never considered.

"Yeah, plans. You going to head back home? You have errands to run? Get that oil problem looked at in your car? You want to try and link up with Luscious?"

"What are you going to do?"

"I'm going to put Morton in the car, and we're going down to my office. But we should probably get started. I've got a one o'clock appointment," I lied.

"So what you're telling me is I should get my ass out of here."

"Yeah, pretty much."

"Okay, give me just a minute. Hey," she said and pulled her cellphone out of her back pocket. "Can you give me Luscious's number? I need to call him anyway."

I debated for half a second and then figured he was the one who got involved in the extracurricular activities, not me. I gave her the number. She put the phone to her ear and headed up the stairs to the guest room. "Oh, hi. Hey, did you rest up?" she said and giggled then closed the guest room door behind her. I picked up her coffee mug, went into the kitchen, and placed it in the dishwasher. I made a quick grocery list, took out the trash and recycling. I straightened up the spice rack and drummed my fingers on the kitchen counter waiting for her to leave.

Eventually, she came down with Madame under her arm. Her hair was done, she had makeup on, and there was a lovely scent of perfume. "Sorry to keep you waiting. I'm all set. Thanks for letting us in earlier this morning." She made it sound like she rang the doorbell at nine instead of four.

It didn't matter. She was leaving. "Glad to be able to help out, Roxy. You and Madame take care. I'm going to check around to see if anyone has heard anything about this Massinni gang, bunch of idiots. Let me know if you hear anything."

"I will, Dev." She took a couple of steps toward me, gave me a kiss then stepped back, struck a sexy pose, and said, "Mmm, nice."

I smiled and just nodded.

"Okay, well, I guess if there's nothing else, I'll be off. Catch you later, and thanks again," she said and let herself out.

Suddenly, there was no TV noise. No one wanting a teaspoon of this and a tablespoon of that. No one fixing a salad and complaining the lettuce wasn't organic. I was tempted to open a beer in celebration, instead, I poured the lukewarm dregs from the coffee pot into my mug and enjoyed the peace and quiet.

When I finished my coffee, I went upstairs to grab my keys off the dresser. I spent twenty minutes picking up towels in the bathroom, closing drawers, scrubbing mascara out of the sink, and adding a new roll of toilet paper. I opened the door to the guest room. Roxy's suitcase was still there. I picked it up with the intention of placing it down next to the front door, but it was light, very light. In fact, it was empty. I opened the drawers to the dresser. She had unpacked and arranged her clothes in all the drawers. I opened the closet door. Two outfits hung on hangers and two pair of stiletto heels, one red and one black, were on the floor.

It looked like she was moving in.

Twenty

Not for the first time Heidi interrupted me. "Dev, I already told you I can't understand you when you're yelling into the phone. Now either calm down, or I'm going to hang up."

I took a couple of deep breaths. "All I'm saying is, your friend Roxy is out to lunch. She was completely unaware of the four guys we chased off last night. Then she shows up at my place at zero-dark-thirty in the morning because she got freaked out by some stupid zombie movie. She climbs into bed with me and—"

"Wait a minute. She climbed into bed with you, and now you're complaining?" Heidi laughed. "Since when did this start?"

"Hey, I didn't even know she was in there until she pushed me out. Her little dog has more common sense than she does. Who rings your doorbell at four in the morning because they were watching some zombie movie?"

"She's used to working nights, Dev."

"Yeah, stripping and then dealing with after-hours entertainment."

"Oh, so now all of a sudden that's a problem. I'll just remember that. Nothing after the sun goes down when you're involved."

"I didn't mean it like that. Okay, okay. I get it, enough of my bitching. Have you learned anything about Sheldon Smeet?"

"Talk about a piece of work. He has not been indicted, yet. But it's a foregone conclusion. He's involved in some really questionable real estate practices, easily a dozen million-dollar homes like Roxy's. Five people have already come forward with separate lawsuits. But the bigger scam is rentals. A number of newer buildings with one or two hundred units, all in the outer ring of suburbs. His bank, Third National, has loaned millions more than they were authorized. There's talk of them going under federal control. Smeet as president and CEO, along with a number of vice presidents and loan officers, are up for indictment. It's only a matter of time."

"Any mention of someone named Dante Massinni?"

"Not that I recall, but why do I know that name? Was he in the legislature or something?"

"Not that I'm aware of, but that doesn't mean he wouldn't fit in. He seems to be behind the eviction notice Roxy received. Some members of his organization were there yesterday morning and another group of people last night."

"What did they want?"

"They wanted Roxy out of there, like immediately."

"What did you do?"

"Asked them nicely to leave."

"And did they?"

"Yes, they seemed to see the wisdom in our request."

"I'm not sure I want to know anything else," Heidi said.

"Okay. So where is Sheldon Smeet now? Does he still show up at the office? Is he even allowed in the building."

"That's one of the many questions. From the reports I've read, he hasn't been seen for probably seventy-two hours. Three days. I do know he's had to surrender his passport, so theoretically he can't leave the country. That said, I don't think it would be too hard for him to charter a plane to Mexico, South America, or somewhere in the Caribbean."

"Well, if you hear anything else, let me know."

"I will, and thanks for helping Roxy. I know she's kind of crazy. She always has been, but she's my oldest friend."

"Yeah, well, another night at my place and I'm going to send her over to you."

"I'll make it up to you, Dev. I promise."

"I'm going to hold you to that. Keep me posted," I said and hung up.

Twenty-one

y phone rang later that afternoon. Louie had just suggested we head over to The Spot for a little libation.

"Haskell Investigations," was how I answered.

"Hi, Dev, you watching the news?" Luscious said.

"No, how's it going? Did Roxy ever get in touch with you?"

"Yeah, she did. As a matter of fact, she just hopped into the shower. You watching the news?"

"No, I'm at the office. Why? What's going on?"

"A five-alarm fire up in North Oaks is what's happening."

"You're kidding. Her place is burning?"

"I'd say, at this point, it's pretty much already destroyed. Firefighters from a number of the northern suburbs."

"What channel are you watching?" I said and turned my computer back on.

"KARE Eleven. They're doing a live bit. If you go on YouTube and input North Oaks fire, you can probably get it."

"I'm doing that now. Hang on." I got on YouTube, input North Oaks fire, and a moment later, the KARE Eleven site came on and immediately began playing. The video lasted a minute and twenty-seven seconds. Another video of the fire was in the Up Next column.

"Yeah, I've got it on now, Luscious. I'm guessing what they're showing is where the entry used to be. Other than the oil slick on the gravel, there's nothing I'm seeing that would suggest it's Roxy's place."

"The house is toast, Dev. Someone must have set it on fire this morning. That's a quiet road, no close neighbors. The place could have burned for a couple of hours before anyone noticed. Someone breaks in, squirts an accelerant all over, and lights it. About all they can do is try to contain the fire, hopefully stop it from spreading into the woods."

"Has Roxy seen this?"

"Yeah, we were watching it in bed."

In bed. In the middle of the afternoon. Good for them, I guess.

"She's talking about going up there once she's dressed. I suppose I'll go with her," Luscious said.

"I'll head up there in a bit, once the rush hour calms down. No sense in hurrying. I'm thinking we're not going to be able to get that close with all the fire equipment."

"That's the same thing I told her, but she wants to get up there. Can't say as I blame her. I guess the place came furnished, but she still had a lot of personal items, clothes that sort of thing."

"I'd say there's a pretty good chance all of that has been destroyed, Luscious."

"I suppose, good thing you invited her over last night."

"Invited her? Luscious, I didn't invite her over. She was on my front porch at four in the morning ringing the doorbell. Tell you the truth I was more than a little surprised she didn't call you and get directions. I guess she didn't have your phone number. But I didn't invite her. I wouldn't try and sneak into your territory."

"Mmm, thank you, Dev. That makes me happy. I'll see you up there," Luscious said and hung up.

"Sounds like that maybe wasn't the best of news," Louie said.

"Well, it looks like, after all the bullshit of the last forty-eight hours, Roxy's place is in the process of burning to the ground."

"Arson?"

"That would be my guess. Not that it's confirmed by any means, but what are the odds? Someone somewhere is benefiting from this. My guess, it's the Massinni family. They probably wanted to burn the place down all along."

"Maybe," Louie said. "If you did some due diligence on the insurance, that might answer some questions. If it was insured for some number over value, maybe that was the cause, but that just doesn't seem to add up. Why go through all the hassle of getting Roxy out of there only to burn the place down?"

Twenty-two

As I drove up to North Oaks, Louie's words continued to bounce around in my thick skull. "It just didn't make any sense." I had to agree.

The road going past Roxy's place was blocked a half-mile from the last intersection before you came to the bend in the road. There was a patrol car parked across the road with a North Oaks cop leaning against the side of the squad car. He had a McDonald's bag resting on the hood of the squad car, and he was eating what looked like a Quarter Pounder with cheese. When I pulled alongside, he quickly tossed the remainder of the meal into the bag, swallowed, and smiled.

"Sorry, sir. Afraid there's been a fire up ahead. The road is temporarily blocked. Should be opened up by tomorrow morning."

"Yeah, I saw it on the news. I got a call from the woman who lives there." I purposely didn't use the term owner. "I'm supposed to meet her up at the house. I'm a private investigator. I told her there wouldn't be anything to see, but you know how they can be."

He nodded and asked for some ID. I pulled out my wallet and handed him my driver's license along with my PI license.

After a moment, he handed them back to me and said, "Okay. Just stay at least a hundred feet back from the firetrucks. They're in the process of winding down. Two have already left, but there are still hoses and equipment scattered all over, so please be careful."

"Thanks," I said and pulled around his squad car. I drove down along the bend in the road. The moment I saw the first firetruck, I pulled onto the shoulder and parked. I walked toward the scene, thinking as I went that the idiots from last night must have parked back here somewhere and scattered into the woods in an effort to surprise us.

There were three firetrucks still on site. Two of them looked to be more finished than not. The crews were busy wrapping up hoses and stacking equipment. A couple of guys were sharing coffee from a thermos. They looked at me and nodded but didn't say anything. I walked past and stood across the road from where the house used to be. A hose was mounted to a ladder directing a blast of water down below. The only things I could see that suggested a structure had even been there were the two chimneys from the fireplaces in the living room and a sidewalk that suddenly just stopped. Nothing else seemed to be left. Despite the stream of water, there was still smoke rising from the what I presumed would be a pile of rubble.

"Was this your place?" a voice from behind asked.

I turned around to see a man with a weathered face and a white mustache. I pegged him at late forties, maybe fifty. His face had an element of soot that stopped in a straight line across his forehead where his fire helmet must have been. He'd taken his helmet off and now carried it under his left arm. He still wore the coat and boots.

"Hi, my name's Dev Haskell," I said and extended my hand. "I'm a private investigator. I don't live here, but I spoke with the woman who does, and she's going to be meeting me here shortly. Hopefully, in the next thirty or forty-five minutes. I was just up here yesterday. Everything seemed fine."

"A private investigator? What's that about?"

"Nothing to do with this." I pointed to where the smoke was rising. From where we stood just across the road, there wasn't even rubble to see. "You guys have any idea what happened? A gas explosion or something?"

He shook his head. "Too soon to say. The investigators will do some preliminary work late this evening, but they'll really get into it tomorrow. As far as you know, there was no one in the structure?"

I shook my head. "I don't think so. She lived with a little white dog, and they weren't here. No children or elderly folks."

"What's her name?"

"Roxanne LaRue. Like I said, she should be here shortly. I wish I could tell you more. I only met her a few days ago. I'll give you a yell when she comes. Your name is?"

"Schuyler. Mike Schuyler. We should be getting two of these rigs out of here shortly. Best to stay on this side of the road until we're out of here."

"Sure thing, Mike. Nice to meet you. Hopefully, no one fighting the blaze was injured."

"No, knock on wood. Everyone's accounted for. Nice meeting you. What'd you say your name was again?"

"Haskell, Dev Haskell."

"Got it. Take care," he said and walked over to one of the trucks finishing up.

Maybe fifteen minutes later, Luscious and Roxy walked around the bend. Roxy's eyes seemed to get bigger with every step. She had Madame on a leash, and she reached down to pick her up. She held the dog against her shoulder like a baby and looked like she was in shock.

One of the rigs honked its horn, and three guys quickly climbed in. A moment later, it drove off. Two men boarded the other rig, and it looked like it was about to leave. Mike Schuyler was talking to the driver. Both of them were laughing.

"Hey Dev, you been here long?" Luscious asked.

"Hi, guys. Not quite a half hour. That rig over there is about ready to leave. I guess there were five of them here at one time. It's pretty much over. I was talking to one of the firemen. He said they'd have investigators do some preliminary stuff this evening before they really start in tomorrow."

"Oh. My. God. What's left to investigate? It's just a hole in the ground," Roxy said.

Twenty-three

It was dusk before the last firetruck eventually left. We watched as it disappeared down the road before anyone said anything.

"What do you think?" Luscious said.

"Let's check it out," I said.

"You guys go ahead. I think we'll just stay over here," Roxy said. She was still holding Madame on her shoulder. For her part, Madame appeared to be sound asleep.

Luscious and I crossed the road and made our way up the sidewalk to where the entry once stood. The fire crew had placed metal poles at either end and strung black and red plastic tape across the length with the words 'DANGER DO NOT CROSS' in red letters. We ducked under the tape. Once we were past the gravel parking area, the ground was muddy from all the water that had been poured onto the site. We stood at the end of the sidewalk and peered over the edge.

"Oh, man. What a mess," I said.

"There's nothing left," Luscious said.

He was right. Other than a pile of charred rubble, there literally was nothing left. I could make out the burnt remains of a couch and the refrigerator. One of the granite countertops from the kitchen jutted out from the rubble. A porcelain toilet lay on its side. The plastic soil pipe was long gone, no doubt melted. The air still smelled smoky, and I had a slightly charred taste in my mouth.

Beyond the pile of rubble, what remained of the deck was face down and more burned than not. It was in the mud about two feet from the edge of the pond. The gas grill was next to it, bent and smashed. The hinged cover on the grill had snapped off. About twenty feet off to the right was all that remained of the grill's propane tank, just the top but no hose. Obviously, it had exploded in the fire. The cinder block walls on three sides were still standing, but they appeared severely bowed and definitely not safe.

"Well, I guess that pretty much saves us the hassle of having to recover any items. There's nothing left to recover."

"I can't imagine what you're going to tell Roxy," I said.

"Me? Why do I have to be the one to tell her?"

"Because you spent a good chunk of time, yesterday and today, getting up close and very personal with her in the sack. You obviously know her a lot better than I do. Besides, I'm not very good at that sort of thing anyway."

"Is there a way to get down there and get some of my stuff?" Roxy called from the far side of the road.

"Come on. You might as well tell her," I said.

Luscious gave me a look but didn't say anything as we headed back across the road. Luscious reached out and petted Madame asleep on Roxy's shoulder

"Can we use the stairs, or should we go down the hill over on the side?" Roxy said.

"Well, I don't think using the stairs is going to work, they don't exist anymore, and I'm not so sure about taking the hill down there," Luscious said.

"But I've still got a ton of clothes, my laptop, and all sorts of stuff I need to get out of there."

"Well, um, what was it you were saying, Dev?"

After a very long moment, Roxy said, "Dev?"

I shot Luscious a look, then said, "To be honest, Roxy, there's nothing left. Everything is destroyed. The staircase is gone, the kitchen's gone, the bathrooms no longer exist. The TV is melted, your clothes are nothing but a pile of ashes, there's no furniture. The only things left are the fireplace chimneys, and they're going to have to be torn down. Sorry."

"But there must be something left, somewhere."

"I wouldn't bet on it. Just some scorched wood and you can kind of see one of the granite countertops from the kitchen."

"I need to see for myself," Roxy said. She handed Madame over to Luscious and headed across the road.

"You mind going with her, Dev? I don't think Madame should be exposed to that kind of devastation."

"Give her to me."

"She'll be more comfortable with me, Dev."

"Oh my God," Roxy cried as she leaned over the edge.

I ran across the road and grabbed her by the belt loops on her blue jeans just before she began to slip down the muddy slope.

Twenty-four

We were all seated in my living room. Seated wasn't exactly the term. Roxy was stretched out on the couch. I sat on a footstool, and Luscious was nodding off in the wingback chair. He was still holding Madame, and she appeared to be sound asleep. Morton had climbed upstairs almost an hour ago. A plate of crackers and some old cheese I found in the back of my refrigerator were resting on a cutting board on the coffee table in case anyone had been interested.

No one was.

"I just can't believe it," Roxy said for the umpteenth time and took a sip of her vodka and tonic. It was her fourth or fifth glass.

"Well, I think it's time to consider the alternative. What if you and Madame had been caught in the fire? By the look of things, I'd say there was a pretty good chance you never would have made it out. I'm sorry about your clothes and things, but at the end of the day all of that can be replaced."

"Replaced? I lost my graduation prom dress from high school. That can't be replaced. And what about my kindergarten class picture? Where do I get another one of those? Fan mail from big tippers when I danced, it's not like I know where any of those guys live. Well, maybe a couple of them, but not the rest." She shook her head, drained her glass, and held the empty out to me. I tried to ignore it, but she wiggled it from side to side. "Dev, I'm empty."

"Maybe you've had enough. You don't want to wake up with a headache tomorrow, do you?"

"It's too late to worry about that."

"Luscious is already asleep. Maybe if you just closed your eyes you—"

"He's just resting up for later tonight because he knows what's in store. Interested?"

"Let me fill that glass for you," I said and took her glass out to the kitchen. So my life had come to this. I used to joke and say I just wanted my dates drunk enough so they couldn't testify. Now, I wanted Roxy to pass out and just go to sleep. I filled the glass with ice, poured in tonic, added a drop of vodka, and headed back into the living room.

"Here you—" I immediately shut up and quietly set the glass on the coffee table. Roxy's eyes were closed, and she was softly snoring. I turned off the lights, left a lamp on in the hallway, and tiptoed upstairs. Just in case she made it this far, I turned on the lights in the guest room and left the door open. Then I headed into my room and locked the door.

Morton woke me around six the following morning. I got dressed and quietly headed downstairs. Luscious and Roxy were still in the living room, snoring. Only now Luscious was on the couch, Roxy was on top of him, and his jeans were draped over her. I didn't feel like staring. Madame was waiting for us at the back door. I let both dogs out, made a pot of coffee, and filled the food and water dishes. At seven, I went up the street to the restaurant/bakery and bought a cinnamon apple coffee cake.

Luscious strolled into the kitchen a little after eight, fortunately, he had his jeans on. "Mmm, Dev, I could smell that coffee."

"Help yourself, man. Mugs are in the cabinet right in front of you."

He poured himself a coffee and sat down on a stool. "So what do you think we should do?"

"I'm not quite following. What do you mean?"

"You know, with Roxy? What are we going to do with her?"

"No offense, Luscious, but you're the guy who has kind of been in a relationship with her for the past seventy-two hours."

"Relationship might be too strong a word, Dev. I mean we've certainly enjoyed each other's company, but that was more a spur of the moment thing."

"Oh, I don't know, man. She sought you out, and if you don't mind my saying, you certainly seemed to enjoy various aspects of her company."

"Well, yeah, but you know, that doesn't necessarily mean a relationship. It's, I don't know, maybe more like just lucky timing or something."

"Lucky timing?"

"Yeah, like getting a free drink when you walk into a bar 'cause you're the hundredth customer. Or, getting dealt the King of Hearts and suddenly you're throwing down a royal flush and cashing out of the game. You picking up what I'm putting down?"

"Yeah, I think so. But, she's gonna need a place to land, and it would seem to make a lot more sense that she go with you instead of staying here with me."

"I don't have that kind of room at my place, and besides, I got my mother staying with me at the moment."

"Your mom, when did that start?"

"Couple of weeks back."

"She okay? She got some medical problem or something?"

"Humf. She's just fine. She's there because she thinks I need a little direction in my life. And believe me, she's not afraid to give it to me. If you can believe this, last week we had the minister over for dinner. Brother Theo."

"How'd that go?"

"Actually, way better than I expected. He just wanted dinner then told her he was going to have a private chat with me. Of course, she just beamed when he sat me down in the living room. She's watching out the kitchen door, and he places his hands on my head. All he does is, he whispers and says, 'Thanks for having me over for dinner.' Then we pray for a minute or so, and he wants to get my inside scoop on the Vikings season this fall."

"What'd you tell him?"

"I told him to bet on them winning every game until the middle of October, and then they'd be worn out, just like every year." We both laughed at that then Luscious said, "I'm sorry, Dev, and don't get me wrong. I'd love to have her over, but my mother would never speak to me again. Ever. What about your girlfriend?"

"Girlfriend?"

"Yeah. That woman who said they were friends since being little kids."

"Oh, you mean Heidi. Yeah, funny thing, she laughed and made it very clear Roxy staying with her just was not going to happen."

"So what are you going to do?"

"I honestly don't know."

Twenty-five

Against my better judgement, I left Luscious in charge. A little after nine that morning, Morton and I headed down to the office. Louie wandered in thirty minutes later. I'd been watching a woman put on her makeup in one of the apartments across the street, hoping she might drop the towel wrapped around her. As Louie entered, I set the binoculars down on my desk.

"You two are in kind of early. Everything all right?" He tossed his briefcase on his picnic table desk and poured himself a coffee.

"Yeah, everything's fine as long as you don't go into detail."

"What's the news on the fire?"

"They're starting the investigation this morning, probably on site by now. I don't know if they'll ever determine anything. Once the firetrucks pulled out last night, we could get a little closer and take a look."

"And?"

"And there was literally nothing left to look at, not so much as a stick of furniture. The only things remaining were the two fireplace chimneys and a lot of charred lumber. I would guess the chimneys will be torn down in pretty short order. As far as any personal effects remaining, it didn't look too promising. You'd literally have to sift through the ashes to find anything."

"She going to camp out at Heidi's?"

"I only wish. Heidi smiled at me and gave a definite no. I asked Luscious, he and Roxy seem to have something going, but apparently, his mother's staying with him right now, so Roxy there wouldn't work out. Looks like I'm going to be stuck with her for the time being. Say, Louie, you wouldn't want to consider—"

"No, don't even go there."

"You sure? She seems amenable to just about anyone—"

"No, thanks for thinking of me but no."

"Well then, can you help me with this? I want to find this Sheldon Smeet character. Get some answers on that property of Roxy's. You know anyone over at Third National who could maybe give me an idea where he is?"

Louie seemed to think for a long moment then began to fan through his Rolodex. "I know two guys who I think might still be there. From what I hear, just about everyone who's able is jumping ship. One of the guys may have been fired last year but let me check."

Louie read a Rolodex card, punched in the numbers on his phone, then held up his index finger, signaling 'Wait a moment.' Eventually, he shook his head then said, "Hey Jimmy, Louie Laufen here. Long time no see,

I think it's my turn to buy. Give me a call back. I got a question for you."

He hung up the phone, and as he flipped through more cards, he said, "Both these guys are pretty sharp. I hope they haven't bailed out yet. Ahh, here we go."

He dialed and a moment later said, "Hi, Gary, Louie Laufen. Just checking in. You free to talk? What's the word? Yeah, I've heard that. Really? When? Well, are you free for lunch? How about the Crow's Nest? Little before noon? Oh, yeah, that'll work. I'll see you then, and I'm buying."

Louie hung up and said, "Meeting him for lunch. He's a smart guy. He didn't want to say anything in the office, and I can't blame him. We'll meet him for lunch at noon and get the lowdown."

"You sure he'll be okay with me being there?"

"Yeah, he said he's out of Third National at the end of the week and heading to some private firm. Perfect time to get the inside scoop before he has a chance to calm down. He's a good guy, and there's a pretty decent chance he'll have the lowdown on this scumbag, Sheldon Smeet."

Twenty-Six

The Crow's Nest wasn't that far from the office, but we took my Jeep Cherokee anyway. It wasn't a place I went to very often, and when I did, it was always for lunch. The noontime crowd was made up of working folks with a hankering for simple, solid food. There was an end of the workday crowd who began showing up for happy hour around four, but anyone with any brains was out of there by half-past seven. Right around eight in the evening, the crowd changed to shiftless jerks and troublemakers, and even with a solid menu and stiff drinks, most folks didn't need the hassle.

The place smelled of meat and onions frying. We settled into a corner booth fifteen minutes early. Louie ordered a whiskey with a beer back. I was tempted but stuck with water. Gary Peterson wandered in about ten minutes later. He looked somewhat familiar, and I thought maybe I'd seen him on the news or featured in a newspaper article. He was dressed in a grey suit, a white shirt that was unbuttoned at the collar, and a loosened red, white, and blue tie. He waved to us and hurried over to the booth.

"Hey, Louie, long time no see," he said and shook hands with Louie. He eyed me, not suspiciously, and said, "Are you Louie's officemate. That P.I.?"

"Yeah, nice to meet you, Gary. Dev Haskell," I said as we shook hands.

"I hope I'm not under investigation." He smiled but looked like he was only half-joking.

"Nah, you're safe. Well, unless you've been setting houses on fire." All three of us laughed, but Gary gave me a second look that suggested my comment had registered somewhere in the back of his mind. He hung his coat on a hook attached to the booth and slid in next to Louie. He ordered a Coke. We ordered lunch and chatted about nothing for a few minutes. Then Louie said, "I left a message for Jimmy, but I haven't heard back."

Gary shook his head. "Jimmy bailed a couple of months ago. The guy he reported to was a real prick and had it in for Jimmy. You know how squared away he is, and finally, he just couldn't take it anymore."

"Funny, his office number still had his voice message saying he was currently unavailable. I left a message telling him to call me."

"Just another indication of how things are falling apart at the old Third. Two months and you still get his voice message? Time was not too long ago that would have been changed the day before he cleaned out his desk."

"Did he end up somewhere?" I asked.

"He got picked up by a hedge fund, big raise, sterling reputation. I talked with him a couple of weeks back. He sounded a hell of a lot happier. I gotta tell you, all these investigations going on, everyone is wound tighter than a five-day clock. I can't wait for Friday to get here. I'm cleaning out my desk and moving to a financial firm, James and Emmett."

"They're a class act, too," Louie said. "Well done, you."

Of course, I'd never heard of them before. "Supposed to have a good reputation," I lied, not wanting to seem like I was in the dark.

"I tell you it's quickly getting to the point where you're going to be thought of as guilty just by having worked there. Once all the indictments are handed down, you'd be better off telling potential employers you were out of work for three years rather than admit you worked for F-ing Third National."

"Are you expecting a lot of indictments?" I asked.

"First round is most likely going to be five people, but I've got a feeling that's going to be just the tip of the iceberg. It's one of the reasons I'm jumping ship. Well, me and a hell of a lot of other people. That doesn't count Jimmy and the gang that had enough sense to get out two months back. What was a steady drip of good folks leaving has turned into a heavy stream, and it'll become a flood the moment those indictments are handed down."

"Any idea who's on the list?" Louie asked just as our lunches arrived. Louie had some a double cheeseburger with bacon, Gary had a regular cheeseburger and onion rings, and I had two chicken fajitas.

Gary lifted the top on his cheeseburger and smiled. He squirted mayonnaise onto his plate, dipped half the burger in and took a bite. "Mmm, they make the best burgers here. On the indictment list? Certainly Smeet, Eldon Woodward, that jackass Michelson, Tracey, and Kenny Barnes. Two possibles would be Jack Griffin and Madeline Thompson, but I think they'll hold off on those last two until the second round."

"I thought Sheldon Smeet was going to be the only one," I said.

Gary smiled, dipped his burger in the mayo, and took a bite. "Mmm, Smeet is certainly in charge of the criminal empire, but he couldn't have done it without help. A lot of help. They were all very nicely rewarded, and now they're about to pay a very large price. Most of us can't get far enough away, soon enough. It's going to get really ugly, and like I said, the mere fact of guilt by association is going to come into play when you're trying to put food on the table. It's going to be a house of cards, and the folks I just named will be forming a line to cooperate with the federal authorities if they haven't done so already."

"I'm working a case that may have a connection with Sheldon Smeet. What can you tell me about him?"

"Smeet? If someone is in business with Smeet, you look hard enough, their hands are going to be dirty. It's just the way he operates." Gary dragged the remaining half of his burger through the mayo, crammed a large bite into his mouth, and squirted more mayo onto his plate. He chewed for a long moment, thinking.

"Okay, Smeet. First of all, don't underestimate him. Yeah, he's going to be indicted, but it's way overdue, and he's just now getting nailed. He's probably fought off a half-dozen investigations over the last decade. His problem, well not the only problem, but the one that finally got his ass in the ringer is he came to believe he was invincible, untouchable. If he had quit while he was ahead, we wouldn't be here having this conversation. Is he a crook, a cheat, a real jerk? Yeah, absolutely, but the man is not stupid." He took another bite of his burger and smiled. "Mmm, this is just what I needed. Really good."

"Smeet still come into the office?"

"Humf. I'm not sure. If he does, he sneaks in late at night when no one is around, and he heads out before sunrise. I'm only half-kidding. I haven't seen him, and I don't know anyone who has seen him in probably the last month. He's got a lake place up north. I think it's on the White Fish chain, up near Cross Lake. He used to spend a lot of time there, maybe that's where he is now, just waiting for the ax to fall. With today's technology, he doesn't have to be in his office. As long as he's got internet access, he could be anywhere. I do know he had to turn his passport over to the feds. So theoretically, he's still in the country."

"So his lake place might be where he's at," I said.

"Possibly. I mean, I honestly don't know where he is. But the lake would be my guess."

"Would you know the address up there? My client has to send him some insurance paperwork. She wanted to have it delivered to his home, but if he's not there, what's the point?"

"He might be up there. I'm really not sure. Hell, he could be renting a penthouse out in Vegas right now and throwing a big party for all I know."

"The name Massinni ring any bells with you? Dante Massinni?"

"Yeah, warning bells. You investigating that crook?"

"Not really. My client, actually she's just a friend of a friend, and I was helping her with a problem. Anyway, she's got a place up in North Oaks and yesterday—"

"That damn fire, right? God, I can't wait for Friday to get here and I'm officially out of there. I never met this Dante guy, but the reputation isn't what you'd call sterling. That was part of the trouble when Smeet got into thinking he was untouchable. He lined himself up with this character, and by extension, the guy's entire organization. Anyone would find that bastard guilty from the first look you give him. A bunch of million-dollar properties and some very questionable loan practices. On that North Oaks property, from what I hear, Smeet completely bypassed the loan review board and guaranteed funding to someone who could not have qualified. Kind of a version of, if you owe enough money to your lender, they have to work with you. Well, that Massinni character owes more than enough money, and not only does Smeet have to work with him, he more or less controls Smeet. We're all about to see how well that's worked out."

Gary made a show of checking the time on his watch. "Oh, man, I better head back to the office. Don't want to give them a reason to cut the defined contribution to my pension account at the last minute. You sure I can't pay for my lunch?" he said, sliding out of the booth and slipping his coat back on.

"No, Gary, we got it," Louie said. "Glad you're getting out of there before the flood gates open. I pity the folks that try to hang on."

"You're telling me. Dev, nice to finally meet you. Louie's told me a lot of things about you."

"Yeah, well don't believe any of it. I'm really a nice guy." I pulled a business card from my wallet and handed it to Gary. "If you get the opportunity, I'd really appreciate it if you could find Smeet's lake address and give me a quick call."

"Let me think about that. I wouldn't want to be linked in any way to his illegal undertakings," he half-joked. Everyone laughed, and we watched as Gary walked out of the place. He stopped and had a thirty-second conversation with two guys sitting at a table near the front door.

"Man, he's gonna dodge a bullet on this one. I'm glad he's getting out of there and landing with a top-notch firm. He'll be going places, and I don't mean a federal institution," Louie said.

"You think he was involved in any of that Smeet stuff?"

"Gary? No, not a chance. He's a straight shooter. But he was right, anyone who hangs on there is sooner or later going to be tarred with the same brush, and no one is going to want to hire them. I've seen it happen before. You bust your ass and then you're found just as guilty only because you worked there."

"You think he'll call me with that address up north?"

"Yeah, if he can get it, he will. You probably didn't pick up on it, but as long as I've known him, he's been a straight shooter who's aimed for the top. Smeet and his crew held him back for just that reason. He's a straight shooter. There's no love lost, and I wouldn't want Gary pissed off at me."

The bill came, Louie handed it to me, and we left.

Twenty-seven

A call listed as 'Unknown' came through on my cellphone about two hours later. I answered in my standard way, "Haskell Investigations."

"Dev Haskell, please."

"Gary?"

"Yeah, Dev. I wasn't sure that was you."

"Yeah, I'm working two jobs. I answer the phone, and I clean the office."

He gave a short laugh. "I've got Smeet's lake place address for you. I would appreciate it if you would keep this to yourself and not mention it to anyone, not even Louie. There's such an undercurrent of double-cross currently flowing through this place I would prefer not to be a part of it. As a matter of fact, I'm calling you from a payphone just to play it extra safe."

"I can understand that. We were both saying how lucky you are to be getting out of there in time."

"Yeah, I'm thinking I'm going to make it just under the wire." I wrote down the address as he gave it to me, thanked him, and hung up.

I took a pass on Louie's offer to join him over at The Spot. As Morton and I headed home, I kept my fingers crossed, hoping that Roxy had found somewhere to land. No such luck. I pulled into the driveway behind Roxy's Audi I heard music blasting from inside the house the moment I exited the car. She had only pulled a little way into the driveway, so my car ended up blocking the sidewalk. A grocery store circular in a plastic bag with a red rubber band around it was lying on the sidewalk leading to my front porch. The mailbox had four envelopes and two more circulars stuffed in it. The front door was unlocked and open about three inches.

As Morton and I stepped into the house, I could hear the windows vibrating from the music. Roxy was in my front room dancing by herself to some dreadful thing playing on the TV. She wore an earmuff hearing protection device on her head, and she was dancing, shaking her rear from side to side in time to the thundering beat. I have to say she wasn't hard to watch, in a sleazy sort of way. She wore a thong and a t-shirt. I took in the sight for a long moment before I turned off the TV. Roxy did about three more wonderful shakes of her perfect rear before she turned around.

"Oh, hi, Dev. What? You don't like listening to Desperate Bangers?"

"That's the band that was playing? Aptly named."

"They're one of my favorites."

"What'd you do today, Roxy?"

"Do?"

"Yeah. Did you talk to the fire department up in North Oaks? Did you drive up there to check it out? Did you look for a place to stay?"

I looked around the room. A couple of coffee mugs, a plate with the remnants of scrambled eggs and some silverware rested on the coffee table next to the crackers and cheese from the night before. I noticed the glass with the tonic and drop of vodka drink I'd left on the coffee table last night now sat empty. Luscious was nowhere to be found.

"I'm still in shock, and I've been trying to deal with that all day. Right now, I just feel like I'm adrift up in outer space, my safety cord has been cut, and I can't get back to the space capsule."

Oh man. "Is Luscious still here?"

"He got a call from his mother and had to go home."

The guy was over thirty, and his mother still had to direct him, not that he didn't need it. "Did you give him a ride?"

"No, he said he wanted to take the bus. Hey, what's the plan for dinner? Oh, and you're out of eggs and almost out of vodka."

"Thanks. How's the head?"

"Fortunately, I was able to sleep in this morning. Luscious was such a sweetheart. He tiptoed around and let me sleep, and then he kissed me goodbye and left me a note."

"What'd the note say?"

"Just what I told you that he tiptoed around, and he kissed me goodbye. Oh, and he mentioned that his mother called looking for him."

It had all the earmarks of Luscious fleeing the scene after three days of Roxy. I was quickly feeling like I was on my own. "Well look, why don't you clean up that stuff on the coffee table, and I'll see what I can make for dinner?"

"I didn't find a lot in the refrigerator, so you might have to do some grocery shopping. I left a note on the kitchen counter of some things you can pick up for me if you don't mind."

I didn't respond and headed into the kitchen. The dirty pan from scrambled eggs was still on the stove. Thankfully, the burner had been turned off. The sink had a number of dirty dishes in it, and a small but constant stream of water ran from the tap that was not quite completely turned off. God only knew how many hours that had been running. Fortunately, she hadn't plugged the drain, yet.

I opened my refrigerator ready to grab the package of hotdogs. The package was there, but it had been opened, and there was only one hotdog left. It had been unopened when I left this morning. I chalked that up to Luscious. I was more convinced than before that his mother hadn't called, he was just using that as his excuse to flee the scene. Who could blame him?

"I'm gonna hop in the shower," Roxy called from the stairs.

I was just glad to have her out of my sight for a few minutes. I let Morton out the back door to do his business. Madame was stretched out on the back steps, lying in the sun, no doubt thankful she was able to escape the poor attempt at music from the Desperate Bangers.

I sat at the kitchen counter and flipped through the mail. A letter from the Library Foundation, the Minnesota Park Service, someone running for office wanting a 'modest donation,' and then there was an envelope with my name handwritten and no address or stamp. The envelope was cream-colored and looked fancy. It was also perfumed -very nice perfume.

I opened it and pulled out a sheet of matching stationery. There, in elegant, feminine penmanship, was a note. It started with the day's date and read:

'Dear Dev,

Missed you and Morton this morning. I hope you merely forgot and haven't given up on my efforts to assist Morton as he learns the basics. I've time for him tomorrow morning if that would fit your schedule. It's important that we try to adhere to a regular schedule. It will make his efforts all that more productive.

Hope to see both of you soon,

Amanda'

Damn it, Morton probably didn't forget, but I sure did. I looked out the kitchen window. Morton and Madame were chasing one another around the backyard. I didn't have the heart to stop them, and besides, he could sure use the exercise. I headed out to the front of the house heard the shower running, and called upstairs, "Roxy, I'm going over to the neighbors for a minute."

I didn't get an answer and didn't want to interrupt her in the shower, so I headed out the door and around the block.

Twenty-eight

As I approached Amanda's place, I saw her sitting on her porch swing. She waved as I headed up the sidewalk and called, "Well, Dev. I was beginning to wonder what had happened to you. Is Morton all right?"

"Yeah, he's fine, chasing another dog around the backyard as we speak."

"Good, he needs that."

"Thanks for the note. I'm getting more involved in a case I don't want to be involved in, and it just completely slipped my mind this morning."

"How is his attitude?"

"Morton? Same as always. The guy is pretty laid back. I can have him over here tomorrow morning if that still works for you."

"That would be perfect. Oh, where are my manners? Can I offer you a glass of wine?" she said as she set her glass on a little end table. The glass was filled with white wine, and I could tell it was chilled because there was perspiration along the sides.

"Yeah, I'd love one, as long as I'm not intruding."

"Not at all, Dev. Wait here a moment, and I'll be right back." She hopped off the swing and hurried into the house.

The swing was made of oak and looked like it might comfortably seat three. There was an off-white cushion fitted across the length of the swing and three small embroidered pillows to place behind your back. I sat down and tried it out.

"Oh, perfect, great, make yourself comfortable," Amanda said, stepping out of the front door. I started to get up, but she said, "No, no stay seated. It's just perfect, isn't it?" She handed me a chilled glass of white wine. "Sometimes, in the evening, I like to sit here and watch the traffic go by. Maybe chat for a minute or two with one of my neighbors if they're out for a walk. I find it very relaxing."

"Yeah, I have to be honest. I've never thought of putting a swing up on my front porch, but I really like this."

"Of course, your street is just that much busier, and it's also a bus route, so you have even more noise. But here, this is so nice and almost private, even though anyone who goes by can see me."

I took a sip from the glass of wine. It was sparkling. White wine usually wasn't my thing, but it was actually pretty good. "Thanks for the glass of wine. It's very nice."

"You're very welcome. It's from Portugal. It's my favorite in the summer. I have to watch it Two glasses is my limit. It's so nice of you to stop by."

"I've had a crazy couple of days, and I just forgot about dropping Morton off. I appreciate you making time for us tomorrow morning."

"Happy to do it. I enjoy working with Morton. He's an absolute delight."

"Yeah, that's one of the words I occasionally use to describe him."

"Oh, don't be too hard on him. He's got a very outgoing personality, and he's quite curious."

I had to laugh. "What, he told you that?"

"Yes, in so many ways, he did."

"It's like you're the dog whisperer."

"I'll take that as a compliment. They oftentimes acquire the personality of their master. I'd say Morton has acquired yours."

"Oh, sorry to hear that," I said and laughed.

"I meant it as a compliment."

We chatted on for another twenty minutes, never discussing anything of import. Then Amanda said, "Mind if I ask you a business question?"

"No, not at all, what did you want to know?"

"You're a detective, right?"

"Well, technically a private investigator but yeah. I investigate everything from someone's spouse having an affair to maybe a robbery or insurance claims. I have a regular client who has me doing legwork on people who submit job applications to him. I check the routine information to make sure it's correct, credit ratings, that kind of thing. If a case concerns something the police are involved in, say an assault or, God forbid, a murder, I usually won't get involved. If only because I don't want to screw up an ongoing police investigation. What most people don't realize is that, contrary to what you see on TV, investigations are usually pretty slow moving and not all that exciting. I know some folks in the police department and on a rare occasion, I might help them with some aspect of an investigation." I didn't mention my longtime friend, Aaron LaZelle, or Detective Norris Manning, who had been trying for years to find a reason to send me to prison.

"You ever look for missing people?"

"I have."

"Did you find them."

"Most of the time. There have been a couple that clearly did not want to be found, and they were quite good at covering their trail. A few times, there was an issue of chemical abuse, drugs or alcohol, and the individual just disappeared below the radar. I had one where a guy went on a walk, not like around the block, but out west in Utah. He attempted a two-week trek through the wilderness, never to be seen again. He walked through some pretty rough terrain, and no remains were ever found. By all accounts, he was happily married, a college professor, two little kids. I'm thinking he probably had a serious fall, cracked his skull or maybe broke a leg or a hip and, unfortunately, died in the wilderness. No one has found him, yet, but I suspect someday, someone will. I found two girls up north a few years back, college girls, on a winter trek. When we discovered the bodies, they were stripped down to their underwear."

"They were raped?"

"That's what the thought was initially. But they froze to death, succumbed to hypothermia. When that occurs and the body begins to shut down, the natural defense system makes you feel like you're getting hotter. They actually ended up delirious and removed their own clothing. They weren't raped, which brought some relief to the families, but they did freeze to death. The weather at the time was minus forty, not a good idea to go on a seventeen-mile trek."

"Interesting."

"Yeah, in a sad sort of way. You sound like you might know someone who's missing."

She didn't answer for a long moment. "I have a younger sister. It's just the two of us. Our father died at a young age, and our mother raised us, she passed away three, no four years ago now."

"And your sister?"

"Oh, God, where to begin? She was always a free spirit. That term covers a lot of ground. Ever since she could walk, she's gone from one obsession to the next. Cartoons, movies, books, boys, vegan, gluten-free, chemicals. Her latest obsession is, or was, becoming a rock star."

"She go out to Hollywood or Vegas?"

"No, that's the funny thing. She stayed local, sang in a number of different bands, never really found her style, although she had a couple of decent reviews in the newspaper. She made a trip out to Sturgis, played some big gig there. A band from the coast offered her a try-out."

"Sturgis? The big motorcycle rally?"

"Yeah, that was two years ago. She faded from sight about six months after that, as soon as her lease was up on her apartment. I haven't heard from her since."

"Well, two things. If she left once her lease expired, that suggests she had at least the semblance of a plan. Maybe not what you or I would consider, but a plan nonetheless. The second thing would be, if she was serious about following the music thing, maybe she decided she wasn't going to get back in touch until she made it big."

"Your second version sounds more like her thought process, although all this time later, I don't know. Usually, she burnt out in two or three months on whatever the latest great idea was."

"If you want, I could do some checking around."

"You wouldn't mind? I, I could pay you something."

"Don't worry about that. How about we trade time? You work with Morton, and I'll try to track down your sister."

"Okay, yeah that would be great."

I drained my glass of wine. "I should probably head out. I've got a problem to deal with back at home."

"Not Morton, I hope."

"No, a friend of a friend. In fact, she sounds a bit like your sister, only crazier. Anyway, if you could line up some information on your sister, last known address, last job, a photo, whatever schooling she had. Maybe a list of friends, if you know any. I'll look into it."

"Oh thanks, Dev. I'll have it ready and organized for you when you drop off Morton tomorrow morning."

"Yeah, about that, I've got to run up to Cross Lake in the morning, and I may not be back until mid-afternoon, is that okay? Otherwise, I could get someone to pick him up if it's a hassle."

"So not a problem. I'd love the company. How about you don't show up until dinner time. Say six-thirty if that works for you?"

"Sounds great, but are you sure?"

"Positive. I'll plan on seeing you tomorrow morning. I better go get that information on my sister arranged, and thank you, Dev. This means a lot to me."

Twenty-nine

At least the door was closed and locked when I got back to my place. The shower was still running upstairs. Roxy was going to wash down the drain if she didn't get out of there soon. I headed into the kitchen and looked out the window. Madame and Morton were taking a break, stretched out in the late afternoon sun. It looked like they'd run each other to the point of exhaustion. A tennis ball and two chew toys lay on the ground between them.

I opened the refrigerator and took out the sole surviving hot dog, filled a pan with water, and set it on the stove. Amazingly, there were still some Bar-B-Que potato chips left, and I inhaled those then wolfed down the hot dog.

Roxy came downstairs a half-hour later all dressed up. "You already back from the grocery store, Dev?"

"Actually, no. I didn't go. I'm going to be traveling tomorrow. Hey, you think you could get me a copy of your insurance policy?"

"Insurance?" she said, sounding completely clueless.

"Yeah, your household policy. The one covering your personal items, furniture, maybe jewelry, even your yoga mat, things like that. You'll want to get in touch with the company just as soon as possible and let them know a claim is coming through. Make a laundry list of everything you lost. We can probably get an initial report from the fire department in the next week or so. That insurance payment obviously won't cover everything you lost, but it will help you get back on your feet."

"I should probably get one of those, that's a really good idea."

"Wait a minute, Roxy. Get one of those? Does that mean you didn't have an insurance policy to begin with?"

"Well, not yet, but if they're gonna give me some money, I certainly want to get one."

"It doesn't quite work like that."

"That doesn't sound fair. Who's going to pay for all my stuff that went up in smoke?"

"Well, if we can find your friend Sheldon Smeet, maybe he could tell us. You also need to find a place to land. I've got a bunch of guys coming here in a couple of days, and they're going to be using the guest room and probably the couch," I lied.

"Bunch of guys? I know how to make 'em feel welcome and give 'em a trip they'll never forget."

"Not this group, they're all religious ministers."

"Don't kid yourself, Dev. Those are the people who always pay top price."

It sounded like the voice of experience. "Not this group. You better find a place in the next couple of days. Maybe you could land at Heidi's. She's got a couple of spare rooms."

"Heidi? I love her to bits, but she's too tight control. Know what I mean?"

"I might have some idea."

"I'll check some places out. God, if this keeps up, I'm going to have to go back to work. Well, I better hit the road. I'll catch you later."

"I got you blocked in on the driveway, so let me back out. When you get home tonight, can you park on the street? I'm going to be leaving early tomorrow morning, and that way I won't have to wake you up."

"Yeah, not sure where I'll end up, but if I make it back here, I'll park out on the street, not a problem."

I followed her out to her car and pulled into the street then waved at her as she backed out and sped away. It was like saying goodnight to a sixteen-year-old, except Roxy was twenty years older and a lot less mature. I pulled back into the driveway. I stopped just beyond the public sidewalk, so there'd be no room for her to park in the driveway. As I headed back into the house, it dawned on me, I never gave her a set of keys to the place. Maybe that was a good idea and would hopefully serve as an incentive to find someplace else to land.

Thirty

Even though I told Roxy I had an early day, Morton and I were having breakfast in the kitchen at half-past eight. On my way into the shower, I'd checked the guest room. It was empty. I hurried downstairs to put the coffee on and glanced out on the street. Roxy's car was nowhere to be seen. She wasn't on the front porch or sleeping on the couch in my front room. I relaxed in the peace and quiet. I'd filled Morton's and Madame's food and water dishes, made blueberry pancakes for myself, and we enjoyed a leisurely breakfast.

I checked my emails. Sent a message to Louie, reminding him I was heading up north, hopefully to find Sheldon Smeet. I sent a message to Luscious, telling him I was heading out of town and warning him that Roxy was still looking for a place to stay. I double-checked the locks on the backdoor. I locked the front door on the way out and put Morton and Madame in the back seat. They remained back there during the sixty-second drive to Amanda's. They barked, and their tails began wagging as we pulled up in front.

Amanda was sitting on the porch swing, sipping a mug of coffee. She waved to us as we pulled up, and

Morton barked back. I tucked Madame under my arm, hooked Morton's leash, and tried my best to get him to heel on the way up to the front porch. It didn't work.

"Well, hello, Morton. It's so good to see you. We're going to have the whole day together just the two of us. And who is this?" she said, giving Madame a nice rub behind the ears.

"This is Madame. She belongs to the friend of a friend I mentioned yesterday. She didn't come home last night, so I've got Madame. I'm going to have to take her up north with me."

"What? Why don't you leave her with me?"

"Oh, I can't do that. She's—"

"No, leave her. We'll get along fine. It's a lot better than having her in the car for three hours up and three hours back. Honest, Dev, leave her. I'd love it."

"You sure?"

"Yeah, it's so not a problem."

"Okay, if you're sure. I really appreciate you doing this, Amanda."

"Don't be silly. Can I interest you in a cup of coffee?"

"Oh gee, thanks, that's nice, and I would love to, but I should probably head out. It's going to be after the noon hour before I get to my destination."

"Not a problem, do you want the information on my sister?"

"Actually, would it work if we went over it tonight? I'm going to drive, hopefully meet with a guy, and then get back in the car and drive down here. I hate to have that information sitting in the car and if something happened to it, well you know . . ."

"That makes perfect sense. We can go through it over a glass of wine."

"Sounds good. Can I bring anything tonight?"

"Just you and an empty stomach. I'm making lasagna."

"Sounds perfect, I'll see you tonight. Say, just in case, can I have your phone number? If something delays me, I don't want you wondering what in the world happened."

I input her phone number on my cellphone, said goodbye to Morton and Madame, who couldn't have cared less, and headed north.

Thirty-one

It was the middle of the week, the traffic was moderate and growing better the further north I traveled. I'd put in the address Gary Peterson had given me on my cellphone GPS and occasionally heard a response. Usually telling me to continue on in the direction I was headed.

I passed through the small town of Cross Lake and proceeded up a two-lane county road. I passed three different lakes along the way. It was quite apparent that the idea of a lake cabin, at least in this area, was something in the past. The homes I saw were three-story mansions with at least two very expensive boats, gorgeous lawns, and gardens. My memory of coming up here as a kid and fishing for sunfish in a rowboat might as well have included sleeping in a covered wagon.

"Turn left at the next intersection and continue on for one point two miles."

I did just that, checking my odometer for the one point two miles. At just about that point, my GPS said, "Your destination is on the right."

There was a gated entrance that led into a forest of birch trees. The gate was severely smashed where it used to hook up to a steel support. I pulled to a stop, got out, and looked at the gate. It had clearly been rammed by some vehicle. Based on the height and the amount of damage, I guessed a truck or heavy vehicle of some kind had smashed it. A broken chain lay off to the side. There were footprints along with the tire marks suggesting that, after someone had smashed the gate and broken the chain, they got out and pulled the gate open and closed the gate behind them as they left.

I backed up, drove down the road about thirty yards to a slight clearing, and parked. There was a rural mailbox mounted on a post next to the gate. I opened it and took out a handful of envelopes. They were all addressed to Sheldon Smeet at a St. Paul address and then stamped with the date they had been forwarded up here. Based on the stamps, it was three days' worth of mail.

I didn't touch the gate when I slipped through. I stayed maybe ten feet into the woods as I walked parallel to the trail leading in. The trail wound through the birch woods for a good distance. It went up and down four slight rises until I saw a lake in the distance and off to the side what looked like a Swiss chalet. White stucco and beams, three stories tall with a red tile roof. Another lake mansion, this one imported from the Alps.

Lace curtains hung in the multi-paned windows. I knelt down and watched for a long period but couldn't detect any movement. There was one vehicle parked in front of what appeared to be a triple garage. The car was a dark blue Mercedes. From where I was, I couldn't see the model. Whatever the model, it looked expensive. It also looked like it hadn't been driven in a while. There were a number of leaves scattered across the windshield and the hood. After another ten minutes, I slowly approached through the woods, checking for any movement. All was quiet.

I tucked my pistol inside my belt, untucked my shirt to cover it, and walked out of the woods into the parking area. The sun was out, some birds were chirping, and a couple of large flies buzzed around me for a few steps before taking off. Still no movement around the place. I watched for curtains to move in the windows but never saw anything.

I headed for the front door. I walked up a brick path with a small hedge on either side. As I approached the front door, I noticed it was open maybe two or three inches. There were a dozen panes of glass in the door, three across and four up. The lower right-hand pane was broken, leaving a hole large enough for someone to reach inside and unlock the door. I pulled the pistol out of my belt, stepped off to the side, and pushed the door open with my foot. The door creaked as it swung open.

I peeked in, looked left and right, and didn't see anyone. I stepped in cautiously. My ears strained to pick up a sound, nothing except for a few more large flies buzzing around.

The room was two stories high with a large granite fireplace at one end and a second-floor balcony overlooking the room with four closed doors. The fireplace had a large split log mantel that ran its length. Over the fireplace was another painting like the two in Roxy's place. A grey-haired guy with a red nose, Sheldon Smeet. Two brown leather couches sat perpendicular to the fireplace on a blue and red oriental rug. Brass floor lamps stood at both ends of the leather couches, and a coffee table rested between them. The coffee table was a log that had been split lengthwise then stained and polished. A crystal glass with a harp cut on the side and a trace of lipstick around the edge rested on the coffee table.

I stuck my head in the kitchen. Gorgeous cherry wood cabinets hung on the walls. The black granite countertops displayed vodka and bourbon bottles resting next to an ice cube tray. Grey Goose and twenty-five-year-old Rip Van Winkle bourbon appeared to be the brands of choice. There was an office behind the kitchen, a number of files were stacked on a large desk and lay open. The drawers on the desk were pulled open. The computer keyboard was illuminated, but the screen appeared off. I pushed the shift key on the keyboard, and the screen came to life, displaying a box to write your password and log into the computer.

I walked back through the living room and headed up the staircase. There were more flies buzzing around as I climbed the stairs. I picked up an unpleasant smell that grew stronger as I climbed the stairs. The first two rooms I checked were empty and, by all appearances, looked to be guest rooms. Each room had a bathroom attached. The third room appeared to be the master bed-room.

Due to the smell, I knew what I was going to find. A granite fireplace was opposite a four-poster bed with what looked like white silk sheets. The sheets were pulled back at an angle on one side of the bed, just like a fancy hotel would do. Sheldon Smeet, at least I presumed it was him, was seated in a rocking chair in front of the fireplace. His right hand was missing, and the blunt end of his wrist was wrapped in what looked like a blood-stained t-shirt. I had a ton of questions I wanted to ask him, but what was the point? He was dead.

Thirty-two

He was with the Crow Wing County Sheriff's Department. As soon as I found Sheldon Smeet dead in the rocking chair, I was pretty sure I wasn't going to get any answers from him. I walked back to the entrance gate and called 911. It took twenty minutes before the first two cars arrived within a minute of one another with sirens blaring and lights flashing. I had the feeling they may have both been stopped at some coffee shop for a break. Life being what it was, they probably had to leave before their coffee arrived.

The guy talking to me had been the third car to arrive on the scene. He stood maybe six-two or three, blonde hair, piercing blue eyes, and a soft voice. Don't let the voice fool you. He looked like he'd have no problem taking me on with one hand tied behind his back.

"Did you touch anything?" Officer Smolinski asked.

"I touched the return key on the computer keyboard in the office. Other than that, I don't think I touched anything except to push the front door open with my foot."

"And you said you're a Private Investigator?"

"Yes, sir. I've got a license in my wallet I can show you if you want."

"Yeah, might as well take a look."

So far, so good. I planned to remain on my best behavior. I didn't need a hassle, or for that matter, a broken nose. Once I'd called 911, I walked down the road, drove my car back to the front gate, and parked on the shoulder. I put my pistol back in the glove compartment, slipped on the trigger lock, and waited. I handed Smolinski my P.I. license, along with my driver's license and my conceal and carry permit.

"You're carrying?" he said, looking at the permit.

"No, I'm not. I've got a pistol in my glove compartment with a trigger lock. But just in case you guys want to check my car, it's all above board."

He nodded and said, "Tell me what you're doing up here."

I told him about the fire at Roxy's. I said we couldn't reach Sheldon Smeet in his office, and so I decided to drive up to Cross Lake. "As soon as I saw the damage to the front gate and the broken chain on the ground, I became concerned. So I left my car here and walked up to the house. I noticed the window on the front door had been broken, and the door was slightly open. I pushed the door open with my foot, went in, saw Mr. Smeet in that rocking chair in the bedroom, and got out of there as fast as I could."

"You're aware he was about to be placed under federal indictment?"

"I've heard some rumors but nothing more," I lied.

"And he owned the home your client was living in?"

"Yes, I'm not sure of the relationship. She had signed some papers, but there's a real question if she would have any legal responsibility. The attorney who reviewed them found them to be rather questionable."

"Questionable?"

"Well, just for starters, she has no apparent income, and yet he supposedly loaned her one point two million to buy the place. But there's no record of her ever receiving that sum of money, or any money, as far as that goes."

"Seems to have been somewhat of a standard practice for Mr. Smeet. We've been swamped with federal requests, all sorts of paperwork. They wanted an ankle monitor put on him last week, but there had never been a hearing. I don't know. The kind of money they're talking, you'd think he would be a flight risk, but they didn't follow procedure on the ankle monitor, so there wasn't a hell of a lot we could do. Let me just check with the guys inside. Might be a good idea if you went back in there. You got time to do that? It's almost two."

"Yeah, be happy to help in any way I can."

He stepped off to the side and radioed the guys inside. Another sheriff's car pulled up while he was talking. A guy in civilian clothes, jeans, and a wrinkled sports shirt climbed out from behind the wheel. He nodded at me as he walked past but didn't say anything and stopped next to Smolinski.

"Hi Jake, nothing like a day off," Smolinski said once he was off the radio.

"It figures. Nice weather, kids are out with Sally's folks, and this happens. Can this Smeet guy be any more of a pain in the ass?"

"Jake, this here is Dev Haskell." Smolinski handed my license and card back to me. "He's the one who called it in. He's a P.I. down in the cities. Up here to talk to Mr. Smeet about a client and what sounds like another bogus loan."

Jake eyed me up and down and said, "A P.I. down in the cities. What happened, you wash out of the police academy?"

"Dev Haskell, nice to meet you, Jake. I didn't catch your last name."

"I don't think Lenny gave it," he said and ignored the hand I'd held out to shake.

"So Jake, the guys up in the house said we should go up, me and Haskell here."

"What the hell?"

"Just telling you what they said. He was first one on the scene. Be nice to maybe get his side of things. You know, what he noticed and shit."

Jake shook his head and said, "Oh, what the hell's the difference? Yeah, might as well. Give me a minute head start." He took off at a slow jog. The way he ran reminded me of the pace we set doing five miles every morning in the Army.

"Sorry 'bout that. He's a good guy. Just not all that fond of folks from the cities."

"Not a problem, there are days I feel the same way. What branch of the service was he in?"

Smolinski gave me a funny look and said, "Army. How'd you know he was in the service?"

"Just a wild guess. Shall we head up there?"

"Huh? Oh yeah, don't let old Jake get to you. He has that effect on everyone when they first meet him. But after you get to know him, he's a pretty nice guy."

"How many folks decide not to take the time to get to know him?"

"Yeah, I guess there is that."

Thirty-three

We walked back up to the house. Taking the trail was a lot easier than weaving a path through the woods.

"What do you know about this place and Sheldon Smeet?" I asked as we headed down the trail.

"Up until recently, not all that much. There used to be three cabins along this end of the lake, all similar and owned by two brothers and a sister. Last name was Baxter or Traxter, something like that. They were out of Saint Cloud. I think the sister was the youngest of the three, and she's eighty-four or five now. Both the brothers passed away some years back, maybe as many as twenty. With their deaths, the places passed to the sister. Eventually, she couldn't keep her own place up, let alone two more. Last I heard, she was in a rest home somewhere. Anyway, she sold the three places as a package. Smeet bought 'em. Got all three for a pretty good price, and I'm sure she felt she got a good chunk of change out of the deal. He didn't have them for more than thirty days before all three cabins were torn down and construction was started on that place of his."

"Not too many people happy about that. He brought in a crew from someplace in Europe to build this new place. The architect was from Switzerland if you can believe it. This at a time when everyone was begging for work up here, so right off the bat, he pretty much pissed off all the locals. Can't say he's done very much to change that attitude since."

"The quick look around I took made me think of someplace in Europe," I said. "I mean, it looked like a nice place and all but maybe a little too fancy for my tastes."

"I've had to escort two, no wait, three now. Three different process servers out here to serve him."

"And were there any problems?"

Smolinski shook his head. "No, he just took the things without saying so much as a word, stepped back inside and closed the door behind him. I guess you could say he was polite if nothing else. With all this federal stuff going on, and everyone making comments, he may be guilty as all get out, but leastwise, in my experience he's had the sense to remain quiet."

"You aware of a wife or a daughter?"

"No, I wouldn't know anything about that," Smolinski said, shaking his head. The mansion suddenly appeared in front of us. "You know, after all I just said, I still have to admit, it's one hell of a beautiful place. I guess this Smeet fella must have been part of that one percent that have all the money and don't have no taxes to pay."

A window was open on the second floor, and given the one time I'd been inside, I was willing to bet the window was in the master bedroom. Depending on just how long Smeet had been sitting in that rocking chair, they would be in desperate need of some fresh air. When we stepped inside, the two uniformed officers were talking with Jake. All three were standing in front of the fireplace. Jake was shaking his head 'no' and had his cell phone pushed up against his ear.

One of the guys pointed upstairs and shook his head no. Everyone waited in the living room while Jake finished his phone call. Once he got off the phone, he said, "They're on their way. Should be here in the next twenty minutes, just passing through Cross Lake now. Until then, they want us outside. Don't touch anything on the way out."

"Is that your crime scene team?" I asked, heading for the front door.

"Yeah," Jake said. "But this ain't like the big city, Hassle. We don't have our own team. We use the BCA team out of Bemidji. They'll be here shortly. Until then, they want us all outside and like I said, don't touch a damn thing on the way out."

We stood out front for a good fifteen minutes. Smolinski and the other two uniforms were trading stories about people in the office. Jake stood maybe twenty feet away looking out at the lake. After a couple of minutes of listening to tales about people I didn't know, I wandered over to Jake.

"This bastard's got close to a quarter of a million wrapped up in those two boats at the dock, and he's never gonna use them," he said and nodded toward a long 'T' shaped metal dock. The dock sections were white enamel, and the underlying supports were dark green. On the one side was a cigarette boat with a massive engine. On the other side sat a large cabin cruiser that looked like it could easily sleep about a dozen people. The thing was larger than the house I grew up in. Based on the little I knew of Smeet, I couldn't picture him driving either.

"I never thought he'd be the kind of guy who could drive either of those things. I'm kind of surprised. I don't know that much about him, but I basically figured him for more of a couch potato."

Jake looked at me and shrugged. "Neither one of those damn things are appropriate for this lake. It's too damn small. People on this lake like fishing for bass or walleye, and they sure as hell don't need that shit churning up the water. Guys like Smeet, he's too busy stealing hope and money from working folks to learn how to drive that shit. The hot button for him is having someone ferry him around. Jackass, he could probably cruise around the entire lake in twenty minutes and he ain't the only one like that up here nowadays."

"Well, based on the way he looked up in that master bedroom, I'd say you won't have to worry about him. What do you know about that missing right hand?"

"Not a thing. News to all of us. We placed a call into the local hospital, and we're checking Duluth, too. But so far, nothing."

"Yeah, all I know is he was supposed to have screwed a lot of people."

"They get all the suspects gathered together, they'll have to hold them in the Vikings stadium," Jake said and laughed.

"Yeah. My thinking is the real estate scams, the loan problems, his connection with known criminals down in the cities. The hand probably wasn't someone with a bad loan. That was professional or at least semi-pro. The name Dante Massinni, mean anything to you?"

Jake gave me a long look out of the corner of his eye. "I know the name, but that's about it. Not saying he don't have something going on up this way. We just haven't found it. Yet."

"This might be it, killing Smeet. Maybe it's a warning to the half-dozen folks lining up to turn state's witness once they're named in the indictments."

"Could be. Oh, here they are. That didn't take long," Jake said as the BCA van suddenly appeared through the trees and drove into the parking area. The van was large and black, with impresive gold letters 'BCA' on the side of the van. We all walked toward it as the van stopped, and three people climbed out, two men and a woman.

They opened a side door on the van, and as they began to step into blue hazmat suits and pull on latex gloves, Jake told them the location of Smeet's body.

When he finished, they pulled out cases of equipment and headed inside.

Jake looked at me and said, "Dev, why don't we go back to my car. I'll tape your statement, and you can get back down to the cities at a decent hour. It's going to take them at least a couple of hours in there."

It wasn't lost on me that he used my first name instead of calling me hassle. I nodded, said thanks to Smolinski, and walked down the trail with Jake.

I sat in the passenger side of the front seat. Jake recorded our interview on a device he set on the dashboard. I offered nothing special that I'd seen or noticed other than, as far as we knew, I was first on scene. I told him I got the address from a staff member at Third National and didn't give Gary Peterson's name. I mentioned I'd never been here before and, in fact, had never met Smeet in person. When I saw the broken pane of glass in the open front door, I went in. Soon as I saw Smeet, I phoned it into 911. Pretty much end of story.

The interview took all of twenty minutes. We shook hands, said goodbye and I was back on the road just in time to make the evening rush hour traffic. Actually, heading south it wasn't that bad. I only had to slow to about forty. Now the traffic heading north was bumper to bumper and barely crawling.

Thirty-four

I was home fifteen minutes before I had to be at Amanda's. There was no sign of Roxy and, thankfully, no indication she had tried to break in. I took a quick shower, changed, bought a bottle of wine up the block at Solo Vino, and hurried around the corner to Amanda's. She was sitting on her porch swing with her back to me, so she didn't see me until I was in front of her house and heading up the sidewalk.

"Oh, Dev. Taking the long way?"

"No, just grabbed this bottle of wine," I said, handing it to her. Morton and Madame were sitting on the floor next to the swing. Morton's tail was swishing back and forth, but he remained sitting.

"Oh, my God. How did you get him to do that?"

"He's very smart. They both are." She said something and both Morton and Madame were suddenly up, sniffing me. Morton stuck his head under my hand in case I might miss the opportunity to scratch him.

"Would you like a glass of wine? Or, I think I might even have a beer if you'd prefer that."

"A beer sounds great," I said.

"I'll be right back. Settle into the swing and you can tell me about your day when I get back. I'll put this wine in the fridge and get that beer."

She was back in two minutes with a frosty mug and a refilled glass of white wine. She handed me the beer and settled in next to me. She gave a command. Morton and Madame laid down on the porch floor in front of us.

"So you were up in the lake country?"

"Yeah, up and back. I was near the White Fish chain."

"Gorgeous area."

"Yeah, it is, although I haven't been up there for quite a while. Used to go up as a kid when my folks would rent a cabin at a resort. It was a different time back then. Might as well have been a hundred years ago. In those days, we stayed in actual log cabins. Nothing fancy, but we had lots of fun."

"We did the same thing, my folks and my sister and me. I used to love it. Our folks would rent a cabin for a week. When we were little, we played on the beach, and when we were older, we lay out on beach towels and worked on our tans," she laughed and shook her head.

"Yeah, sounds like just about everyone I know. The place I was at today, it used to be three separate cabins. Probably built in the 1950s. Two brothers and a sister owned them. Over the years the brothers passed away, and the sister inherited their property. She sold all three places to a rich guy from down here in the cities. He knocked down the cabins within thirty days and built a mansion. Now there are more mansions on the lake than cabins. It's all really changed."

She took a sip of wine and said, "I know that's what we refer to as progress, but there's a price to be paid for it. It's like we all long for that simpler time, but we'd still like to keep the internet, central air, Netflix, credit cards, it goes on and on."

"What's your schedule for dinner?" I said.

"Do you have to be somewhere? We can eat any-time."

"Oh, no. No rush, but I want to make sure we have time to cover the information you have on your sister."

"How about this? I'm going to put some garlic bread in the oven, that'll just take ten minutes. We can sip and chat, we'll eat dinner, and we can discuss Nancy over dessert. Does that sound okay to you?"

"That sounds just fine."

We chatted on the swing about everything and nothing. I learned that Amanda divorced five years ago, and she reverted back to her maiden name. She taught elementary school, but more or less retired from that three years back. She occasionally did substitute teach-ing, but dogs were her passion, and she currently didn't own one. She liked Morton and wanted to know more about Madame. I gave her a brief history of Roxy and ended up by saying, "Maybe she's a trust fund baby who doesn't have to worry about getting her act together. Which means she never will. I don't know. I'm guessing Madame probably served as a crutch for a limited period of time. That time has passed, Madame is still here, and Roxy has moved on to other things. Roxy's been gone for two days, no apparent concern for Madame, not so much as a phone call. It's pretty sad."

"Oh, poor thing. I was picking something up while we were working, that explains a lot. Say, we're having lasagna and garlic bread tonight. It's not fancy, but—"

"It sounds perfect. To tell you the truth, I can't wait."

"Well then, let's get started." She stood, and Morton and Madame immediately lifted their heads. "Morton, Madame, come," she said, and they went with her into the house. I dutifully followed behind them.

Thirty-five

We were seated in the dining room. A room with a marble fireplace and oak wainscoting about five feet high. The wall above the wainscoting had been painted a cream color. At the top of the wall was an elegant stencil maybe six inches below the cove molding running around the entire room. The wonderful smell of garlic bread drifted out from the kitchen.

Amanda served up the lasagna and garlic bread. It was delicious. She served a nice red wine with dinner. I helped clear the dinner dishes and took them into the kitchen. Amanda dished up two bowls of vanilla ice cream and then covered the ice cream with homemade chocolate topping. The dessert was to die for.

We were seated at the dining room table. Amanda was maybe halfway finished with her ice cream. I was scraping hints of chocolate topping from the sides of my empty bowl with my spoon only because I thought licking the bowl might be bad form. She reached over to the chair next to her and pulled up a white three-ring binder.

"This is the information I have on my sister, Nancy," she said, opening the binder.

The first page was actually an 8x10 color photo of an auburn-haired woman who looked like she would be Amanda's sister.

"She's very attractive. Is that her actual hair color?"

"Yes, she's been a redhead since birth. Our mother was too."

She turned the photo and revealed a birth certificate. "Nancy. She's four years younger than me, so she'd be thirty-seven now. Born here in town at United Hospital." She turned the page, revealing a lacy tattoo. The design had a pink flower at either end and a hummingbird sucking the nectar.

"And she has this tattoo?"

Amanda smiled and nodded at the same time. "Yes, not the stupidest thing she's ever done, but it's in the top ten. Right up there with the time she shaved her head, although the hair would grow back, or she could always wear a wig."

"And you told me she was a singer."

"One of the many things she's done. Here's a list of the bands she sang with, at least the ones I could remember," she said, turning to the next page. "I only knew some of these people by their first names, so I don't have any way of getting in touch with them. I do know that some of these groups no longer exist. It's a very transient business."

"If you've got the band names that'll help. At the end of the day, it's very much like a small town. It's amazing who knows who."

She turned another page. "Here's a list of the guys she dated. To suggest she was in a long-term relationship with anyone would be incorrect. Maybe ninety days was more like it. I'm not aware that there was ever anything like abuse. For whatever reason, she just didn't stay with any guy for very long."

"Any chemical problems you're aware of?"

She shook her head. "No. I mean, did she have too much to drink now and then on a night out? Yeah, sure. After all, she was singing in bars and clubs. What guy wouldn't enjoy a redhead who's had too much to drink? But I would never call her an alcoholic if that's what you mean. Did she do drugs? She smoked a joint from time to time. Again it was the nature of the biz she was in. But hard drugs? Not as far as I know. Nothing like ecstasy or those kind of things, at least not that I'm aware of."

"Did she live with you?"

"No. She and my husband got along very well. I think they enjoyed one another. When we divorced, she was genuinely sad. She hated to see it happen and tried to talk me out of it."

"Where did she live?"

"Where didn't she live would probably be the shorter list." She turned another page. There were almost a dozen addresses on the list. "These are just the places I can remember. The first five or six she was in with two or three people sharing a flat, guys and girls. Probably, the last four or five places she was in an apartment by herself. Small places. A couple were efficiency units.

She never lived in anything larger than a one-bedroom. I can safely state that they were not the best places. Certainly not in the best neighborhoods."

"And this list is more or less in order? She moved from one to the next?"

"Certainly the last three, maybe four."

"She must have been moving every three or four months."

"Yes, always to a better place. At least that's what she said. I don't know if she ever signed a lease. I doubt it, given the frequency of her moves and the places she rented. I mean, it got to the point where she was too embarrassed to invite me, and I certainly didn't want to go. I remember one of the places, this one," she said, pointing to an address on East Seventh Ave. "It was originally a duplex, and at some point, got converted into six units. When I got there, this fat guy was passed out in the hallway. I said, what the hell is this? I mean we had to step over the guy, literally, because he was in front of her door. And she says, 'Oh relax, that's Arthur. He's always doing that.'"

"Arthur, nice."

Amanda suddenly teared up and sniffled. "That was the night I told her she could move in with me. She wouldn't have anything to do with that idea and actually was very upset I'd even mentioned it. We quickly grew apart after that night."

We chatted for a while longer. It was almost nine when I said, "Amanda, I can't promise anything other than I will do my best to try and find her. Okay?"

She nodded, sniffled once more and said, "Thank you. I really appreciate it."

"Let's see what I can find. I better get these two home. After a strenuous day at school, they're probably exhausted."

"Is this Roxy person at your house?"

"I hope not, and if she is, she doesn't have a way to get in. Fortunately, I didn't give her a set of keys, and she never asked for any."

"I wonder if it would be all right if Madame spent the night here. I've got a bed she can use and food and water dishes. You can bring Morton around tomorrow morning, and we'll work again."

"Oh, that's really nice of you, but you don't have to do that."

"Oh, Dev, I really want to, honest. Actually, after going over this information about Nancy, I could maybe use Madame's company."

"Well, yeah. I don't have a problem with it, and God only knows what Roxy is up to."

"Great, I'll plan to see you boys in the morning." She reached down and gave Morton a thorough scratching on his head. He wagged his tail back and forth and groaned happily.

Thirty-six

I turned on the lights when we got home. There was no sign of Roxy, which I guess was a good thing. Morton and I were both tired. By the time I went upstairs to bed, Morton was already asleep. I set Amanda's three-ring binder on my dresser and hit the sack. I was out within three minutes but not for long.

I woke to loud, furious pounding on the front door. Morton whined and slipped his head beneath a pillow as I pulled on my jeans, grabbed my pistol, and hurried down the stairs. I turned on the light in the entryway.

There, waving at me through the front door, was Roxy with two other women. One girl carried a bottle of vodka, one carried a bottle of wine, and Roxy had a twelve-pack in each hand.

They were dressed like street people. Not the homeless type, but like women working the street. Short skirts about the length of one of my t-shirts, if I'd been wearing one." Oh, thank God you were up. I was afraid we weren't going to get in," Roxy said as she strutted past. Her two girlfriends followed.

"I wasn't up. I was sound asleep," I said. My statement appeared to fall on deaf ears. The woman carrying the wine bottle rolled her eyes and ran her tongue over her upper lip. She leaned toward me and gave a soft sexy growl as she walked past following Roxy into the kitchen.

"Hey, Roxy, I had kind of a long, hard day, so keep it quiet, okay. Ladies?"

"Don't you worry, baby," the woman who growled a moment earlier said. "You won't hear a sound." Then she laughed out loud, and the other two idiots joined in. I went back upstairs to bed.

It was after two in the morning when I'd had enough. Morton's head was still under the pillow. I could feel the bass from the music downstairs vibrating on the bedroom floor. I pulled on my jeans again. This time, I grabbed a t-shirt, and once that was on, I slipped my pistol into my waistband. There were four people passing a joint around in my entryway and drinking beer out of the can. Cheap beer. Lousy beer. I'd never seen any of them before. A crowd of people was crammed into the front room, clapping and whistling as some blonde-haired bimbo stood on my couch in a red thong, drinking a half-pint of vodka. She was shaking her surgically enhanced figure for everything she was worth, and I stared for a long moment.

"You got it, baby. Show us how it's done," some drunken woman shouted and pulled her top off over her head, almost falling down in the process. A couple was on the floor in front of the fireplace groping one another, but everyone was too involved in egging on the dancer on the couch to take notice. I stepped over the gropers and headed into the kitchen. Roxy was sitting on the kitchen counter in her unbuttoned blouse and mini-mini skirt, sharing kisses with two guys. One wore a green nose splint, and the other had on a pair of black cowboy boots with silver metal toes and heels. A strange contraption was wrapped around his lower jaw. Both had beards and ponytails, and although they looked familiar, it took me a long minute to recognize them.

Jimmy and Tony Massinni. What the hell? In my kitchen? Playing grab all you can get with Roxy while she sat there slurping out of a martini glass. I couldn't decide who I should shoot first, the two brothers or idiot Roxy? My money was on Roxy.

"Hey, Roxy," I yelled over the noise.

"Wait your turn, dude. We're just getting started," Jimmy Massinni said without looking up. I was about to put my gun to his head when I heard loud pounding on the front door. I hurried back out to the entryway. The four fools smoking the joint had suddenly disappeared, probably to watch the stripper who was now in the process of bending over and accepting slaps on her rear. If she got one, she got at least a dozen slaps across the backside, from men and women. I'd have to deal with that in a minute but first the pounding on the front door.

I looked out at the door at two uniformed police officers about to pound on the door again. I quickly opened the door.

"Mr. Haskell?" one of the officers said. "We've received a number of complaints about excessive noise. I'm afraid we're going to have to ask everyone to vacate the premises, present company excepted."

"Thank God you guys are here," I shouted. "Just a minute, let me turn down the damn music." I stepped into the front room and turned the music off. *Thank God, peace, and quiet,* I thought, as everyone groaned and turned toward me.

"Oh man, what'd you have to do that for?" said some fool in a faded black t-shirt and a jean jacket with the sleeves cut off.

"Officers, please help me get these people out of here. I'll start with this one," I said and grabbed the guy with the jean jacket, dragging him toward the front door.

"Hey man, you can't do this. I got rights. This is brutality, dude."

"I'll show you brutality." I took hold of his collar and belt, hurried him into the entryway and slammed him into the door frame. "Now get out of my house and don't come back."

He grabbed onto the railing leading down the steps and headed for the street. The two cops stepped inside. One leaned over to me and said, "I think if you just ask nicely everyone will leave."

"Tell you what. There are two guys in the kitchen, one with a nose splint and the other with his jaw wired. Jimmy and Tony Massinni, if you could nicely ask them to leave while I clear out this front room, that would be great."

"Massinni, like in Dante?" one of the cops asked.

"Yeah. They're his sons or nephews or something. If I go back there, I'm liable to hit them with a frying pan or worse."

"The thought is tempting," he said, and they hurried back to the kitchen.

"Okay, folks. Party's over. I don't care where you go, but you can't stay here. Come on. Time to leave." I heard a couple of empty beer cans get tossed onto the floor. There was a good deal of grumbling, but people started heading for the door.

A drunken woman in the corner glared at the guy holding her purse and said, "Don't you tell me what to do."

He dropped her purse on the floor and headed out the door.

The blonde who'd been standing on the couch stripping had her top back on and her jeans draped over her shoulder. She gave me a wink as she headed into the entryway. Beer cans, booze bottles, cigarette butts, a thong, and a pair of red heels were scattered around the room.

"I can find my own way outta this dump, so get your hands off me before I call my damn lawyer and get your ass fired," someone growled.

I glanced into the entryway as the cops led the Massinni brothers out the door.

Roxy staggered out of the kitchen. Her blouse was unbuttoned, and her skirt was hiked up to her hips. She sloshed what was left of her martini onto the wingback chair and said, "You cops don't have anything better to do than ruin all the fun?" She went to take a big gulp but the glass was empty.

"Hey, Roxy. Go on up to bed and rest up. You're out of here in the morning."

"Oh, really. Well, maybe I'll just leave here tonight. What do you think about that, Mr. I'm So Important?"

"I think that's an even better idea. Go on, get out."

"Oh, you can just bet I'm leaving," she said and staggered toward the front door. "Oh, hey Dev. A little hint of what you're missing." She kissed her hand, then bent over and mooned me as she slapped herself on the rear. I figured I must be getting old because that didn't make me try to talk her into staying. Instead, I followed her out the door and watched while she weaved from side to side on the way to her car and then struggled to unlock her car door.

The two cops were standing in the driveway watching the crowd disperse. The Massinni brothers were nowhere to be seen. There was another squad car parked on the street with its flashing lights on.

I stepped out onto the front porch and called to the cops in the driveway, "Hey guys, that woman trying to get into the red car is extremely intoxicated and should not be driving."

"We're just waiting for her to unlock the door and get behind the wheel, then we'll give her a little ride down to detox."

It was another minute of drama before Roxy finally got the driver's door open. The two officers calmly strolled over to her car, opened the door, and pulled her out from behind the wheel. She screamed something and apparently kicked one of the officers.

She was suddenly face down on the hood of the car with her hands cuffed behind her back. As they led her to their squad car, one of them looked up at me and grinned.

"DUI and assaulting an officer. She'll be going away for a while."

"I'm warning you two, let go of me. I got friends who'll make you wish you never did this. You hear me?"

The officers put her in the back seat then smiled and waved as they drove off. I could see Roxy screaming at them as they drove past. No doubt they were recording her rant, and it would be presented at her trial. I stepped off the porch and walked over to the car with the flashing lights. There was a sergeant sitting behind the wheel.

"Excuse me, but did you get all that on your dash camera?"

"Every second," he said and smiled.

Thirty-seven

I locked the front door and cleaned up the front room. I filled a trash bag with beer cans, six or seven half-pint bottles, a pizza delivery box, and two McDonald's bags. It was after three by the time I was finished picking up. I was exhausted and headed back upstairs. Morton was nowhere to be seen, but then, who could blame him?

As I drifted off to sleep, I was vaguely aware of hearing Morton beneath the bed. A little while later, he climbed into my bed and leaned against me. I woke the next morning almost pushed out of bed again. It took me a long moment to focus on the digital clock, just a little after eight. I drifted back to sleep for fifteen minutes before I opened my eyes again. Now I could hear Morton snoring. Only it didn't quite sound like him. My first thought was Roxy, but she was probably still in police custody. I rolled over and stared at the blonde woman who'd been standing on my couch, stripping. What was worse, now that I had a chance to focus on her, she looked familiar. Unfortunately, very familiar. Swindle Lawless. And she was in my bed.

I was almost afraid to touch her.

"Swindle. Hey Swindle, it's time to wake up. Swindle?"

She rolled over on her back, spread her legs beneath the covers, and with her eyes still closed, said, "Go ahead and help yourself just don't wake me."

I slipped out of bed, grabbed my clothes, ran into the bathroom, and locked the door. I took a long shower, making sure to double scrub any portion of my body that may have inadvertently come in contact with Swindle.

It had been a couple of years and probably three or four name changes since I'd last seen her. Standing on the couch, stripping for the party crowd, and then hiding under my bed. Clearly, not much had changed. What was she doing here? How did she know Roxy? Or more importantly, how did Roxy know Swindle?

Which reminded me, Roxy. I dried off, got dressed, and hurried downstairs. I put the coffee on and then called Heidi.

"Dev? Is everything okay?"

"Thought you might like an update. Your close, personal friend, Roxy, was arrested this morning a little after two AM."

"What? What do you mean she was arrested?"

"Just what I said. Arrested for DUI and assaulting a police officer, but those are just the charges I'm aware of. I suspect there'll be more to come."

"Assault. What did she do?"

"Assaulted one of the two officers, kicked him actually. Then she threatened them. Shouting that she had friends who were going to make them wish they never arrested her. Hello? You there, Heidi?"

"I don't believe it."

"Well do, and I would guess they've got pretty good documentation. There was a sergeant parked on the street, and he told me he got it all on his dash camera. I would guess she's going to be doing some time on this one."

"Isn't there anything you can do?"

"I suppose I could call the city prosecutors office and offer to give eyewitness testimony against her."

"Dev, there's the possibility she could be sentenced on these charges and—"

"Yeah, and when I called you and told you she was a major pain, you couldn't be bothered. She brought a bunch of people over late last night to party, just a small crowd of maybe thirty to forty deadbeats I've never even seen before. The cops showed up at two in the morning because of all the complaints from my neighbors. Some woman was standing on my couch wearing just a thong after stripping for the crowd. Meanwhile, Roxy is enjoying herself sitting on my kitchen counter letting two guys paw her."

"What?"

"Oh, yeah. Aren't you interested in who the two guys were?"

"You knew them?"

"In a manner of speaking. It was the Massinni brothers, Jimmy and Tony."

"Wait a minute. Aren't they the ones who served her with the eviction notice?"

"You got it. Apparently, they can grab hold of a lot more than just eviction notices. Of course, now, thanks to Roxy, they know where I live."

"I don't know what to say."

"You don't have to say a thing, Heidi. In fact, it might be better if you didn't say anything. But I wanted you to know what happened last night because, if I get a call from her, I'm going to hang up."

"Oh, I'm so sorry. I had no idea. What in the world?"

"I'd say she's over the edge. That's all I've got. Just be careful. You were right. You don't want her staying with you. I gotta hang up and deal with the next problem. You take care, Heidi." I heard footsteps coming down the staircase, and it didn't sound like Morton.

Thirty-eight

Swindle strutted into the kitchen wearing a St. Paul Saints t-shirt of mine and her thong. "So you again, I knew there was something I liked. You enjoy yourself last night?" She struck a pose that made me want to squirt her with a garden hose.

"For your information, Swindle, we didn't so much as touch last night except when you tried to push me out of bed. You hid upstairs in my bedroom once you finished dancing on my couch and the police arrived."

"How'd you like the show?"

"I didn't. I didn't see you dance, and I didn't recognize you. I—"

"We can fix that right now. Put on some music, lover boy, and let's make it happen."

"I got a better idea. Why don't you get dressed and head home?"

"Oh, are we upset? Feeling left out? I've got a little something in mind that'll cure all of that for you, baby."

"No thanks, Swindle."

"Who told you about that name? I ain't been Swindle for years."

"And I haven't seen you for years."

"It's coming back to me now. You a cop?"

"No, I'm—"

"City council?"

"No."

"I know you from somewhere, just give me a minute here. I killed a lot of brain cells last night. Where was the first place we did it? I'm thinking you look familiar. You the guy who liked the whipped cream?"

"Believe me, Swindle, we never did it, and I sure as hell don't plan—"

"Sounds to me like you know what you've been missing out on."

"Swindle, for the love of God, I haven't been missing out on anything. Now go on upstairs and get dressed so you can get out of here."

"Sure, you don't want to try? Tell you what, I can make you happy in under two minutes. Works every time. You just get that can of whipped cream and I'll—"

"Swindle," I shouted. "Go get your clothes on and get out of my house."

"Oh, now I know—"

"Swindle, go, now, or I'm going to throw you out."

"You like it rough, don't you? Whatever turns your crank, honey."

"Go."

"Okay, but it's your loss, crabby. Go ahead, check around, you'll hear how good everyone says I am."

"Last chance. Get out of my house."

She strolled out of the kitchen then called as she climbed the stairs, "Come on up if you change your mind."

I opened a cupboard and took out the aspirin bottle. I poured two into my hand then washed them down with lukewarm coffee.

Swindle was back downstairs about twenty minutes later. Her jeans looked to be spray-painted on, and her top was cut off and frayed about mid-chest, just barely covering her medical enhancements. She was barefoot.

"You want to share some of that coffee?"

"Not really, but I'll pour you a mug if you promise to leave as soon as you finish it."

"Works for me," she said and settled onto a kitchen stool as I filled a mug with coffee and slid it across the counter to her.

"So don't tell me," she said after taking a sip, "but ain't you one of them disbarred attorneys?"

"No."

"You still a lawyer then? I could use—"

"No, I've never been a lawyer. I'm not a cop. I don't serve on the city council or work in the mayor's office."

"Well, then how do I know you?"

"It was a long time ago. I forget how we met. You about finished with that coffee?"

"Honey, I'm just barely getting started," she said and raised her eyebrows suggesting God only knew what.

I pulled her coffee mug back across the kitchen counter and set it in the sink. "It's time for you to go, Swindle."

"Well, excuse me for trying to make you happy."

"Time to go," I said.

"You didn't happen to see a pair of red heels lying around somewhere, did you?"

"No, I didn't," I lied.

"Ah, well, doesn't really matter. Damn things didn't fit anyway."

I walked her out to the front entry and opened the front door for her.

"Last chance," she said.

"Just go, please."

"Okay, but it's gonna be your loss. You'll be missing out on a time to remember." She walked down the sidewalk and hurried to catch up with a guy walking his dog. "Hi there, what are you up to today?"

I closed the front door and locked it just as my cellphone rang.

Thirty-nine

I answered as I headed toward the kitchen.
"Hi Dev, just checking to see if you were still planning on bringing Morton over this morning."

"Oh, hi, Amanda. I'm sorry. I've been dealing with a bit of a problem over here."

"Everything all right?"

"Yeah. We're finally getting back to normal. What time is it?" I said as I headed upstairs to find Morton.

"It's a quarter-to-ten," Amanda said just as I heard a noise from the guest room. Fearing it might be someone else from last night I hurried down the hall. Morton was in the process of doing his morning stretch. Someone's powder blue thong, or what was left of it after Morton had chewed it, was lying on the floor.

"Oh sorry, I had no idea it was that late. Morton is just up, and I'm going to let him out and we'll—"

"Listen, Dev, if it's all right, I'd love to work with them over at your place today. It would be an added dimension for both of them to experience training in the area they're most familiar with."

"Yeah, that's fine. I was planning to check on some of the apartments you had on Nancy's list. Tell you what, give me twenty minutes and you and Madame come on over."

I hung up, let Morton out the back door, then ran to the front door and peered out to make sure Swindle wasn't still hanging around. Fortunately, I didn't see her and hurried up the block to the bakery/restaurant. I got two caramel rolls and ran back home.

Amanda was at the door five minutes later. As she stepped into the house, I caught her wrinkling her nose.

"Smell something funny?"

"Mmm, maybe it's—"

"It's a long story is what it is. How about some coffee and a caramel roll while you listen? Morton's out in the backyard. You can let Madame out. How did she do last night?"

"Just fine, there seems to be a little spring in her step today. Any news from that Roxy person?"

"That's a big part of my story. Come on back to the kitchen."

Madame and Morton proceeded to chase one another around the backyard while I gave Amanda the update on Roxy's return and arrest. She didn't interrupt once while I told her the story, although her eyes seemed to grow wider and wider. I neglected to mention Swindle hiding under my bed or my waking up next to her.

"So this Roxy person has been arrested?"

"Yeah, I phoned one of her friends this morning to give her an update, and I guess if she wants to post bail, she can. But Roxy is out of here for good. In fact, I'm going to take all her clothes out of the guest room, pack her suitcase, and leave it on the front porch."

"Well if she kicked a policeman, won't she go to jail?"

"Theoretically. I suspect her friend will post bail. She'll have to get an attorney. She'll certainly go to trial, but that might be six months or even a year down the road. I just don't want to deal with her. Lesson learned, or should I say relearned, no good deed goes unpunished."

"I wonder what this means for Madame."

"Yeah, interesting. She never mentioned her. Didn't ask about her when she arrived and didn't bother to look for her. Madame is a lot better off without Roxy in her life, believe me."

"Apparently, it just seems so sad, so worthless."

"Yeah, it's too bad. You sure you don't mind staying here and working with these two today?"

"No, not at all. Like I said on the phone, I think it will be a good experience for them."

"Okay, well, I'm going to head upstairs and pack Roxy's suitcase. I might call her friend and see if she'd like me to drop it off. Otherwise, I'll just leave it out in the front yard with a sign on the thing that says free."

"Oh, Dev, that would be mean. Don't do that."

"Yeah, I know, but I'd love to do it. More coffee before I get going?"

"That would be very nice if it's not too much trouble. I'm going to head out back and start working them so you can take off."

"Not a problem." I filled her mug and headed up to the guest room. Roxy's suitcase was in the closet. I emptied the dresser drawers, tossed in both pairs of heels and the two outfits hanging in the closet. Then I phoned Heidi and ended up leaving a message. It was a little easier getting Roxy's suitcase down the stairs than it had been bringing it up, but not by much.

I looked out the kitchen window and watched Amanda for a moment. She was in the backyard with Morton and Madame. Amazingly, she was giving hand signals, and Morton was actually following them. I wheeled Roxy's suitcase out to my car and tossed it into the trunk. I grabbed the three-ring binder off my dresser and headed over to Heidi's.

Forty

Heidi was just getting into her car when I pulled up. She saw me in her rearview mirror and waited, lowering the window as I approached.

"Heidi, glad I caught you."

"Have you calmed down yet?"

"I'm getting there. I've got Roxy's suitcase in the trunk of my car. Do you want it?"

"Actually, I was just on my way to see about getting her released."

"There's a change. Usually you're doing that for me. Are you planning on bringing her back here?"

She gave a little sigh. "No. The more I thought about it and decided with no plan, and after what you dealt with last night, I can't have that chaos going on in my life. I have enough to deal with just keeping an eye on you, and I don't want to deal with her staying with me."

"You have any thought on where she can go? I don't want her coming back to my place. In fact, I won't let her in."

"I have a colleague at work who owns a number of apartment buildings. He has some vacancies, and he's agreed to rent to her."

"Are you going to be paying the freight?"

"That's none of your concern."

"Okay, fair enough. You want me to put her suitcase in your trunk? Right now, it's packed with just about every item she owns."

She seemed to think about that for a moment and finally nodded. "I suppose you better. She's going to need it sooner or later. Besides, if I give it to her today, maybe that will send the message to her that you're finished, and I'm about to be."

She pressed a button, and the trunk popped open an inch or two. I lifted it up as I walked past and back to my car. I opened the back door, eased the suitcase down to the street, and wheeled it over to Heidi's car. I took a deep breath, hoisted the thing into her trunk, and closed the lid.

"Okay, you're good to go. When you see her, you might tell her I'm not answering my phone if she calls. Everything she owns is in that suitcase, so there is no reason to contact me ever again."

"Thanks a lot, crabby," Heidi said then raised her window and drove off. I watched her disappear down the street. Not so much as a thank you or an apology for the absolutely worthless person she stuck me with. I had to smile. Payback, compliments of Roxy, was about to begin.

I opened the three-ring binder on the passenger seat and turned to the page with all the apartments listed. I knew approximately where the last one was. This was the duplex that had been turned into six units. I wondered if fat Arthur was still there sleeping in the hallway.

I pulled in front of the place fifteen minutes later. The house looked like a 1920s construction in a neighborhood of similar structures. It probably wasn't that great a house when it was built, and a century of wear and tear had done nothing to improve things. Currently, it was covered with grey aluminum siding. Some of it appeared to be rusted in spots or maybe that was just from the nails they'd used. There was a section of siding that had been torn off on the front corner next to the porch. It wasn't a large area, no more than two feet long and three feet high. Based on the condition of the wood beneath, it looked like the aluminum siding had been missing for a number of years.

The roof consisted of grey, asphalt shingles that looked very worn and needed replacement. There was a brick chimney jutting from either side of the house and extending above the roofline just a foot or two, suggesting they were non-functional and probably capped on top. The worn wooden porch floor appeared cracked and splintered in places. It had been painted grey at some point, but only hints of the paint remained. It was a busy street, and I had to wait for a number of cars to pass before I opened the door. I walked up to the front porch. The front door was metal and had been painted white back in the Eisenhower administration. Years of grime surrounded the doorknob and boot marks scuffed the lower portion of the door. There used to be a window in the upper half of the door, but now the area was covered by a sheet of plywood. Someone had scrawled four-inch high illegible graffiti with a black marker. I tried the doorknob, and the door opened, so much for security.

The hallway smelled like spoiled meat. The doors on either side of the front entrance were labeled 1 and 2 with adhesive numbers that had been applied crookedly. I climbed the creaking staircase to the second floor. There were three doors labeled 4, 5, and 6 with the same adhesive numbers. A plastic garbage bag was in the hallway outside unit five. The bag was open, and I could see remnants of what appeared to have been a roast chicken, clearly the reason for the spoiled meat smell. I walked back downstairs and to the back of the staircase. The door leading to the basement was labeled 3. The term dive bounced around in my head. Obviously, nothing had changed in the nineteen months since Amanda's sister Nancy had lived here except that fat Arthur wasn't asleep in the hallway. I walked back outside, sucked in some fresh air, and headed for my car.

The next three places I checked out were pretty much the same. Cheap apartments that were costing the tenants too much no matter what they were paying for rent. That made four buildings I checked out, covering nineteen month's worth of Nancy's accommodation. I was debating going onto the next place when my cellphone rang.

I checked the screen, Amanda. My first thought was, *'What in the hell has Morton done now?'*

"Hi, Amanda, everything going okay?"

"Dev, Dev, they shot her. They drove by, and they shot her," she screamed.

"Amanda, calm down. What happened. Who's been shot?"

"Madame, a car just drove by and shot a bunch of times. They shot Madame. They shot her."

I had the car in drive and pulled a U-turn across the middle of the street. A horn blared on one side, and tires screeched on the other. I didn't wait to see if everyone was okay. I just accelerated and picked up speed. Four blocks, later I came to a red light. I sped down the right turn lane, looked left and right and ran through the light. I passed two cars on the right and headed up the hill, leaning on my horn to get people out of the way.

"Dev? Dev?" My phone was lying on the passenger seat, and I heard Amanda's voice.

"I'm on my way, Amanda. Call the cops," I shouted then leaned on my horn as two guys stepped into the crosswalk. They had the right of way but fortunately stepped back and just gave me the finger as I shot past. I took a right on Kellogg Boulevard and sped up the hill, running two more lights. I whipped around a woman making a left-hand turn onto Summit and a half block later shot through the red light as I made a right turn onto Selby. I leaned on the horn and ran the stop sign at Western. A block later, I jumped the curb, pulled across the boulevard, and skidded to a stop on the sidewalk in front of my place.

I could see Amanda kneeling on the front porch. Her back was to me. I pulled my pistol and scanned the street. Just two girls on bikes riding past heading towards downtown, fortunately, I don't think they saw my gun.

"Amanda? You okay?"

Forty-one

Along with Madame lying on the porch floor, there were two bullet holes in my front window. "They shot her, Dev. Someone shot her."

"Are you okay?"

"She's bleeding, Dev. They shot her."

Amanda was obviously in shock. Morton was pacing back and forth whining. Madame was breathing, but her eyes were closed. The entrance wound was on the left side of her chest, and what looked like an exit wound was maybe three inches back on her left side. The exit wound didn't appear to be that large, so it didn't appear to have been a hollow point round.

"Get Morton into my car," I said.

"They shot her, Dev. They shot—"

"Amanda, move," I shouted. "Get Morton into the car. We're taking her to the doctor."

When I shouted, she blinked a couple of times and suddenly was back in the here and now. "Come on, Morton," she said, hurrying off the porch and running to the car. Morton was at her side.

I gently picked up Madame. She easily fit in my hands. She whined a little but didn't open her eyes. I hurried off the porch and across the lawn. Morton was already in the backseat, and Amanda was settling into the passenger seat.

"Can you hold her while I drive?"

She placed her hand's palm up on her lap, and I carefully placed Madame in her hands. I hurried around to the driver's side, fired up the car, and backed into the street before my door was even closed. Fortunately, no cars were coming. I made another U-turn, bounced up over the curb and on the sidewalk for a few feet then sped down the street. The vet I take Morton to was just two blocks away, and I knew they did surgery there. I ran the stop sign, making a left onto Western Avenue then took the first right onto Marshall Ave and skidded to a stop. The vet was just across the street from where I was double-parked.

Amanda looked like she was going to open her door, and I said, "Stay there. I'll get her." I hurried around the car, opened Amanda's door, carefully slid my hands underneath Madame, and lifted her. "You got Morton," I called over my shoulder and ran across the street. Fortunately, a woman was coming out the door, and when she saw how I was carrying Madame, she stepped back and held the door for me.

I ran into the small lobby and past the receptionist counter. "Sir?" the receptionist called as I ran past.

"This dog's been shot. Call Tommy and tell him I'm in the prep room," I said as I hurried down the hall. The prep room was three doors down. It has an examination table with a white paper lining over the cushion. The door was open just a couple of inches. I gave it a hip check and hurried in. I laid Madame on the examination table. She was still breathing. Her eyes remained closed, and when I carefully removed my hands, she didn't make a sound. I watched her breathe for a long moment before I headed for the door to find Doctor Tommy. I didn't have to go very far.

Tommy was dressed in a white lab coat, and he was pulling on a pair of latex gloves as he hurried down the hall. "Dev, what do you got?"

"Bichon Frise shot in the chest with a small-caliber round, maybe twenty-five minutes ago. She's breathing. There appears to be an exit wound."

He brushed past me and hurried to Madame. "Where'd this happen?"

"Over on my front porch. Someone drove past and fired a few rounds. One hit Madame, two hit my front widow. I don't know the caliber, just a quick look and with the lack of blood I'm hoping she can survive."

Tommy nodded and hit a button on the desk phone. "Carol," he said, "I'm in prep. Get Christine in here. Tell her we'll need . . ." He went on to mention a half-dozen items then hung up. "Dev it's going to get busy in here. You can do the most good out in the lobby right now. I'll call you if we need you."

His back was to me, and he opened a drawer and pulled out a syringe wrapped in plastic. He tore off the wrapping and tossed it in a corner. He squirted a portion of the contents into the sink and proceeded to give Madame a number of shots around the entrance and exit wounds.

"I'll call you if we need you, Dev. Get your ass into the lobby," he said without looking up just as the woman who must have been Christine hurried past me carrying a metal tray loaded with a number of items.

I walked out of the prep room and back down the hall. As I entered the lobby, the receptionist looked at me and said, "Everything okay?"

I shrugged and said, " I guess we'll see. She, she couldn't be in better hands right now. Just say a prayer," I said as tears began to well up in my eyes.

She nodded and said, "You can wash up in the restroom." She nodded at the unisex sign on the door.

I looked at my hands. The palms were bloody. "Oh, yeah, thanks," I said and cleared my throat to get rid of the lump. I took a deep breath as I headed into the bathroom, careful to open the door using just my fingertips. I soaped up, washed and rinsed my hands a half-dozen times before I dried them off under the warm air drier. I checked myself in the mirror and took a deep breath to calm down. When I came out, Morton and Amanda were seated in a distant corner.

"You okay?" Amanda said as I headed toward them.

"Yeah, I guess we'll know better once we hear what the doc has to say."

"At least you got her here. I didn't know what to do. I couldn't think. I've been past this place a million times, and it never even registered with me to get her in here."

"Can you tell me what happened?"

She shook her head. "I'm not sure. We were sitting out on the porch. One minute we're taking a break, they're just sitting, and the next minute the front window was cracked. I heard a noise from the street, but all I saw was this great big black car suddenly speed up."

I thought for a moment before it dawned on me. "Did the car have a bumper sticker? Red letters on a white background that said MILF Hunter?"

"I can't be sure. MILF Hunter? M.I.L.F right? I've seen that word before, but I don't know what it means. I think it's some kind of political group."

"Political?"

"Yeah, like Minnesota International Liberation Front or something. That's just my guess. You know, the first letter of each word," she said.

"The first letter?" In my head, I was in the process of spelling out Minnesota and International.

"Yeah, MILF. Why? What does it stand for?"

"Back up for a second. You said the car was black?"

"Yeah, black and big. An SUV."

"You remember a stripe on the side of the car, close to the bottom of the doors?"

Amanda nodded.

"And did the taillights extend up almost to the roof of the car?"

"Yes, but how did you know all that?"

"It was a Cadillac Escalade. And it had a bumper sticker that said MILF Hunter?"

"Maybe. I can't be sure. But what is that? Some political organization? A labor union? What?"

"MILF, Amanda. It's the trendy abbreviation for Moms I'd Like to Fuck."

"What?"

Forty-two

After twenty minutes of trying to explain MILF to Amanda, I more or less gave up.

"God, that is so awful. And how did I get to be so out of it? So you know these MILF people?"

"You mean the moms or the shooters?"

"The shooters. I don't want to go near the moms."

"If it's the guys I'm thinking of, they're brothers. I don't really know them. But I'm pretty sure I know who they are."

"But why would they shoot at your house? I mean, I've heard about these drive-by shootings before, but I never, ever thought I would actually be involved in one. What in the world?"

"These two idiots were part of that rabble the police evicted from my house last night."

"Oh my God, and stupid me, I was in such shock. It never occurred to me to call the police. We should do that now," she said, reaching for her phone.

"No, no, please don't call the police. I don't want to get them involved."

"Dev, believe me if you don't report this to the police, these hoodlums are going to think they can do absolutely anything they want to you and that you'll be powerless to stop them. I mean, they shot Madame. They could have shot Morton or even me. What if there had been a child walking by or someone pushing a baby stroller? If they did something like this, they aren't going to stop. Dev, you can't let them get away with this."

"Oh, believe me. They will not be getting away with this."

She shook her head. "I hope you're not thinking of taking the law into your own hands. That makes you no better than they are. In fact, in a way, it makes you even worse, because you know better, and they, well, they're just awful people."

"I promise I'll be good and behave," I said. Amanda looked like she didn't believe me. "What I intend to do right now is wait and make sure that Madame will be okay. Then, we're going to get you home and get you calmed down."

"I'm calm, Dev."

"Yeah, you are, but let's be honest, it's been a crazy morning for both of us," I said and gave Morton a long rub behind his ears. I spent the next half-hour paging through two Sports Illustrated magazines while Amanda lost herself in a book of Dog Breeds.

I may have been paging through the magazines, but I didn't read anything. I just kept going over everything

I planned to do to the Massinni brothers. Tommy eventually came out of the prep room, walked over, and sat down in a chair across from us. His white lab coat was bloodstained.

"What's the word?" I asked.

"Is she going to be okay?" Amanda said.

"Good and yes," Tommy said then ran both hands over his face and took a deep breath. "Thank God you got her here when you did, Dev. Another sixty minutes and things might not have gone so well, but she's going to be fine. It's going to take a while for her to heal, but she will. She's young enough. You were right Dev, small caliber, thankfully. She's still anesthetized, but you can peek in if you'd like to. I'd like to keep her here for forty-eight hours, just to watch her and play it safe. I'm not expecting any problems. But I want to be sure."

I nodded and said, "I can't thank you enough, Tommy."

"Like I said, it's a good thing you got her in here when you did. Tell me again how this happened."

Amanda told him in about three sentences. Fortunately, she left out the part about identifying the car by the bumper sticker. The last thing I needed was Tommy filing something with the police. We chatted on about how crazy some people were for another ten minutes, and then we peeked in at Madame for a moment before we left.

My car was still double-parked across the street but somehow had managed to escape getting a parking ticket or worse, getting clamped or towed. I pulled in front of Amanda's house, walked her up to the door, and gave her a kiss on the cheek.

"Thank you, Amanda. If it weren't for you, I don't think Madame would have made it. It sounds like she's going to be all right after some recovery time. She's lucky to have you in her life."

"Do you think that woman will want her back?" She appeared on the verge of tears as she asked the question.

"I think she won't even ask, and if she does, I'm not going to tell her a thing. Madame has been through enough after today. She doesn't need Roxy coming back into her life."

"Thanks, Dev. I'm going to walk back down there later to check on her."

"Would you like to come over for dinner tonight?"

"Oh, gee thanks, not that I wouldn't, but right now I'm feeling really drained. The whole event is just so unbelievable, and as bad as it is, it could have been so much worse." She shook her head and suddenly looked exhausted.

"Okay, well, rest up and let's talk tomorrow morning."

"That sounds good," she said, not looking all that happy. She unlocked the front door, pasted a smile on her sad face, gave a little wave, and closed the door behind her. Morton and I drove around the block, and I parked in the driveway.

Forty-three

orton sniffed around the porch floor where Madame had been lying and gave a little whine. I looked at the two bullet holes in the front window. I found the third one about two inches from the window and another one about six inches above the floor. That last one was most likely the round that had hit Madame. I guessed that as the Massinni's drove past, it was probably idiot Jimmy behind the wheel. So Tony fires a round, and Jimmy immediately stomps on the accelerator. The rest of the rounds go wide, probably as their Escalade leaps forward. Fortunately, none of them hit Amanda or Morton.

I walked into the house and headed for the front room. Morton wandered back to the kitchen. It only took a minute before I found the two rounds that struck the front window, they were embedded in the far wall of the room. I got a paring knife out of the kitchen and dug the rounds out of the plaster wall. They were definitely small caliber, thankfully. No telling what the damage would have been if they'd been a .39 or .45 caliber round. I placed the rounds in my pocket then hurried down to the basement, grabbed a two-gallon bucket of taping compound, a plaster knife, and went back upstairs. In less than a minute, I had the holes filled. I called a contractor I knew and told him about my front window. He said he'd be over at five to check it out.

We hopped back in the car, and I drove down to the office. Louie was nowhere to be seen when we arrived. The coffee was on, but there was only about a half-cup left in the pot. God only knew how many hours it had been sitting there. Against my better judgement, I poured it into my mug and sat down at my desk.

I opened the middle desk drawer and pulled out the Massinni brothers' driver's licenses. I logged onto my computer and brought up Google maps. The brothers shared the same address, which came as no surprise. After all, who would want to live with either one of them?

The house was over on the East side of town. It was located just east of Lake Phalen on Atlantic Street, a mere two blocks from the lake. I input the address and brought up a picture of the house. The house, which was sitting on the corner, was a split-level stucco and brick structure that looked like it may have been built in the mid-1960s. Interestingly enough, in the picture, a black Cadillac Escalade sat in the driveway, although it appeared to be a couple of years older than the vehicle they were currently driving.

The place looked like too nice a residence for the Massinni brothers to own, and I figured Dante probably had something to do with it. I looked up the Ramsey

County property taxes for the address. Sure enough, Dante Massinni was listed as the owner and taxpayer. The home was listed as a 1A-residential homestead and a single-family dwelling. No doubt the neighbors were thrilled having the Massinni brothers living next door.

My phone rang, and I answered, "Haskell Investigations."

"Hello Dev, Aaron LaZelle."

"Aaron, how are you? Long time no talk." My friend Aaron is a lieutenant with the city's police department. We'd known one another since we were kids. He heads up the city Homicide section, and unfortunately, there was no doubt in my mind why he was calling.

"Yeah, it's been far too long, Dev. I'm thinking we should grab dinner sometime. Maybe tonight if you don't have anything going. You're not busy tonight, are you, Dev?"

"No, no tonight would be great. I got nothing planned."

The tone he'd used sounded more like a father talking to an idiot son. When he asked the question about being busy tonight, the unspoken statement was cancel anything you have planned, numbskull.

"How does Shamrock's sound? Say five-thirty, burgers and a beer, and we'll be in there just before the evening crowd hits?" Aaron said.

"Can we make it six-thirty? I got an appointment with a contractor at five-thirty."

"A contractor? What are you having done? Kitchen? New bathroom?"

"Nothing that romantic. I'm thinking about new windows, double glazed. Hoping to cut down the heating bills next winter," I lied.

"It's always something, isn't it?" he said. "All right, I'll see you at six-thirty. Don't be late."

"Looking forward to seeing you, Aaron," I said just before he hung up.

Shit! Someone obviously reported the shooting. My money was on Amanda. She probably called the police once I dropped her off. I searched my memory trying to remember if I'd actually mentioned the Massinni brothers to her. I didn't think I had. Our discussion was more centered on the term MILF.

No doubt Aaron had seen some 'shots fired' report, recognized my address, and was going to get involved. That was okay, at least to a point. I wasted time on Facebook for fifteen or twenty minutes. At five, we got in the car and headed home.

Forty-four

I went to high school with Mike Casey. He was a contracting rep for Andersen Windows now, and he had installed all new double-glazed windows in my place five or six years ago. I was waiting out on my front porch when he pulled up five minutes early. He waved at me as he climbed out of his van and headed up the sidewalk carrying a briefcase.

"Hey Mike, thanks for coming over. How's it going?"

"Good, Dev, good. How about you?" he said as he climbed the steps and held out his hand.

"Just like always, Mike, fine if you don't go into detail," I said as we shook hands.

"Hilarious. You're a piece of work, man." He glanced at the front window. "Oh, oh, when the hell did this happen?" He stepped over to the window and rubbed his little finger around both bullet holes. "Bastards. Hopefully, no one was hurt."

I shook my head and said, "No. No one was hurt."

"Any idea who did this?"

"Nope, just some dirtbag driving by, I guess."

For just a moment, a look registered on his face that suggested he didn't believe a word. "Thank goodness no one was injured. Let me get this measured out." He reached into his briefcase and pulled out what looked like a cellphone instead of the tape measure I had expected. He ran it from right to left across the top and then from top to bottom down the right-hand side. He repeated the process, only this time, instead of going across the glass, he ran it over the outer edge of the wooden frame.

"Okay, that should do it. You know, Dev, for not too much money, we could install bullet-proof glass."

I was about to laugh and say no, then said, "What's the time frame?"

"With the bullet-proof? I'd say a week, give or take a day. We'll use a solid steel frame, but you'll never be able to tell the difference. The frame is primed, and you can paint it the house color using latex paint. I'm guessing that's what you used," he said, taking a step back and looking at the trim color and then the siding. He noticed the two bullet holes in the siding. "Four shots? What'd you do to piss this asshole off?"

"You got me. Like I said, I've no idea who it was. Haven't bothered anyone of late. I'm hoping it's just some jerk driving by and doing it for a laugh. Maybe showing off for a girlfriend or something."

"Yeah, sounds like the kind of guy I'd like one of my daughters going out with.... not."

"They dating already?"

"No, thank God. The thirteen-year-old is acting like she's sixteen and thinks she's ready. She and her mother are usually at odds over something. Her younger sister is just quietly watching the battles and filing the information away. Our son is ten now, and he's a typical boy, oblivious."

"I don't envy you. I can imagine how I'd be once a daughter started dating."

"I got that part covered. Already told the thirteen-year-old. On her first date, the guy can just come over to the house, and the three of us can sit on the couch watching a movie. I get to pick the movie, and I'll be sitting in the middle between them. I figure that will probably scare any idiot boys off until she leaves for college and then what I don't know won't hurt me."

"Yeah, Mike. Good plan. I don't see any problems with that at all."

"You'd be amazed at the number of fathers I tell that to, and you can see the wheels start to turn in their head."

"Look at all the things we tried on dates in high school."

"Oh please, don't even go there. I don't want to even think about it. Hey, so as long as you're continuing this lifestyle, I'm recommending the bullet-proof glass."

"Yeah, I suppose you're probably right. Okay, go ahead and do it. You said a week?"

"Give or take a day. You in any special hurry? I can put a rush on it, but I'd have to charge you."

"No. Normal turnaround time will work just fine. You got time for a beer or something?"

"I'd love a beer, but I'd better not. I got two more stops to make. Can I get a rain check?"

"The door's always open, Mike. Maybe after you do that installation, if you got time."

He closed his briefcase, and we shook hands goodbye. I gave him a wave as he climbed in behind the wheel and drove off. Just a little before six, I decided to head down to Shamrock's for my meeting with Aaron LaZelle. At least if I got there early, I could choose the table.

Forty-five

I parked on a side street about a block behind Shamrock's and walked in the back door. The place was
filling up, but I spotted two open tables. I was
headed for one when someone called my name. I turned
and saw Aaron already sitting at a table by the front window. He raised his beer glass and pointed toward the bar.
I got a beer and headed over to the table.

"Aaron, good to see you, man. It's been too long." I
set my glass down and shook hands then pulled out a
chair and sat down. I had the feeling Aaron was studying
me the entire time.

"Yeah, been way too long," Aaron said. "So tell me,
Dev, how are things going?"

"Oh, I suspect a bit like you, maybe not so intense,
but somewhat the same. You know, different day, same
old shit."

He smiled, nodded, and took a sip. "Yeah, of course,
most of my friends keep me informed about things going
on in their lives, and that seems to work as a moment of
sanity for me. You know, just knowing they're safe and
everything is going okay. What do you think, Dev? Do
you keep me informed?"

I glanced at the clock on the wall. "Aaron, I'm almost fifteen minutes early. I've only been sitting here for all of about ninety seconds, and you're already starting in on me."

"And just how long was I supposed to wait, Dev? Four shots fired in the middle of the morning at your house. Two hit your front window. You're lucky these guys didn't shoot you. Who in the hell did this? What the hell did you do to make them do this? And why, in God's name, didn't you tell me? Damn it."

"I don't know who it was, Aaron. I don't—"

"Stop right there. If you're not going to tell me the truth, don't say anything else. I don't need to be lied to."

"Aaron, I'm not lying. I don't know who did it. And by the way, how did you find out about this? I didn't file a report."

"Yeah, that's another thing. I'm aware you didn't file a report. I guess just another day in the life, why bother to let the police know? I know this might be tough for you to comprehend, Dev, but when someone fires four rounds on a busy street, in the middle of a big city, you might not be the only person endangered. Yeah, I know you slept through worse in the mid-east, but this is Saint Paul, Dev. Go ahead and call us crazy, but we're kind of uptight about jackasses shooting guns in our city. And the last thing we need is another jackass deciding to settle the matter in his own way. So hear me loud and clear. You are not to respond in kind. Any questions?"

"Oh, so now all of a sudden I'm a jackass?"

"No, not all of a sudden, you've always been one. Okay, I've said my piece. You know what you're going to order?"

"My usual, the bacon bourbon chicken sandwich. So how did you find out about this?"

"A neighbor filed a report."

"Did she mention four shots were fired and two hit the window?"

"First of all, I don't know if the person who filed the report was male or female."

"Bullshit," I said and now was almost positive Amanda had ignored my request and filed the report.

"And, for your information, no, she didn't mention how many shots were fired. I went over to your house this afternoon as soon as I read the damn report. I saw the damage to your front window and the two bullet holes in the siding."

"Well, the good news is, I called Mike Casey, and he came out and took the measurements for a new window."

"Mike Casey? How's he doing? I haven't seen him in years."

"We didn't talk for long. He had two more appointments. He's doing fine. Three kids, one is thirteen, and it sounds like she's doing just what she's supposed to do. She's driving her parents nuts."

"What kind of glass are you getting?"

"If it makes you feel any better, I'm going with the bullet-proof he recommended."

"Good, and yes, it does make me feel better. You think this might have something to do with some woman you've been seeing. Maybe some incensed husband or a nutcase boyfriend?"

"I've been too busy of late to get into any trouble along those lines."

"I don't know, complaints in the middle of the night about noisy parties. A squad car having to evict everyone. Apparently two of your new best friends turn out to be those worthless Massinni brothers. Just a warning, it's only a matter of time before those two are sent back to prison."

"I should have known you got hold of that report. Gee, imagine my surprise, they've got prison records."

"What the hell are you doing partying with those two losers?"

"Well, before you get back up on your high horse, let me explain why those two were in my place." I went on to tell him about the Roxy debacle. We ordered dinner. It eventually arrived, and with all of Aaron's questions, I still wasn't done with the story. I finished halfway through our meal, by which time we were both on our second beers.

"So where is this Roxy person now?" Aaron asked and stuffed two more of my French fries into his mouth.

"I'm not sure, and I don't really care. All I know is, I'm not going to have to deal with her anymore. Heidi went down this morning to see about posting bail."

"Not going to happen," Aaron said.

"Why not?"

"If she's charged with assaulting an officer, they'll keep her behind bars for at least seventy-two hours, and then she'll have a hearing where bail will be set. She's not going anywhere for at least another two days at the very earliest. Depending on her record, I'm guessing bail will be set at a hundred grand, and that's if it's a first-time offense. Your friend Heidi will have to come up with ten percent, unless she goes to a bondsman. Either way, she's on the hook for a hundred grand."

"Humf, I know I wouldn't want to be responsible. That Roxy is just crazy enough to try to cut and run."

"And you said she was tied up with Sheldon Smeet?"

"Not in so many words, unless that's what he was into. He took her out to Vegas for a couple of nights, and they partied. Like I said, he gave her the keys to this place that just burnt down. I'm not convinced he wasn't setting her up right from the start. I'm willing to bet he had her figured as being naive, and oblivious, and now she's suddenly in way over her head."

Aaron shook his head. "Makes the lowlifes I deal with look pretty good. This woman sounds like she had every opportunity in the world and threw it all away."

"Not far from the truth."

When we parted after dinner I picked up the tab. On the one hand, it bothered me that Aaron knew as much as he did, but on the other, it was nice to know someone like Aaron had my back. I decided The Spot might be the place for just one more.

Forty-six

I parked along the side of the building, and after chatting a minute or two with three guys smoking outside, I entered through the side door. Mike was tending bar, and he gave me a wave as I stepped in. I walked down the bar to an open stool and sat down. There was an empty whiskey glass in front of the stool, but no one was standing around when I looked, so I figured whoever it was had left.

"Good to see you, Dev. Where you been the last couple of days?"

"Working, Mike, no rest for the wicked."

He laughed and said, "No one would know that better than you. What can I get you?"

"I think a Summit IPA."

"Coming up," Mike said and poured me a glass. He slid the glass across the bar and walked down to the other end to fill someone else's order.

Suddenly a familiar voice said, "Thanks for saving my place, Dev." I turned around, and there was Louie, all smiles.

"Louie, sorry, didn't know this was your stool. I just saw the empty glass and figured whoever was here had left." I hopped off the stool, and Louie sat down.

"So how was your day?" Louie said as he raised his empty glass and caught Mike's attention.

"You don't want to know. Let's just say crazy and leave it at that. I was in the office this afternoon, but I'm guessing you had a trial or something."

"Actually, my day was probably just as crazy as yours. By the way, I saw your friend Heidi down at the county jail."

"Oh really, what did she have to say?"

"Never had the chance to talk to her. She was with some high-priced lawyer who would never admit to knowing me. She didn't look very happy. Is she in any kind of trouble?"

"No, other than she's suddenly been saddled with Roxy. Her childhood friend who is a major pain in the butt."

"This is the same woman that's staying with you?"

"Past tense, she was staying with me. After throwing a party at my place that had the cops showing up around two in the morning, she cleverly managed to get arrested for a DUI. Then, in the process of getting arrested, she assaulted a police officer right in front of my place. Heidi told me she was going down there with the idea of posting bail. I had dinner with Aaron LaZelle earlier tonight. He thought it would be at least three days before they released her, and he said she's probably looking at something like a hundred grand for bail."

Louie took a sip of his fresh drink and nodded. "Yeah, and that's provided she doesn't have a record."

"That's pretty much what Aaron said, too."

"Anything remotely resembling a prior offense, either DUI or assault, and she'll be looking at six months to three years."

"I don't know her prior history, but what you're saying pretty much mirrors what Aaron was telling me. I took Roxy's suitcase stuffed with all her earthly possessions over to Heidi this morning and told her I'm done with Roxy. She said she was just on her way to post bail. I don't know if she had that attorney lined up before or maybe she went down there, got the bad news, and then got ahold of him. Funny he wouldn't tell her she was looking at a minimum seventy-two-hour lock up."

"I'm blanking on that guy's name, but he's out of his element. You want to do an international trade deal he might be your guy, but DUIs and assaults, he'd just as soon not get his hands dirty. I'm sure he's not afraid to charge though."

"That is *so* not my problem. I washed my hands of Roxy as of last night. I wish her the very best of luck, and I hope I never see her again."

"Buy you another?" Louie said.

I thought for a moment and said, "No, it's been a long day, and I think the best thing I can do is just head home. You in the office tomorrow?"

Louie took a sip and nodded. "Yeah, unless something comes up, I should be in around nine or so."

"See you then," I said. I headed out the door, waved good-bye to Mike as I left, and hopped in my car. I drove past my street and up Amanda's, hoping to see her sitting on the porch and maybe stop. No such luck. The lights were off, the house was dark, and either she was already in bed, or she was out. I drove home and parked in my garage. For just a nanosecond, I wondered where Roxy's car was and then smiled when I remembered it had been towed.

I went into the house, let Morton out the back, and when he came back in, we both headed upstairs to bed. I turned on the TV and promptly fell asleep. I woke sometime in the middle of the night, turned off the TV, and slept until seven-thirty the following morning. We had a leisurely breakfast. I rolled the trash and recycling bins out to the curb, and we took a quick walk around the block and past Amanda's. She wasn't out on her porch, and I thought it was too early to ring her doorbell, so we went home.

Forty-seven

At nine, I phoned Amanda, but my call dropped into her voicemail after two rings. "Hi Amanda, it's Dev. Just checking in. I didn't know if you wanted to work with Morton this morning. Give me a call if it's convenient. I'm going to check on Madame this morning. If there's any change, I'll let you know."

I put the leash on Morton, and we walked over to the vet. When we walked in, the receptionist was all smiles. Morton immediately sat when we stopped at the counter.

"Hi, Dev. Here to check in on Madame?"

"Yeah, how did she do last night?"

"She's just fine. Let me just get the doc out here. He can give you an update, and then you can check her out." She picked up the phone and punched in two numbers. After a moment, she said, "Hi. I've got Dev Haskell and Morton out here. Okay, I'll tell him," she said and hung up.

"Everything okay?"

"Yes." She nodded. "He's just finishing up with someone, and he'll be out. Is it okay if I give Morton a biscuit?"

"Yeah, sure, you'll have a friend for life."

She reached into a large cookie jar behind her desk, pulled out a dog biscuit, and stepped around the reception counter. Morton immediately stood and started wagging his tail with his tongue hanging out.

"Oh, good boy, Morton, good boy." She half-tossed the biscuit, which Morton grabbed in mid-air and inhaled in three quick bites.

We sat in the lobby for no more than five minutes. Morton focused on the receptionist in the event there might be a second treat.

I was paging through a year-old magazine when Tommy appeared and said, "Hi, Dev. Come on back. She's doing just fine." As we walked down the long hallway, he gave me the update. "She had a quiet night. She's doing fine and is up and around. I'd like to keep her for one more night just to be sure, but I don't expect any problems."

He opened a door at the end of the hall, and we walked into the room. There were four dogs in there, all with plastic cones around their necks. Madame was in the back in a large kennel. She was lying down pawing a chew toy, but when she saw us, she immediately got up and hurried to the front of the kennel. Morton's tail began wagging, and he stuck his nose through the fencing. Madame responded in kind.

"You'll have to keep the cone on her for maybe ten days until she heals. Keep an eye on it. Thus far, she's healing nicely. I'll want to take a look at her before you remove the cone. Amanda was in last night and again earlier this morning. I told her the same thing.”

“Yeah, she was pretty upset. Not that I wasn’t, but she seemed to be in a bit of shock yesterday.”

“Well, she seemed fine this morning. I told her a little softer diet for the next four or five days wouldn’t be a bad thing, and there’s a standard antibiotic she can get across the counter that wouldn’t hurt and might just speed up the healing. I wrote it down for her.”

“I’ll leave that in her hands. Oh, I meant to ask, did you happen to file a report on this incident with the police?”

“The police? No, we didn’t. We rarely do. I figured you would do that. I suppose we can if you want me to.”

“No, it’s already done. I just wanted to be sure that, if you did file, they didn’t look at this as two separate incidents.”

Tommy nodded. “Not to worry. We haven’t filed anything.”

“Good, thanks, Tommy. Listen, we’ll get out of your hair. You’re going to keep her overnight again?”

“Yeah, just to be on the safe side. I mentioned it to Amanda. She said she’d be here tomorrow morning when we opened.”

“Thanks again, and she apparently likes the chew toy.”

“Yeah, well, Amanda brought that this morning. Good to see you, Dev. Glad everything worked out.”

"A testament to your skill, Doc. Many thanks." We shook hands, and I had to give Morton a couple of strong pulls on the leash to get him to follow me out of the room. Madame barked a good-bye, and we walked up the street past Amanda's. I rang the doorbell, but she didn't answer so we headed home, climbed in the car, and drove down to the office.

Forty-eight

Louie was in the process of working his way through a stack of files when we arrived. He looked up and said, "How's it going?"

Morton headed for his bed and lay down. While I poured a mug of coffee, I said, "Amazingly, we had a quiet night. You need a refill?"

"Yeah," Louie said and set his empty mug on the edge of the picnic table. "Any word on the shooting victim?"

"We just came from there. She's doing fine, and they're going to keep her one more night just to be on the safe side. Amanda is going to be picking her up first thing tomorrow morning."

"Hear anything from Heidi?"

"Nope," I said and sat down behind my desk. "I'm guessing she got the word Roxy will be a guest of the county for at least another forty-eight hours. Not much she can do until then, and honestly, I don't want to get involved."

"Probably wise," Louie said and went back to his files. I opened the three-ring binder on Amanda's missing sister, Nancy, and paged through to the list of people she sang with and the places they performed. I saw no point in looking at more filthy, dive apartments or former single-family homes that had been converted into multiple units.

I turned on my computer and went onto Facebook. I worked my way through the list of fifteen names, looking for a matching Facebook site. I found four local names that matched the names on my list and sent them each a message, asking if they could give me any information on how I could connect with Nancy Williams. I lied in the message and said I wanted to speak with her regarding a singing contract.

"You going to be here for a couple of hours?" I asked Louie.

"Longer than that," he said without looking up. "I have to get through these files by the end of the day, and I'm going at a snail's pace."

"Would it be okay if I left the boss here?" I nodded at Morton half-asleep in his bed. "I've got to go to a half-dozen bars and see if they know anything about Amanda's sister. I don't want to leave him sitting in the car for any length of time."

"Not a problem. You mind filling his water dish before you go? I'm going to be focused on these damn things, and I won't be paying attention."

"You got it." I filled Morton's water dish. He glanced up at me for a brief moment when I set the dish down, but he didn't raise his head. Instead, he just took a deep breath and closed his eyes. Apparently, it was nap time. I was jealous.

The first place I went to was The Music Cafe. A nice enough place over on Payne Avenue. I'd been there a few times, but contemporary jazz wasn't really my thing. I walked in with the 8x10 of Nancy in my hand and went up to the bar. It wasn't quite noon, and there were maybe a dozen people in the place. Two of the usual types were seated at the bar staring at half-empty glasses of beer and looking neither left nor right. Every place seemed to have one or two of these guys.

"Hi, what can I get for you?" the bartender asked with a smile. He was an average-sized guy with dark hair except around the temple where it had started to grey. I pegged him at mid to late forties. He wore a white shirt with a button-down collar open at the neck and a black vest.

"Is there a manager I can speak with?"

The smile quickly faded. "No, she's not here at the moment. Is there a problem?"

"No, not really. Maybe you can help me." I handed him the 8x10. "I'm hoping maybe someone might have a way I could get in touch with this woman. Her name is Nancy Williams. She sang with a couple of different jazz groups but probably used a stage name. I have a client who would like to extend a contract to her, but we can't find her. I know she performed here at least once or twice."

He looked at the photo for a long moment and slowly shook his head. "No. No, can't say as she looks familiar. You want to hang on for a moment? Let me check with someone else."

"Yeah, please do."

He walked to the end of the bar and called a woman over. She appeared to be waiting tables, but there were only two tables occupied, so she had some time at the moment. She walked over and studied the photo for a good half a minute before she shook her head no, and he headed back to me.

"Sorry," he said. "She doesn't ring a bell with either one of us. How long ago was she here?"

"At least two years ago."

"Oh, well there's part of the problem. We've acts here seven nights a week. A lot of times two or sometimes even three in a night. No offense, but they all run together after a while."

Unfortunately, it made sense. I took out a business card, wrote 'Nancy Williams' across the top of the card, and handed it to him. "If you could give that to your manager when she comes back, maybe the name might ring a bell."

He looked at my card and then up at me. "A private investigator. She in some kind of trouble?"

"Trouble? No, just the opposite. Apparently, she sent a demo tape to my clients some time ago. They think she'd be the perfect fit for some big recording they've got lined up, and I've been trying to find her. No luck so far. I'm just hoping she's still local and hasn't signed with someone else."

He nodded, suggesting my explanation made sense.

"Thanks, appreciate the help. If you could just pass that card on to the manager."

"I'll be sure to do that. Good luck finding her," he said as he slipped my card into a vest pocket.

Forty-nine

I had no better luck in the next three places. Everyone was nice, but no one recognized Nancy's photo, let alone her name. The last place on my list was the Voodoo Lounge over in Minneapolis. I'd heard of it, but I'd never been there. The place was on the edge of downtown, about a half-block away from where things started to turn pretty seedy. Just down the block was a strip joint, and across the street from there was an Adult Toy Shop named Fantasy Garden with a red light that flashed 'Open 24 Hours.'

I parked on a side street and walked around the corner to the Voodoo Lounge. The building was a two-story red brick structure with a large red stone block at the top of the building with the year 1894 carved into it. A sign on the dark blue door posted the hours and read, 'Open 5:00 pm until 2 am.' It wasn't quite four in the afternoon. I pulled on the door, and it opened, so I decided to take a chance and stepped inside.

The place was dark. Dim lights illuminated an oblong bar in the center of the room with tables and chairs throughout the room. All the walls were exposed brick and covered with posters of jazz groups I'd never heard of. The one exception was the curved wall behind the small stage. The wall was painted the same dark blue as the front door. A neon sign that said 'VOODOO LOUNGE' hung on the wall. A piano and three chairs sat on the stage.

"Hey, sorry, man, but we won't be open for another hour," a guy said as he stepped through a swinging door on the far wall. He carried a stack of three green plastic trays that were filled with drink glasses. He set the stack of trays on the bar before he turned to face me. He wore jeans and a navy-blue t-shirt with an image of the 'VOO-DOO LOUNGE' neon light across the front. He looked to be about my age. His hair was trimmed and thinning on the top.

"Sorry to bother you. I was hoping the manager might be here."

"I'm the manager, the head bartender, and the owner, and if I owe you any money you're going to have to get in line."

"No, no nothing like that. I'm looking for someone, and I wonder if you could help me. She sang with a number of different jazz groups. She used a number of different stage names, and I've been trying to find her."

"You a cop?" he said and pulled one of the trays off the stack and set it on the bar.

"No, a private investigator, actually. Dev Haskell's my name," I said and held out my hand.

He nodded but didn't shake my hand. "So why do you want to find this woman? What's she done?"

"She sent a demo tape to my clients some time ago. They've got a recording gig lined up, and they think she would be perfect for it. The problem is, they can't find her. That's why they hired me, and I've been having the same kind of luck. We know she sang here at least a few times. Unfortunately, the most recent date I have was at least two years ago. I've got her picture here," I said and held out the 8x10 photo.

"You got some identification?"

I pulled a business card out of my wallet and handed it to him.

"You got a driver's license?" he said, looking at my card.

"You sure you're not a cop?" I joked and handed him my license. At least he smiled at my attempt at humor. He compared the name on my driver's license to my business card and handed the license back to me.

"Let me see that photo."

I handed the photo to him and said, "Her name is Nancy Williams, although she performed under a number of different stage names."

He studied the photo for a long moment. "Yeah, Nancy Williams. I remember her. I think she used the stage name Delilah. Yeah, from what I remember, she was pretty good."

"Oh, man, you're kidding me. I can't tell you how many folks looked at that image and didn't recognize her. Delilah? How long ago was that?"

"Umm, maybe six months back. Let me just lock that front door and then come on back to my office. I can find out when I cut her a check if you got a couple of minutes."

"I got as long as it takes. You got more of those glasses to carry out?"

"As a matter of fact, I do. You go through that swinging door, there's three more trays on the counter just inside the kitchen. If you could haul them out here and set them next to these three while I lock the door, that would help."

I hurried towards the swinging door and stepped into the kitchen. There were two guys in the kitchen dressed in white smocks and wearing VOODOO LOUNGE baseball caps. The kitchen smelled wonderful. One of the guys was stirring a tall metal pot, and the other was cutting up what looked like about a hundred sausages on a cutting board. The three trays of glasses sat just inside the door on a steel counter. I nodded at the guy stirring the pot, picked up the trays, and headed back out through the swinging door.

"Come on back to my office. What'd you say your name was?" he said as I set the trays of glasses on the bar.

"Haskell, Dev Haskell."

"You from around here, Dev? I don't recognize your name."

"I'm from over in Saint Paul."

"Oh, sorry to hear that," he said. We wound our way around tables and headed for a hallway marked toilets. There were three doors in the hallway labeled Ladies, Gents, and Private. He opened the door marked Private, and we stepped into a fairly neat office. "Why don't you take a seat while I get this up on the computer," he said, pointing to one of two wooden chairs in front of his desk.

He sat down behind the desk and pressed a button on the side of the computer screen. It made a musical sound a moment later, and he said, "This should just take a minute to get online."

I looked around the office. There was a framed photo of an older couple just above the credenza. The woman had salt and pepper hair and a fancy pink outfit. She was wearing a corsage. The bald man next to her was wearing a suit and tie with a boutonniere in the lapel of his suit coat. There was a framed photo next to it, six guys in army universal camouflage uniforms standing out on what looked like a highway or maybe even a runway. Their arms were over each other's shoulders. They were all grinning and giving whoever was taking the picture the finger. There were signatures across the photo.

"Just a second here and I can bring this up."

"You were in Iraq," I said, staring at the photo.

He sat back and looked at me. "How'd you know that?"

"I was at the same party. Your picture, is that you second from the left?"

He didn't look at the photo, but he said, "Yeah, 2011. We were finally going home. What a cluster fuck."

"That outside Sather Air Base in Bagdad?"

"Yeah, you were there too?"

"Yeah, home in 2009 and the term cluster fuck doesn't do it justice."

He smiled and said, "Name is Jack Davies, Dev. Nice to meet you. Let me print this off for you." He made three clicks with his mouse and a small, compact black printer with the label 'brother genuine' fired up on the credenza behind him. A moment later, he handed me a copy of the check. It was made out to Nancy Williams in the amount of three hundred and fifty-seven dollars. The address listed on the check receipt was up in North Branch, Minnesota. The check was dated February 12 of this year.

"North Branch? What the hell is she doing up there?"

"Right now? She's probably looking after her new baby," Jack said.

Fifty

I headed back to the office. It was the beginning of the peak time for rush hour traffic on Interstate 94, and after waiting fifteen minutes to get onto the entrance ramp, I inched my way into the bumper to bumper traffic and drove the next few miles at a slow jogging speed. I took the first exit into St. Paul and drove all the way down to Randolph Avenue, where I took a left and headed down to the office. What was normally a twenty-minute trip from Minneapolis took about forty-five minutes at this time of day, add to that close to a hundred curses yelled at drivers for not doing what I wanted them to do.

Louie was still in the office. Just two files remained in the pile of files to be read. Morton was awake and popped his head up as I entered. He stood, gave his post-nap stretch, groaned, and walked over for a scratch behind the ear.

"Everything go okay? Morton give you any trouble?"

"Not a problem. He woke up maybe fifteen minutes ago and fooled around with that chew toy."

"Looks like you've gone through a good portion of those files."

"Yeah, another forty-five minutes and I should be finished. Can I interest you in a beverage after that?"

"Yeah, I think so. That'll give me a chance to check out some things online," I said and settled in behind my desk. I clicked on my computer, waited for a minute, then got onto the website for the property tax records up in Chisago County where the town of North Branch was located. I input the address on the Voodoo Lounge check for Nancy Williams and wrote down the name of the property owner. The owner was listed as an LLC, a Limited Liability Company. In the case of the North Branch property, the name was Cedar Park Apartments, LLC. I brought up google maps and input the address for the Cedar Park Apartments. The image of the building that came up looked like a decent two-story brick building maybe twenty years old. Just from the google image, it looked a hell of a lot better than the dives she'd been living in here in Saint Paul. I clicked to an overhead shot. There was a parking lot along the south side of the building. I counted ten parking spaces. At the time the photo had been taken, there were only two cars in the parking lot.

I googled Cedar Park Apartments, LLC, and the same address came up as the building. "Hey Louie, can I ask you a question?"

"You already have," he said, closing the file in front of him and reaching for another one.

"I'm trying to find the address for an LLC that's listed as the owner of an apartment building. The building address is what comes up. I have my doubts whoever owns this building also lives there."

"It'll be easier if I just look it up rather than take the time to tell you and then wait for you to screw it up so I can fix it. What's the name of the LLC?"

"Cedar Park Apartments, LLC. It's up in North Branch."

"Minnesota, right?" he said as he tapped his keyboard.

"Yeah, Chisago county."

"Bringing it up now, just a minute." He clicked a couple more keys. "Yeah, here it is, a guy named Arvid Lindgren. You want an address?"

"Yeah."

He grabbed a pen and wrote the address on a yellow legal pad. When he finished, he tore the sheet from the tablet. I started to get out of my desk chair.

"No, no just stay there," he said and quickly folded the sheet of paper into a paper airplane, which he sailed over to me. It landed perfectly on my desk.

"I'll bet you a whiskey you couldn't do that again."

He tore another sheet off, folded it, aimed carefully, and tossed the airplane. It landed about six inches from the first one. "You want to bet again, double or nothing?"

"No, I'll quit while I only owe you one."

"You owe me two, one for getting the information in the first place and the second for the bet."

"Fair enough."

I opened up the first paper airplane. Arvid Lindgren had an address on Main Street in North Branch. Probably an office, which was even better than a home address.

Fifty-one

We were seated at the far end of the bar, close to the side door. Louie was on his second whiskey. I was nursing my first beer. Morton was seated at the foot of my stool waiting for me to hand him the next salted pork rind from the bag.

Louie took a sip and said, "Based on the version you just told me, it suggests this Roxy needs someone to help her get her act together."

"She probably needs a number of people, and what do you mean my version?"

"Well, the facts as you know them."

"Look, no matter how much money she has, she always spends more. She'd much rather go out to Vegas with some lowlife like Sheldon Smeet and offer herself up for three days in some pricey hotel room than get a job and work for a living. She's got the maturity of a ten-year-old and a real knack for ending up with the wrong type of people. And those are her good points."

Louie looked at me over the rim of his glass for a long moment while he sipped his drink. He licked his lips as he set the glass down and said, "You know, Dev, you're getting to be a really crabby old guy."

"Crabby? I extended myself and offered this woman a place to live while she gets her feet back on the ground. I offered to interact with the fire department and learn what their investigation will discover, if anything. I did all this for free because I'm a nice guy. I didn't want her in my bed, even though she tried. I didn't charge her for food. I let her take an hour-long shower every day. I took care of her dog after she abandoned the poor thing. And how does she thank me, the crabby old guy? She throws a party for about forty people I've never seen before, with the exception of the Massinni brothers, who were going to try to kill me. Stop me when I get to the point where I'm the bad guy, here."

"I know all that, Dev, and if it makes you feel any better, for a change, you're not the bad guy. I'm just suggesting this woman has some issues and probably needs some professional help is all."

"Professional help. Yeah, perfect, she can lie in a room on a couch once a week for the next twenty years and tell the professional how screwed up she is and it'll only cost her the modest amount of two hundred bucks an hour. What she needs is a couple of swift kicks in her otherwise perfect ass."

"Am I sensing some hostility following a possible rejection?"

"What? Are you nuts? Louie, are you seeing a shrink?"

"Why do you say that?"

"Because you're not making any sense here."

"I'm merely suggesting there are more than two sides to every story and your view of the facts, as you see them, is simply one of a number of sides."

"Stop it. My head is hurting. Besides, I've got to take off. I want to check on Madame at the veterinarian clinic. With any luck, Amanda can take her home tomorrow morning, and that will be one less thing I have to worry about. There you go, crabby me, taking care of everything. Speaking of which, what's your schedule tomorrow?"

"Tomorrow? I'm in first thing in the morning. I've got a mid-afternoon court date, and I need to prepare."

"This have anything to do with that two-foot high stack of files you were working through today?"

Louie nodded. "Yeah, my on-again, off-again client, Otto Rugglen."

"Otto? The guy who was sued last year after building that house that collapsed?"

"One in the same. Yeah, he violated city code on the size of floor joists, so they were insufficient to begin with, and then he forgot to support them properly on one of the walls. As soon as the buyers moved their furniture in, the place collapsed, literally like a house of cards. He was lucky no one was killed."

"He go to jail?"

"No, fortunately, maybe. He was fined six figures, returned the money from the sale, lost his contractor's license, and is required to pay for the rebuild. Of course,

I'm the bad guy on the whole deal because I didn't get him off scot-free."

"So why are you taking him on as a client again?"

"Because he pays. Because I require fifty percent of my fee upfront before I even think about pouring him so much as a cup of coffee. Besides, his reputation precedes him, and no one will take him on as a client, so he's stuck having to pay me. In other words, Ir's like he's my government check, except he's not the government."

"And what's he charged with this time?"

"Contracting without a license. I think in his mind, losing his license was a good thing. He figures it means he doesn't have to pay the licensing fee, and he doesn't have to get city permits to do any projects. I'm in court on Monday arguing the city has no grounds. I'll do my best, then I'll lose. Otto will end up with a hefty fine and a bill for my hefty fee."

"God, it sounds depressing."

"You kidding? I wish I had fifty more clients just likc him. Always in need and I can charge them fifty percent upfront."

"Yeah, just think, if this keeps up you might actually be able to afford a desk."

"Very funny."

"Hey, I better run. I want to check on Madame at the vet, and I need to get there before they close. Thanks for your help on that North Branch Address."

"My pleasure, thanks for the drinks. I'm in the office all morning if you want to leave Morton there."

"I'll keep it in mind. Thanks. Come on, Morton. Let's go see Madame." At the sound of her name, Morton was up in a flash with his tail wagging. We hurried out the door.

Fifty-two

We drove up to the veterinary office and were able to park right in front. The lights were on inside. I clipped the leash onto Morton's collar, and we hurried in. Tommy was out at the receptionist counter, writing something in a file. When we walked in, he looked up and smiled.

"Well, look who's here. Come to check on the patient?"

Morton's tail was waving back and forth. Tommy chuckled and reached into the dog biscuit jar. "Here you go, Morton, doctor's orders." Tommy tossed the biscuit in Morton's general direction. He snatched it just before it hit the floor.

"How is Madame doing?"

"She's fine, making good progress. Come on back and see for yourself." We headed back to the kennel room. Madame was the only dog in there. When Tommy opened the door to the room, she ran to the front of her kennel and began barking, excited to see us. Morton hurried over, and they immediately began rubbing noses between the slats.

"She'll be able to go home in the morning. I ran some tests on her an hour ago. She's healing nicely but still tender. She'll be excited to get home but see if you can't keep her calm. Maybe stay away from having her run around with Morton for a week or so. The stitches she's got are dissolvable, so they should begin to disappear in ten to twelve days. Once in a while, there may be a remnant that lasts longer, sometimes up to a month or even two. Don't worry, that's normal."

"And the plastic cone?"

"Let's see how she's doing in two weeks."

"She'll be staying with Amanda, so Madame will be getting excellent care."

"Yeah, Amanda was in first thing this morning, then again at noon, and maybe just an hour ago. I've given her the same information. Nice lady."

"Yeah. I don't know her that well, but she seems nice. I'm just sorry she and Madame got involved in all this."

"It's going to work out fine, Dev. It just takes time."

"Well, very much appreciated, Tommy. We'll get out of your hair and let you head home. Now you be sure to send me a bill."

"Already taken care of."

"Amanda?"

"Actually, no. Just some good Samaritan who sent a note that said he heard about it from neighbors and wanted to pay the bill."

"Really? Did he leave a name?"

"No. It was a cashier's check. I could maybe call the bank and see if I could find out who did it. We just added it to the deposit and dropped it in the night box."

"Don't worry about it, Tommy. As long as you've been taken care of."

"Thanks, Dev. Call with any problems or concerns."

I put Morton in the back seat, and we drove the two blocks up the street to see if Amanda might be sitting out on her front porch. The porch was empty, and the lights were off inside. We turned at the corner and headed home.

I was seated at the kitchen counter, eating some slices of pizza I found in the back of my refrigerator. Morton was in the backyard, aggressively guarding the property against a pair of squirrels. I clicked onto Facebook to see if anyone had responded to my message looking for a way to connect with Nancy Williams. I had two responses.

The first one, from a guy named Delton, who was a bass player, said he knew of no way to connect, but wasn't it great someone wanted to have her do a recording?

The second one was from a woman named Tenesha. She said she had been friends with Nancy on Facebook, but all communication had ceased four or five months ago. On a whim, I looked up Nancy Williams again on Facebook. Nothing had changed in the last twenty-four hours. A woman in New Zealand, a woman in California, and another in St. Louis. All three appeared to be at least fifteen years older than Amanda's sister. I looked up Amanda's site and scrolled through her friend list. Nancy wasn't listed. It looked like my only option was to drive up to North Branch in the morning and knock on the door of the apartment in the hopes she might still live there.

I ate the last piece of pizza. I got Morton in the house and watched a movie on Netflix that I'd already seen. I went up to bed around eleven. Morton was already asleep.

Fifty-three

According to my digital clock, it was three-thirty in the morning. My lower intestinal track was rumbling, and I was not feeling the best. I lay in bed, waiting for the discomfort to pass, but it only seemed to grow worse. In short order, it became very apparent what the outcome was going to be, so I hurried into the bathroom to spur things along. I left the light off in the hopes I wouldn't completely wake up, and I could get back to sleep. I was feeling substantially better after twenty minutes thank goodness.

I went back into the bedroom, vowing never, ever to eat pizza again unless it had been delivered that same day. Morton was snoring. But now I was wide awake. My choices was to lie in bed and listen to Morton snoring as the minutes slowly passed, or I could get dressed and have an early breakfast.

I was just buckling my belt when I heard what sounded like glass breaking downstairs. It was loud enough that it made me pause for a brief moment. My first thought was Morton had knocked something over, but I could see him asleep and snoring on the far side of the bed. I slipped my shoes on, took my pistol off the nightstand, and hurried downstairs. The light from the flames on the front porch were bright. I stepped out the front door just in time to see a set of taillights racing up the street. It was dark, flames were running up the side of my house and across the porch floor, but I identified the taillights as belonging to a Cadillac Escalade. The Massinni brothers. It had to be.

I ran back into the kitchen, grabbed the fire extinguisher off the back counter, and hurried out to the porch. It smelled like gasoline, and there was what looked like pieces from a broken mason jar scattered across the porch floor. I hit the flames on the floor first then put out the flames running up the siding. It took less than a minute to extinguish the flames with the foam. I kept spraying the area until the extinguisher was empty.

Thank God the pizza had that effect on me. My place is a hundred and forty years old with cedar siding. The whole place would have gone up in about ten minutes. Obviously, the Massinni brothers were going to have to be dealt with.

I let the foam dry out on the porch and made an early breakfast. Morton came down around seven-thirty, and I let him out. After he ate, I walked out to the porch and swept up the broken glass and dried foam as best I could. I dragged the garden hose around to the front and hosed the last remnants of foam off the porch. Nothing really looked like it would have to be replaced, but both the porch floor and a good portion of the front siding would definitely have to be primed and repainted. Thankfully, using a mason jar for a firebomb hadn't been very effective.

At a quarter-to-nine, I drove down to the office with Morton. Louie wasn't in yet, so I made a pot of coffee, sat down, and called Luscious. I gave him an update on Roxy, cautioned him to be careful about taking a call from her or offering her a place to stay. He thanked me for the information, and then I got to the real point of my call. Luscious said he would make sure he was free later that evening.

Louie arrived about a half-hour later, and I left him in charge of Morton, or was it the other way around?

Fifty-four

The town of North Branch is just a forty-minute drive north of Saint Paul up Interstate 35. It was a pleasant enough drive with the majority of the traffic heading in the opposite direction toward the twin cities. I pulled off the Interstate, took a right at the top of the rise, and headed down Main Street in North Branch. My GPS alerted me to Arvid Lindgren's address. It was right next door to a small coffee shop named The Snook.

The building, in fact the entire block, consisted of one-story brick structures. Arvid's office looked like it might be one of the more recent structures dating back to around 1940. There was a large window that looked in on a young woman sitting at a metal desk with a green linoleum top. She was in the process of sticking stamps onto a stack of envelopes.

I stepped into the office. She was pretty, with bright blue eyes and blonde hair. She wore a white sport shirt with a U of M logo. The three buttons on the sport shirt were all undone. Her shorts appeared to be sprayed on. On one corner of the desk rested a beige phone that had to be twenty-five years old. There was a laptop next to the phone. An iPhone with a sparkly pink cover rested within easy reach next to the stack of envelopes. I figured she might be Arvid's daughter, probably home from college for the summer and forced to work in her father's office. No doubt counting the days before she could flee the scene, the slave labor, and get back to her cool college pals.

She said, "Good morning. How are you?" When she smiled, she flashed sparkling white teeth.

"Hey, how's it going?"

"Oh, you know," she said in a tone suggesting very boring.

"Is Arvid in?"

"No, sorry, he's in court this morning. Is there anything I can help you with?"

"I hope so. I'm looking for one of his tenants, a woman named Nancy Williams. She sent one of my clients a demo tape maybe a year ago. She sings jazz. My client is producing a record, and they want to offer Nancy a contract, but we can't seem to locate her. I know she was renting an apartment from Arvid at the Cedar Park Apartments around the first of the year. I'm just trying to find out if she's still there so we can send the contact to her, or better yet, my client could call and give her all the details."

"A recording contract?" She grinned, and her eyes widened.

"Yeah, apparently, she's just the voice they were looking for. They literally went through hundreds of demo tapes, and hers was the best, hands down."

"Cool. I've met her a couple of times, but she never mentioned the singing."

"Well you know, like so many things, it's a tough business, and she was always working other jobs to pay the bills. But her real love was singing jazz, and now it looks like that one in a million chance is here, if we can find her."

She nodded and said, "Do you know where the Cedar Park building is?"

"I have the address in my GPS."

She smiled and said, "Just take a left one block past the stoplight, four blocks later it's on the left side."

"One block past the stoplight, the one just down there on the corner?" I said and pointed down Main Street.

She rolled her eyes and said, "Yeah. It's the only stoplight in town." She made a face that suggested, *Can you believe it?*

"Are you in college?"

The smile immediately returned. "I'm down in the cities at the U. I'll be starting my junior year in nineteen days." Clearly counting the days until she could escape.

"Sounds great. What's your name?"

"Margareta Lindgren," she said and flashed another smile.

"Listen, thanks for your help, Margareta. I'll tell Nancy she has you to thank for the contract."

"Tell her I want a signed CD."

"I'll do that," I said and headed out the door. I climbed in the car and checked the time. It was almost eleven. If Arvid was going to be back to the office in the afternoon, that gave me maybe two hours before his daughter told him the wonderful news about Nancy's recording contract and he took her head off for revealing a tenant's personal information.

Fifty-five

Margareta's directions were spot on. I took a left one block past the only stoplight in town, and four blocks later, there was the Cedar Park apartment building looking just like the image I'd seen on Google maps. I pulled into the parking lot. Today there were three cars in the lot. Since the spaces weren't numbered, I pulled into one and parked.

I got out of the car and went in the front door. I entered a small lobby with a bank of eight mailboxes set into a wall. Each mailbox had an apartment number on the small locked door but no last names. There was a phone on the wall next to the security door. I pulled on the door handle just to see if the door would open, but unfortunately, it was locked.

I lifted the receiver on the phone, and a screen lit up that read apartment 1. I pressed the downward arrow on the keypad, and 'Apartment 2' appeared, then 3 and so on. I moved the list back up to 'Apartment 1' and hit the pound key. A moment later, the phone began to ring. After six rings, it dropped me into voicemail. The recording was a woman's voice who gave her name as Eunice. She sounded elderly. Apartment 2 was Gary and Grace, also not home. Apartment 3 was Kate, and she wasn't home either.

Apartment 4 was answered on the second ring by a man. "Yeah," was all he said. I immediately had a vision of a guy in need of a shave and a shower, wearing a strappy t-shirt, and drinking a can of cheap beer, not his first, for lunch.

"Hi, I'm calling for Nancy Williams."

"You got the wrong number. She's up in five," he said and hung up.

I scrolled to apartment 5 and hit the pound sign. The phone rang four times, and I was starting to deflate just as a voice answered that sounded exactly like Amanda.

"Hello," she said, and I could hear a baby crying in the background.

"Nancy Williams?"

There was a long pause before she said, "Who is this?"

"My name is Dev Haskell. I'm a friend of Amanda's."

"Is she okay?" There was a note of fear in her voice.

I thought for a nanosecond about saying yes to her question, but maybe that was all she wanted to hear and she'd hang up. So I said, "She survived a shooting."

"Oh my God. Is she in the hospital?"

"I'd like to come up and tell you about it, if—"

"I'm in unit five," she interrupted. The security door suddenly buzzed, and I heard a loud click as the door unlocked. I pulled the door open and headed up the stairs. The hallway walls were painted a cream color, and the carpeting was beige. There was no one passed out or asleep in the hallway. A door on the left opened just as I got to the top of the stairs, and a woman with red hair stepped halfway out the door. She was holding a small baby, also with red hair. Not surprisingly, she looked just like her picture, and there was no doubt she and Amanda were sisters.

"Hi, Nancy, my name is Dev Haskell," I said as I held out my hand.

She nodded and said, "Is Amanda all right?"

"Yes, she's fine."

She scrunched her nose and said, "I thought you just told me she survived a shooting. What are you trying to pull here?"

"I'm not trying to pull anything. That part is correct. She did survive a shooting just two days ago. She wasn't shot. It was a drive-by shooting, at my house as a matter of fact. Four shots, but fortunately, they missed her. Would it be all right if I came in?"

"I'm sorry, what did you say your name was?"

"Haskell, Dev Haskell. I'm a private investigator, and I live just a block away from Amanda. She was at my house, working with two dogs when the shooting occurred. I wasn't home at the time, and in all honesty, the bullets were probably meant for me."

"I'm sorry, um, yeah, please come in. I was just getting ready to feed my baby. Please ignore the mess."

I knew what a mess was, and Nancy's apartment wasn't a mess. The place wasn't large. There was a small kitchen with a living room off to the side. The living room had a couch, a chair, and a cabinet with a TV. I guessed it was a one-bedroom apartment based on the two doors down the short hallway. One would be the bathroom, and the other would be the bedroom. Everything was neat and in its place. Even the baby blanket on the floor with the three little toys was neatly arranged with the toys lined up. There weren't any dishes in the kitchen sink or on the counter.

"Let me just get his bottle out of the microwave before he throws another fit."

"What's his name?" I said.

"Stefan Michael," she said as she took the bottle out of the microwave and headed for the couch. "Grab a seat and tell me what happened."

"I'm guessing your little guy is maybe a month old," I said, settling into the chair next to the couch.

"Not bad. He'll be six weeks on Sunday. Please, tell me about Amanda."

I gave her a brief version. I mentioned Madame getting shot while Amanda was working with Morton and Madame. I didn't mention the Massinni brothers or the fact that I hadn't seen Amanda since I dropped her home after Madame's surgery.

"I want to emphasize that Amanda did nothing wrong. In fact, due to her quick thinking, that little dog has been saved and will be well looked after by your sister. She, well actually the two of them, were simply in the wrong place at the wrong time."

"Incredible," Nancy said, shaking her head.

"Yeah, as awful it is, she was very lucky."

"No, I mean yes, she was lucky. But this happened once before, with her husband."

"Her husband? I thought they were divorced."

"They were, or, well, they were in the process of getting a divorce. They met in a restaurant to discuss the settlement. He was one of those narcissistic types. Everything always revolved around him. Anyway, they met downtown in a restaurant to discuss who got what and when. Surprise, surprise, it turned out he basically wanted everything. They never did come to an agreement, and they weren't more than ten feet outside the restaurant when some guy comes out of nowhere, puts a gun to Sally's head, and shoots him. Right there, on a busy downtown street, at one in the afternoon. Then he calmly hops on a motorcycle and disappears."

"They never arrested anyone?"

"No. There were all sorts of witnesses but no definitive description. There was mention of some Italian gangster guy, but nothing was ever proven. If you're an investigator, you should check it out. I'm sure it's, what do they call it, a cool case?"

"You mean a cold case?"

"Yeah, that's the term."

"And his name was Sally?"

"That was his nickname. His full name was Salvatore, Salvatore Brazzi."

My head was suddenly spinning, and I said. "Do you remember the name of the gangster they thought might have been responsible?"

She shook her head as she lifted Stefan onto her shoulder and began to pat him softly on the back. "No. It was five or six years ago. I mean, if I heard the name I'd probably recognize it, maybe."

"How about Massinni, Dante Massinni?"

Her eyes grew wide. "Oh my God. That's the name. That's him. That's the bastard, but they could never prove anything. But how did you even know that?"

Fifty-Six

I was back in the office before one. Louie was loading files in his briefcase when I walked in. "Oh, Dev, great, perfect timing. I'm about to head out. Got a call this morning, and there's a meeting in the judge's chambers before we go to trial."

"Is that good or bad news?"

"Good, I hope, keeping my fingers crossed. The prosecution is hopefully going to make an offer that would save both of us some time, cost my client money, and maybe see him in the workhouse for a bit. I know that sounds harsh, but frankly, it's a much better deal than he'll get if we go to trial. Much as I enjoy charging him for the representation, you would think sooner or later he'd get the message and begin to obey the law. He just seems to be one of these guys who think the rules don't apply to him. But enough, how'd things go up in North Branch?"

"Honestly, better than expected. I talked with Amanda's sister, and—"

"Really? You found her?"

"Yeah, it wasn't that hard at the end of the day. She wasn't exactly hiding. Turns out there were some family issues, not the least of which is she delivered a baby six weeks ago, and she's been gainfully employed for twenty months. Some stuff on Amanda's side, too. But all in all, I think things worked out a lot better than I could have hoped. She gave me a business card with her phone number and wants Amanda to call her, so that seems positive."

"Great. What's the word on Madame?"

"As far as I know, Amanda has her. I was about to call the veterinary clinic and find out."

Louie closed his briefcase, said goodbye, and headed out the door. I wished him luck in the judge's chambers. I got on the phone and called the clinic. The receptionist answered.

"Hi, this is Dev Haskell calling to see if Amanda Williams was able to pick up Madame."

She actually laughed. "Oh yeah, she was waiting outside when we arrived to open up. She's got a page full of instructions, an antibiotic cream to apply morning and evening, and a three-week prescription of antibiotic pills to be given with Madame's feeding."

"Madame was doing well?"

"Let's just say she was very happy to be leaving. Yeah, she should be fine as long as she takes it easy. At the end of the day, the recovery just takes time. Given the injury, she was very fortunate."

"Thanks for the update and all you guys have done. Please pass on my thanks to Tommy."

"You take care, Dev. And say hi to Morton for us."

I hung up and said, "She said to say hi to you."

Morton gave me a strange look.

I called Aaron LaZelle next and left a message. I went online and Googled Dante Massinni. He was listed in a number of real estate deals over the years. All sorts of multiple unit complexes out in the suburbs. Large complexes, a hundred and twenty, or two hundred and forty units. Nothing really listed that pegged him as a bad guy. I looked up Salvatore Brazzi, Amanda's husband. There were a couple of newspaper articles covering his murder and the investigation. They basically reiterated what Nancy had told me. He was killed in broad daylight. His killer hopped on a motorcycle and fled the scene, and no one was ever charged. Talk about a dead end.

I heard the stairway creaking on the other side of the office door and thought Louie's meeting in the judge's chambers either went very well or was awful. The door swung open and a red-faced Fat Freddy Zimmerman staggered in followed by Tubby Gustafson, flushed-faced as well.

Tubby leaned against the doorframe to catch his breath before he said, "Honest to God, Haskell." He gulped audibly a couple of times. "You better get an office on the first floor or find a building with an elevator if you know what's good for you."

"Last time I checked, you didn't have any vacancies, Mr. Gustafson."

"And nothing's changed, I don't need the kind of problems you'd bring with you. You can't be serious. You moving in? Next to decent people? I'd lose all my current tenants by the end of the week."

Fat Freddy pulled out a chair for Tubby. Once Tubby was seated, Freddy dropped himself in the chair next to him. I was afraid the chair would collapse into a pile of kindling, but thankfully, it held together.

"So, it would appear you've got some serious house-keeping to take care of," Tubby said. His statement brought a smile to Fat Freddy's red face.

"Housekeeping?" I said and looked around. Morton was curled on his bed, with his back to us and his paws draped protectively over his head.

Tubby shook his head and looked at Fat Freddy. "At no surprise, he remains clueless. It never ceases to amaze me, Haskell. Exactly how in God's name did you even make it this far?"

"Oh, you know me, I just stumble along somehow."

Tubby shook his head in disgust. "Your client's home was burned to the ground while she was spending the night with you."

"First of all, she—"

Tubby held up his hand, cutting me off. "Please. If I might be allowed to continue with this laundry list of incredibly stupid behavior. This innocent woman has her home burnt to the ground. In the process, she lost all her personal possessions. Your way of helping is to evict her, call the police, and have her arrested. While she's in jail, you begin a dalliance with another innocent soul who barely survives the gunfire that wounds that cute little dog she loves so much. All because she's foolish enough to attempt to help the likes of you. As if she hasn't already had enough to deal with in her life. Then, you throw your hands up and insist it's up to her to nurse the little dog back to good health. All the while refusing to report the incident, and the Massinni brothers, to the proper authorities. But then, I suppose this is simply nothing more than a glimpse into your otherwise irresponsible, unproductive life."

"That's not exactly the way things happened, Mr.—"

"Silencio, Haskell," Tubby shouted. "You're already on thin ice, here. Once again, it appears I'm about to pay a steep price due to my association with the likes of you."

"A steep price?"

"Yes, a steep price, a very steep price. Obviously, by offering guidance and assistance, it would appear I condone the irresponsibility you seem to wallow in."

"Seem to wallow in? What, exactly would you have me do?"

"The Massinni brothers could do with a wake-up call. And I don't mean inviting them back for another party where some woman is stripping on your couch."

"I intend to meet with the Massinni brothers and discuss their behavior this evening."

Tubby shook his head and looked over at Fat Freddy. "I should have listened to you, Frederick. You warned me. Told me it was a waste of my precious time. I should have listened." Tubby took a deep breath and shook his head. "We may as well go. It's like pissing into the wind."

Fat Freddy jumped up and pulled back Tubby's chair. Tubby groaned as he stood. He shook his head in disgust and headed for the door. He stood with his back to me for a moment then turned and said, "You know, Haskell. Oh, what's the use? Why do I even bother? The door, Frederick, please, before I lose my mind. Honest to God!"

Fat Freddy opened the door, and Tubby headed for the stairs. I could hear the stairs begin to creak as Tubby headed down. Fat Freddy turned toward me, gave me the finger, and hurried out the door. I watched out the window as they crossed the street and climbed into their black Cadillac Escalade. The same type of car the Massinni idiots drove, minus the bumper sticker. Fat Freddy held the door as Tubby climbed into the back seat and pulled out his cellphone. Fat Freddy closed the door, looked up, and gave me the finger again. He climbed behind the wheel, and they drove off.

Fifty-seven

y phone rang as I watched Fat Freddy run the red light and turn onto the entrance ramp to the Interstate.

"Haskell Investigations."

"Dev, Aaron LaZelle. You called." He sounded busy.

"Yeah, Aaron, thanks for returning my call. I wondered if you could set it up for me to review a cold case file."

"A cold case file? Yeah, I suppose I could, maybe. What do you want to look at?"

"Nothing that would solve anything, if that's what you're wondering. You remember Amanda Williams?"

"It's ringing a bell but help me out."

"She's the person who filed the drive-by shooting report. Where the dog got shot on my front porch."

"Yes," he said, drawing the word out to suggest something like, *'So what is this about?'*

"This has nothing to do with that incident, at least not directly. But the case file I want to look at is the murder of a man named Salvatore 'Sally' Brazzi. He was shot downtown back in—"

"In the middle of the day. By some guy who climbed on a motorcycle and drove off. I had just made detective a couple of years earlier. I remember the shooting, although I wasn't involved in the investigation at all."

"Yeah, well, it turns out my friend, Amanda Williams, she was married to the victim, Sally Brazzi. They had met at a restaurant to discuss dividing assets in their upcoming divorce, and he was shot outside the restaurant."

"Really? Did she tell you this?"

"No, as a matter of fact, her sister told me. Amanda never mentioned anything to me. I'm thinking she probably worked very hard to put the whole episode behind her. To tell the truth, I really haven't spoken to her, or seen her, since the drive-by at my place."

"Interesting. Yeah, okay. I guess I can set that up. I'll alert them down at the front desk and the file room. What time are you thinking of coming down?"

"If it works, I'd like to be there in, say, the next forty-five minutes or so."

"That works. I'll set it up. Be sure to give me a yell once you've reviewed the file."

"Thanks, Aaron," I said, but he had already hung up.

It was a warm summer day, so rather than leave Morton locked in the car, I took him for a quick fifteen-minute walk around the neighborhood. Once back in the office, I filled his water dish and headed down to the central police station. I parked across the street from the station in a gravel parking lot that originally was the location of a factory that manufactured washing machines. The city had planned to pave the lot six or seven years ago but had diverted funds every year since. Now, it would probably cost twice as much. I avoided two large potholes that were filled with water and looked deep enough for kids to swim in. I parked at the far end of the lot next to a limestone brick wall, the only remaining remnant of the factory that had once covered the lot and probably employed a couple hundred people.

The desk-sergeant nodded when I told him why I was there. He handed me a form Aaron had filled out and said, "Go down one level. You know where the elevators are?"

I nodded and headed out a side door. I pressed the down button, and the door on one of the elevators opened immediately. I stepped inside and pressed the button for B-1. When the door opened again, the file room was right across the hall.

I handed Aaron's slip to an officer behind the counter. He asked for identification, and as I pulled out my wallet, he typed something in on his computer. He checked my driver's license and nodded. "Be just a few minutes. Grab a seat in cubicle three, and I'll bring it to you," he said.

There were a number of small cubicles against a far wall. Two of them were occupied. I settled into number three. The cubicle had grey fabric walls and a grey Formica counter with a black wastebasket positioned beneath the counter. The chair was on wheels, and I pulled it out, sat down, and waited.

It was more than a few minutes wait, not that I could do anything about it. After about ten minutes, the officer came in with the file, actually a box of files. I had to fill out and sign a form listing the file numbers then return the form to him. I pulled the cover off the box and set it off to the side. I pulled the stack of files from the box, seven in all, and began to page through them one by one. There were 8x10 photographs of the crime scene, including a number of photos of Salvatore Brazzi lying on the sidewalk.

He was face down and mostly on the sidewalk. His right arm and what was left of his head hung over the curb and rested in the street. You could see the edge of a tire and a portion of a bumper on a white car in some of the images. There was a relatively small bullet hole in the back of his head. His forehead appeared to be mostly gone, and a trail of blood ran along the street gutter and into a sewer grate a foot away. I would guess he was dead before he hit the ground. If they determined the round had been a hollow point it wouldn't have surprised me.

There were a number of witness statements, including one from Amanda, who was listed as Amanda Brazzi. She was unable to describe the assailant other than to say he wore blue jeans and she thought he might have had dark hair, but she couldn't be sure. She did not see the motorcycle he rode away on.

The witness statements weren't much better, and any of the statements that provided information seemed to contradict one another. Sunglasses and no sunglasses. Some said he wore blue jeans, and two were definite he wore dark slacks. Three people said he wore a short-sleeve shirt, and two thought he had long sleeves rolled up above his elbows. Boots, tennis shoes, and black loafers were on his feet. He rode a grey, black or, in one statement a red motorcycle. Everyone seemed to agree there was no license number on the motorcycle. Two people mentioned he had the word 'EVIL' tattooed on the fingers of both hands. Small wonder the police never made an arrest.

In one of the files, there was a statement by Dante Massinni, dated a week after the murder. But the statement was more of a background thing, really only from the standpoint that Brazzi had been an investor in one of Massinni's real estate projects. He was neither the sole investor nor the largest. No other mention of Dante Massinni was in the file.

Salvatore Brazzi did have a record. He had been charged with assault in a bar six years earlier, but the charges were ultimately dropped, which suggested to me some sort of pretrial settlement. After two hours of going through the files page by page, I didn't find anything. In fact, I walked out of the file room with even less than I'd arrived with. I had visions of Dante Massinni being hauled in and interrogated in a windowless room with an attorney at his side who kept saying *'Don't answer that.'*

On the contrary, he was interviewed by two detectives in his office who simply asked him questions regarding Salvatore Brazzi.

I delivered the box of files back to the officer behind the counter and took the elevator up to the main floor. I told the desk sergeant I needed to see Aaron LaZelle. He made a call up to the Homicide section, and a woman in civilian clothes arrived twenty minutes later to escort me upstairs.

Fifty-eight

She was a detective with the last name of Rogers, dressed in blue jeans and a black blouse with an ID card hanging around her neck and a badge attached to her belt. She gave the distinct impression she had more important things going on in her world than stopping everything to escort me up to the homicide section. I asked her four general questions and thanked her for taking the time to escort me as we rode the elevator up to the fourth floor. She responded with four one-word answers and a grunt. Not exactly what you'd call pleasant.

She input a code on the keypad next to the door and stepped into the Homicide section office. I quickly followed before the door closed behind her. "His office is over there in the corner, knock first," she said without looking at me and headed for her desk.

I nodded at a couple of people I recognized and got a nod back. Fortunately, I didn't see Detective Norris Manning. The guy hated me and would have gladly put me in a chokehold and cuffed my hands behind my back, just on general principles.

I knocked on Aaron's office door. The door was partially open, but I couldn't see much, the frosted glass panel in the door didn't help.

Aaron half-yelled, "Come on in, Dev." He was seated at his desk behind three stacks of files. His coat was off, and his shirt sleeves were rolled up on his forearms. His tie was loosened, and the top button on his shirt was undone. He had a file open in front of him. "Grab a seat, and I'll be with you in a minute," he said without looking up. Ten minutes and two phone calls later, he finally looked up at me and said, "You went through the Brazzi file?"

"Yeah, didn't learn anything and to be honest, I wasn't even sure what I was looking for. With all the contradicting witness statements, other than the fact that the shooter was a guy, and he rode off on a motorcycle with no license plate, I think there might have been only a couple of statements that corroborated anything another witness said."

Aaron sat back and nodded. "Yeah, it's a classic. We actually use it as an example in our classes. Not only the fact that the crime was in the middle of the day, but I think, with one or two exceptions, no one had been drinking. It was just people minding their own business, moving from point 'A' to point 'B,' and no one saw the same thing. On the one hand, it's truly amazing, and on the other, unfortunately, not that unusual."

"I suspected Dante Massanni might have had a larger roll, but he was just interviewed in his office, answering a few questions about Brazzi. When I first read he was interviewed, I thought they were going to finger him, instead, he just happens to control the fund that Brazzi was an investor in. And Brazzi wasn't even the largest investor."

Aaron nodded and said, "Hence the term, cold case."

I debated telling him about Tubby Gustafson stopping by but decided against it. I said, "That detective Rogers you sent down to escort me up here did not seem like a very happy camper."

"Mmm, she's one of my best. Nothing really gets past her. You didn't hit on her, did you?"

"Are you kidding, and put my life on the line? She'd have me cuffed and in an interrogation room in no time. No doubt she'd call in Manning just to soften me up. I didn't see him out there by the way. Please tell me he transferred to Denver or LA or someplace out of state."

"Sorry to disappoint. He's just out of the office this afternoon. I don't know, Dev, you just seem to bring out that kind of reaction in all sorts of people."

"Come on. We both know the guy has it in for me. He'd love to see me behind bars."

"Don't limit it to just him, Dev."

"Thanks, Aaron. Am I good to go?"

"Yeah, sure. I was just curious if you'd find anything in that file. Not to speak ill of the dead, but the sense around here was it was simply going to be a matter of time before Sally Brazzi was either killed or locked up, and then it happened."

"All I saw was an assault a few years earlier that ended in a settlement before the trial. Like I said, even if he had some kind of beef with Massinni, he wasn't the biggest investor in whatever the project was."

"That particular project was two hundred apartments up in Maple Grove, and you're right, he wasn't the biggest investor. But he may have been the biggest pain in the ass."

"How so?"

"Complaints, threatening to pull out. At one point, he reneged on a contract for sinks and toilets. Apparently, not an easy guy to work with. Very impressed with himself."

"That's exactly the term his sister-in-law used to describe him. How do you know all this? Nothing like that was in the file."

"It's in there, but because it was hearsay and speculation, it was in a separate file. You would have found it if you'd gone through the detective's notes."

"Detective's notes? There wasn't a file in there labeled Detective notes."

"Sure there was, you just missed it. Eight files in the box. Did you even count the files?"

"As a matter of fact, I did. There were only seven, Aaron."

"You sure? Just seven files?"

"Honest, that's all there were, seven. Nothing else and certainly no file labeled Detective's Notes."

Fifty-nine

I was back in the office just after four. Louie was sitting with his feet up on the picnic table, sipping a can of beer. Two empties were on the floor next to the wastebasket just eight feet away. Clearly, two beers had done nothing to improve his aim. Morton was focused on a chew toy and completely ignored me.

"Hey, how did the meeting in the judge's chambers go?"

"Unfortunately, about like I expected. The prosecution made a decent offer, evenings in the workhouse and a more or less modest fine. Of course, my client, always above the law, wanted nothing to do with it. I think once he told the prosecutor to, 'Shove it up her fat ass,' all bets were pretty much off the table. The judge fined him at which point he told the judge to stick it. He's in the county jail for the next forty-eight hours to allow him some time to reflect on his speech pattern. All deals have been pulled off the table, and on Tuesday of next week, we can expect to feel the full weight of the city attorney's office. Should be fun," Louie said, meaning anything but. He drained his beer, wound up, tossed the can, and missed by a mile. It bounced off the wall and rolled under my desk.

"You want one?" he asked, walking over to the refrigerator.

"No, I better not. I'm going to be working late tonight."

"Someone's wife involved in extracurricular activities?"

"No, time for a little come to Jesus meeting with the Massinni brothers."

"What are you thinking?"

"Just a little chat, explain my side of things. Hopefully, set the record straight."

I picked up the phone and dialed a number. Luscious answered on the third ring. "Hello?" I could hear what sounded like a cartoon playing in the background.

"Luscious, it's Dev. You still free later tonight?"

I pictured him in a chair holding the remote. Something like a dish of ice cream or a box of doughnuts would be on his lap." I can be," he said as the background noise gradually disappeared.

"Good, I'll swing by around nine. Your mom still visiting?"

"Mmm-hmm," he said. Obviously, his mouth was full.

"Okay, I don't want to disturb her by calling you so just wait for me outside."

"Nine o'clock, you said?"

"Yeah."

"See you then," he said, and the cartoon noise came back up just as he disconnected.

Morton and I drove to Amanda's on the way home. She wasn't out on the front porch, so I pulled to the curb, got out, and rang her doorbell. I rang it three times and never got a response, so I got back in the car and drove home.

I was waiting for Luscious outside his place a little before nine. I'd been parked in front for less than five minutes when he stepped out of his building wearing black bib overalls, a black t-shirt and a black balaclava rolled up on top of his head. The overalls were in some black designer camouflage pattern. He waved and headed for my car. He climbed in and said, "Evening, Dev." He pushed the seat back as far as it would go, and he still looked like there was barely enough room for him. He oozed over the seat and onto the console. When he buckled up, it looked like he was tightly cinched into the seat. Waves of flesh hung over and hid the seatbelt.

"You ready for some late-night work, Luscious?"

He nodded as I pulled away from the curb. The car suddenly had a decided pull to the right as we headed over to the Lake Phalen area. Along the way, I explained to Luscious that I just wanted to discuss the shooting of Madame and the firebomb thrown on my front porch with the Massinni brothers, and he was there merely to moderate and keep the conversation at a civil level. However, if things started to get out of hand, he had my permission to crack a couple of skulls.

We hopped on the Interstate and drove over to the Eastside. I turned onto highway Sixty-One, took the Wheelock Parkway exit, and drove around the lake to Larpenteur Avenue and from there onto Atlantic Street. The Massinni's corner house was at the end of the block. I pulled around the corner and parked. We got out of the car, walked up the driveway, and rang the doorbell. No answer. It must be part of my karma that no one is home when I ring the doorbell. We walked back to the car, climbed in, and waited.

Sixty

Luscious fell asleep around a quarter-to-twelve and was snoring by midnight. The Cadillac Escalade pulled into the driveway a little after one. I shook Luscious awake. "Hey, they're finally here, man."

"Oh, I must have closed my eyes for a minute. What time is it?"

"It's after one. Come on. Let's go." As we climbed out of the car, we could hear the doors slam on the Escalade, and we heard them talking. A moment later, the Escalade beeped, signaling the doors had been locked with the remote fob.

"She was all over you, Tony. I could tell."

"She just wasn't my type. Besides, it was a long flight. I just want to get some sleep. We don't have anything going on in the morning, and I'm not answering the phone if the old man calls." The second voice had slurred words but not from too much alcohol. It was Tony, the brother with the broken jaw. They probably weren't going to be too excited to see Luscious and me.

We cut across the lawn, and as we came around the corner, we saw Escalade parked in the driveway, and the front door to the house had just closed.

"Might be best if I announce our arrival," Luscious said. Before I could say anything, he pounded thunderously on the front door, then placed a massive index finger over the peephole in the door.

A moment later, the door flew open, and Jimmy Massanni shouted, "What in the hell do you think—"

Luscious grabbed him with both hands, lifted him off the ground, and effortlessly tossed him back into the house, where he slammed into his brother Tony. The two of them stumbled over their suitcases and landed on the shag carpeting.

"Just what the . . . Hey, now you two just wait. We ain't done nothing to you. Honest, we ain't seen your gal since the cops kicked us out of your party," Jimmy said.

"And we didn't know she was yours," Tony added. He still had the wire contraption around his jaw, and as he spoke, they both pushed themselves back three or four feet across the chocolate-brown shag carpeting.

Something wasn't right. The room, supposedly the living room, was completely devoid of furniture other than a table lamp that rested on the floor in a corner next to the picture window. Not so much as a footstool in the entire room. A number of silhouettes on the walls indicated where framed objects had once hung. The place was depressing if nothing else, and the shag carpet screamed 1970.

I looked at the suitcases. They had luggage tags labeled MSP, for Minneapolis-St. Paul airport. "Where have you guys been?"

They glanced at one another and then Jimmy said, "We left town after your party. Honest, we didn't know that Roxy chick was your woman, and we sure as hell didn't know that was your house."

"So how did you end up there?"

"We saw her with some fat guy in a bar. Nice enough guy," Jimmy said.

"Yeah, he bought us drinks, told us this Roxy was looking to party, and he gave us the address. No offense, dude, but she was really coming on to us in the bar. We figured she was, well you know, maybe offering up her services if we backed off on the eviction. Funny thing was, her place had already gone up in flames. Still, she was really coming on to us, you know. I mean people was looking at us, staring. It had all the makings of a memorable night."

"So why'd you guys set her place on fire?"

They looked at one another. "Set it on fire? You gotta be kidding. Come on, dude. The old man is furious. He's on the hook for hundreds of thousands. We didn't burn it. We just wanted to get her out of there," Tony said.

"Yeah, that's a big part of the reason we left town. The old man is really pissed off. And, hope you're not offended, but your woman there is nuttier than a fruitcake," Jimmy said.

I glanced at Luscious, but he didn't seem to have a reaction. "This fat guy. What'd he look like?"

"Fat."

"Yeah, real fat."

"He have a name?"

"Freddy," they said in unison.

"Where'd you go if the old man was so mad?"

"Florida, but it was too damn hot, so we flew back today. We just arrived."

"We had to fly standby, but we couldn't get on the five o'clock flight. So we had to wait until the flight at ten," Jimmy said.

"Anything to get out of that heat," Tony said.

There's a surprise. It gets hot in Florida in July. "You got a ticket?"

"Got my boarding pass right here," Tony said. He reached into his back pocket and pulled out the boarding pass.

I looked at the thing. They weren't kidding.

"One more question, either of you know what a mason jar is?"

Blank looks from both of them.

Luscious slept as I drove back to his place. It was just as well. I needed some quiet time to sort everything out. I pulled to the curb in front of his building then reached into the backseat and gently shook him on the knee. "Hey Luscious, we're back at your place."

"Mmm-mmm, what time is it?"

"It's late."

He stretched and slowly climbed out of the back seat. I hung onto the steering wheel as the car rocked from side to side. He waved good-bye, and I watched until he'd stepped into the building before I left.

Fat Freddy and Roxy? I replayed Tubby Gustafson's visit earlier in the day. How did Tubby know about Madame getting shot? For that matter, how did he know about Amanda? About four shots being fired? About the firebomb? How did he know Swindle Lawless was stripping on my couch or that the Massinni brothers were in the house? How did he know Roxy was in jail, or that she was even staying at my house? And then, Fat Freddy is out with Roxy? And they just happen to run into the Massinni brothers, and Roxy puts herself on display on my kitchen counter? Add to that, I suddenly had an idea of who the good Samaritan was who paid the tab on Madame's surgery. He was anything but good and none of this was making any sense.

Sixty-one

The following morning, Morton and I were in the office at half-past-nine. I called the North Oaks Fire Department and asked for Mike Schuyler. I ended up having to leave a message. I picked up the beer cans scattered around the wastebasket and under my desk. I made a fresh pot of coffee. Louie wandered in after ten, looking worse for the wear. He was wearing the same suit as yesterday. All the wrinkles suggested he'd slept in it. He'd apparently forgotten to shave.

"How did your evening go, Louie?"

"I closed The Spot if that gives you an idea. Any coffee?"

"I put a fresh pot on a half-hour ago."

"Thank God," he said. He dumped the remnants of his mug into the sink in the back closet. He filled his mug, took a hearty sip, and settled in behind his picnic table desk. "So how did things go at your little come to Jesus meeting?"

"I'm even more confused than before." I went on to give him the short version of our discussion with the Massinni brothers. I told him about Tubby's visit earlier yesterday and the fount of information Tubby had. "The more I think about it, the more I get the feeling I've just been a pawn in some giant game, and I still can't figure out the rules."

"Well, that's probably your first mistake. Obviously, there are no rules."

My phone rang, Mike Schuyler returning my call. "Haskell Investigations," I answered.

"Dev Haskell?"

"Hi Mike, thanks for returning my call."

"Not a problem. What can I do for you?"

"I'm wondering if you had any results from your investigation on that five-alarm fire up there."

"The Sheldon Smeet residence. Yes, we do. If you can hang on for a moment, let me bring it up on my screen." I waited, thinking it was interesting he referred to it as Smeet's residence, confirming what I found, there'd been no title transfer to Roxy. "Yeah, here we go," he said, coming back on the line.

"Anything there on the initial cause of the fire?"

"Based on the speed and the extent of the damage—" Schuyler began.

"The place is a total loss, right?"

"Correct. What we found is the fire began in the main, first-floor bathroom. An appliance was plugged in, which overheated next to a number of hairspray cans that served as an accelerant."

"Define your term, a number."

"At least a half-dozen. Frankly, once the appliance overheated, a curling iron by the way, it appears to have been set in the middle of at least six cans of hairspray. The result was horrendous. Had the structure been occupied at the time, the fire maybe could have ultimately been controlled, but that's a very big maybe, and as you know, it wasn't the case. Add to that the fact that the security system had been suspended due to lack of payment, so there was absolutely no 911 alert. What you end with is the perfect storm or, in this case, the perfect fire. The first call came in just a little before seven a.m. That was a visual sighting of flames from a driver passing by. Based on the timeframe and the design of the house, a frame building essentially hidden from view, it suggests the blaze had more than enough time to envelop the entire structure. By the time we arrived on the scene, really all we could do was make sure the fire didn't spread to the surrounding wooded area."

"Total destruction," I said.

"Absolutely. I find the curling iron and the large number of hairspray cans perhaps unique but not something that could ever be considered an intentional setup."

"Either that or someone was very smart."

"Perhaps," Schuyler said. "Either very smart or incredibly stupid. It's a bit of a toss-up."

"Anything else you can tell me?"

"No sir, that's pretty much it in a nutshell."

"Much appreciated, Mike. You and your crew stay safe."

"You do the same, Dev. Hope to meet again under more positive circumstances someday."

"If we do, I'll buy the first round."

"I'll remember that," Schuyler said and disconnected.

"What's the news?" Louie asked. He was in the process of pouring another mug of coffee.

"Only that Roxy is either really stupid or a hell of a lot smarter than anyone gives her credit for."

Sixty-two

I basically accomplished absolutely nothing during the rest of the day. Morton and I left the office early, tiptoeing out so as not to wake Louie. We drove past Amanda's house and surprise, surprise, there she was, sitting on the front porch. She didn't wave as we approached, but I parked in front of her house anyway. I left Morton in the car in case Madame was out on the porch. I didn't want the two of them getting all excited and causing some damage to Madame's wound.

"Long time no see," I said as I walked up the front sidewalk.

"Hello, Dev." Her voice suggested she wasn't exactly thrilled to see me.

"How's the patient doing?"

That brought a quick flash of a smile to her face. "Much better, improving every day."

I climbed the steps, and there sat Madame at Amanda's feet. She wore the plastic cone around her neck, and if you looked at her, you'd never know she'd been shot just a few days ago. There was an uncomfortable moment of silence, and then we both said one another's name at almost the same time.

"Amanda?"

"Dev?"

"Ladies first," I said.

"Look, Dev, I hope you don't think ill of me, but I've just needed some time to myself to think about the future. I think you are a wonderful, kind person, and you can be a lot of fun." I could hear the tension in her voice, and I'd been dumped by enough women to know where this was going.

"I sense the word, but, is coming."

"Well, that's just it, Dev. You can be a lot of fun, but, I think it would be best for Madame and me if we brought the beginnings of any relationship to a close. As much fun as you might be, getting shot at four times at the very least has to give me pause. And frankly, without going into any detail, I've been through this before, and once was more than enough. I like things structured, quiet, organized, planned, and none of those things are you. That's not a criticism by the way. It's just a fact. You're not going to change, and I'm certainly not, so I'm hoping we can part as friends. I'll gladly pay for Madame's surgery, by the way. I think it's the very least I—"

"Don't worry. It's already taken care of."

"Are you sure?"

"Yeah, don't worry about it."

"Oh, you are a very kind person," she said and slowly rose off the porch swing. She gave me a peck on the cheek and quickly sat back down before I could wrap my arms around her.

"I did happen to find your sister."

Her eyes grew wide. "Nancy? You did? Is she all right?"

"Yeah, as a matter of fact, she's more than all right. Your nephew's name is Stefan Michael."

"Nephew?"

"He'll be six weeks old on Sunday." I pulled out my wallet and handed her the business card Nancy gave me. "She'd like you to give her a call. She's living up in North Branch in a very nice apartment where no one sleeps in the hallway. She's had an IT job for over a year and a half."

"Oh my God, my God. And she's okay?" she said as a tear rolled down her cheek.

"Yeah, she seemed fine. Nice lady. Give her a call."

"Oh, Dev this is so wonderful. I, I don't know what to tell you. You have to . . . please send me a bill for your time."

"That's okay. Consider it a little gift for having to put up with me."

"Oh, I feel so terrible, but thank you. Thank you so much."

This was her chance to jump up and hug me. Maybe suggest we tour her bedroom. Instead, she said, "I'm going to call her right now. Come on, Madame, come." She hurried into the house and closed the door behind her.

I was left standing alone on her front porch. After a long moment, Morton barked a couple of times from the back seat of the car. "Coming," I said. I slid in behind the wheel and drove home.

Sixty-three

My phone rang just as I was about to phone in my pizza order. It was Heidi. "Haskell Investigations."

There was a slight pause. "Since when do you not know it's me calling?"

"I'm trying to be professional."

"Yeah, right. Hey, you busy tonight?"

"Maybe, I guess it depends."

"Are you trying to make this difficult for me? Why don't you come over? If I recall I was going to make helping Roxy worth your while."

"I could use that right about now. How about I see you in an hour? I'll get cleaned up and pick up a bottle of wine on the way."

"One hour and don't be late," she said and hung up.

I grabbed a quick shower, picked up two bottles of wine at Solo Vino, and hurried over to Heidi's. I was wearing dress slacks, a lightly starched shirt, and decent shoes. I handed her the two bottles of wine when she opened the door. She was barefoot and dressed in shorts and a t-shirt.

"Well, just look at you. Who knew?" she said.

"See the difference is, you always look great, but I really have to work at it."

"You're sweet," she said, leaning in to kiss me. "Sometimes."

I followed her into the kitchen. She set the bottles of wine on the counter and took two frozen pizzas and placed them back in the freezer.

"We're not going to eat?" I said.

"Not right now, darling. Come on." She took me by the hand and led me into her bedroom. The shades were down, the drapes were pulled, and three candles were lit on her dresser.

"You didn't want to eat right away, did you?" she asked as she untucked her t-shirt.

"Don't worry about it. I can wait."

It was almost eleven when Heidi finally took the pizzas out of the oven. Amazingly, they weren't burnt. She was in a silk dressing gown, and I was in my boxers and a t-shirt. I refilled the wine glasses as she cut the pizza. Having worked up an appetite, we finished the first piece rather quickly. Heidi threw another double cheese and sausage slice on my plate and helped herself to one more pineapple bacon. She took a sip of wine and said, "I got Roxy released today."

"Where is she staying? I need to talk to her."

"Calm down and relax, Dev. It's kind of crazy. She's got a job out of town, Vegas actually. She flew out there this afternoon with a friend who's got connections."

"A friend? And wait a minute, doesn't she have a court date coming up?"

"I mentioned that to her, but she didn't seem too concerned. At some point, it's not my problem or yours for that matter."

"Who was this friend?"

"It just gets crazier. Just a minute. She gave me her card." She walked over to a chair by the door, picked up her purse, and rummaged around. "Yeah, here it is. Get this. Her name is Candi Cane." She laughed and handed me the card. A red and white striped boarder ran around the edge of the card. 'Candi Cane makes all your wishes come true!' it read and then listed a website address across the bottom and the words 'Private Video & Downloads' below that. I glanced at the copy for a brief second before I focused on the color picture. The name might have been Candi Cane, but the picture was Swindle Lawless.

"I know this woman. She's nuts."

"Why am I surprised?"

"What, that she's nuts?"

"No, that you know her."

"She was the woman stripping on my couch when the police arrived. She's certifiable. I know her as Swindle Lawless, but she's had at least half a dozen names before this Candi Cane. And Roxy took off to Vegas with her?"

"Yep," Heidi said and took another bite of pizza.

"You don't seem too upset."

"It's a problem I can't fix. I've finally come to the same conclusion you have. As much as I love my child-hood friend, that person doesn't exist anymore, and I need her out of my life. So, good riddance. She promised to pay back the bail money." She shrugged, climbed off her stool, and carried both our plates over to the sink.

"Hey, I wasn't finished."

"Just talking about her stresses me out. Fill up the glasses and let's go back to bed."

Sixty-four

Heidi kissed me goodbye at some ungodly early hour, told me to lock the door on my way out, and headed off to work. I drifted back to sleep and woke a little after seven. I drove home, let Morton out, and hopped in the shower. We were down at the office before ten. I sat at my desk shaking my head as I thought about Roxy skipping her court date and heading out to Las Vegas with Swindle Lawless. As I was shaking my head, I happened to glance out the window just in time to see a black Cadillac Escalade pull up across the street. What could be worse? The Massinni brothers here to give a response to my recent visit with Luscious. But then the driver's door opened. Fat Freddy Zimmerman slid out, opened the rear door, and my question was answered. Tubby Gustafson was worse.

I watched out the window as they crossed the street. The stairs begin to creak a moment later. Morton, lying on his bed, suddenly looked up and whined. I thought about locking the door, but a hip check from Fat Freddy would probably knock it off the hinges so why bother? The staircase noise grew louder, I heard a groan, and suddenly a red-faced Fat Freddy stumbled into the office. He was followed by a gasping Tubby.

"You two guys getting some morning exercise?"

Tubby looked like he wanted to say something, but he couldn't catch his breath.

Freddy stumbled toward my desk and pulled out a chair for Tubby. Tubby groaned as he settled into the chair, pulled the red silk handkerchief from his pocket, and mopped his brow.

"Honest to God, Haskell. Honest to God," he gasped.

I waited a long moment before I said, "What can I do for you, gentlemen? Sheldon Smeet is dead. The house in North Oaks is a pile of ashes. You've scared Roxanne LaRue out of town. You're in the process of putting Dante Massinni out of business, and you paid the veterinary bill for the surgery on the little dog you shot during your drive by."

"That was a mistake. We didn't mean—"

"Shut up," Tubby shouted.

"Yeah, I thought so. So what do you want from me?"

Tubby seemed to think for a moment. "How does a new office in a building with an elevator sound?"

I leaned back in my chair and thought. *I had an apartment building across the street full of young women who never remember to pull the shades. The Spot bar is within crawling distance. Louie's in here with his picnic table desk. The other option would be Tubby and Fat*

Freddy having ready access to my office.' Gee, let me think.

"Thank you, Tub…, err, Mr. Gustafson. But keeping my office here seems to work out just fine."

Tubby shook his head. "I suppose I shouldn't be surprised, Haskell. It's one of the many reasons you'll never get ahead. You don't update. You don't adapt. You know what you are, Haskell?"

"Content, satisfied?"

"Why do I bother, Freddy? Why do I try to help? Haskell, you simply continue to muddle on in one big circle. Never learning. Never growing. It's funny really, someone so stupid he can't read the writing on the wall. One more individual the rest of us don't have to compete against. Suit yourself," he said and groaned to his feet. Fat Freddy was suddenly on his feet and pulled Tubby's chair back. "I'll never understand," Tubby said and waddled out the door.

Fat Freddy chuckled and gave me the finger as he followed Tubby out. I put my cellphone to my ear and pretended to be on a call as they exited the building. I didn't look out the window until I saw them pull away from the curb and head up the street toward the freeway.

I had a couple of beers at The Spot with Louie. We chatted about everything and nothing. I didn't mention Tubby's new office offer. I fed Morton from a bag of pork rinds, and it was dusk when we headed home. I pulled the car in the garage, and we headed toward the front door. The smell hit me as we climbed the steps to the porch. Fresh paint. It suddenly dawned on me that the porch floor and the siding around the front window were freshly painted.

I hadn't been in the house for ten minutes when the doorbell rang. Morton barked, and I followed him out to the front door. There was a guy I didn't recognize standing on the porch. He did not look friendly. I opened the door maybe six inches, placing my foot behind it just in case he attempted to barge in.

"Can I help you?"

"You Haskell?"

"Yes."

"Mr. Gustafson would like to see you."

"Actually, I was just about to go to bed. I wonder if he wouldn't—"

"He wants to see you now."

A black Cadillac Escalade sat at the curb, and the passenger window suddenly lowered. "Get in the damn car, Haskell. If we were going to shoot you, it would have already happened," Fat Freddy said.

"Come on. Let's go," the guy at the door growled. As we walked out to the Escalade, the rear door opened. I was about to get in when the thug said, "Wait a second." He quickly patted me down then half-shoved me into the car. I climbed into the back seat next to another unsmiling thug. The guy who rang my doorbell climbed in behind me.

As soon as the door closed, Fat Freddy said, "Okay, Liam. Let's go." As we headed down the street, Fat

Freddy turned and said, "Word to the wise, Haskell. Don't argue, don't complain, don't be your usual pain in the ass self." He turned around and stared out the window. No one said anything for the rest of the fifteen-minute drive.

Sixty-five

Tubby lived in a large brick mansion located behind an eight-foot high brick wall and wrought iron gates. The driver entered some code on his cellphone, the gates swung open, and we drove up a circular drive and stopped in front of the double front doors. A big old Harley Davidson was parked off to the side. Another unfriendly looking thug stood just inside the front doors.

"Wait for us, Liam. This won't take long. Alright, let's go," Fat Freddy said as he oozed out of the passenger door.

The thug next to me opened the door then turned and said, "Hurry up, Haskell. Mr. Gustafson is waiting."

We headed into the brick mansion. Fat Freddy led the way, and I followed, flanked by the two unsmiling thugs. We walked through a large entryway with a marble floor and a large wooden staircase leading up to the second floor. We followed Freddy down a hallway. He stopped at the second door and knocked. After a moment, a gruff voice said, "Come in." And Freddy opened the door.

The room was dimly lit, lined with bookshelves, and smelled like old books. Who knew Tubby could read? There was a fireplace at the far end of the room, and above the fireplace was a painting of Tubby standing next to a chair holding some rolled-up documents. I'd seen the painting before, or at least a version of it at Roxy's place, just before the fire. Only that had been a painting of Sheldon Smeet. In this work of art, Tubby was about a hundred pounds lighter, his potato sized nose looked normal and wasn't red. So much for artistic interpretation.

Tubby Gustafson sat behind a large antique desk, staring. Finally he growled, "Sit down, Haskell."

"Good evening, Mr. Gustafson," I said as I settled into one of the chairs opposite his desk.

"Spare me," he said and took a sip from the crystal glass on his desk. I noticed the glass had a harp cut into the side and behind Tubby was a matching crystal de-canter. Eight glasses were arranged around the decanter. Eight glasses plus the one in front of Tubby made nine. I suddenly knew where the tenth glass probably was. In an evidence bag with the Cross Lake police, and it had a lipstick smudge along the edge.

"What the hell are you staring at, Haskell?"

"Nothing sir, other than the lovely office you have. I've never been here before."

"That's right, you haven't. After our earlier conver-sation today, and against my better judgement, I decided I should thank you."

"Thank me?"

"Yes, for saving the life of that LaRue woman."

"Saving her life? Roxy? But I didn't do—"

"Silencio, you moron," Tubby shouted. He glanced over at Fat Freddy. "Standard rule when dealing with this idiot. One more interruption and I want you to cut off his finger and shove it down his throat."

Fat Freddy nodded and reached into his pocket. He pulled out his black switchblade and pressed the button. A blade suddenly snapped out.

"You are here to listen, Haskell, not express your thoughts. I've no interest, and Lord knows you can't afford to use your limited brainpower. Now, as I was saying, I wanted to thank you for saving the life of that LaRue woman."

I apparently made a move that suggested I might speak.

Tubby held up a hand, pointed at me, and said, "You've been warned."

I nodded and assumed a more humble pose.

"Much better. As I was saying, if it weren't for you, she might still be in town. Fortunately, with the aid of a former employee, she's left town. Fleeing a court date and in the process making it impossible for her ever to return safely to this state. Were it not for your meddling with the fools in the Massinni organization, eliminating their attempt to provide security at her home, we may never have had the opportunity to set it on fire. But you took care of that. And, of course, the icing on the cake, she's arrested for assaulting a police officer literally seconds after you threw her out of your house."

He picked up the envelope on the desk and slowly waved it back and forth as he said, "Wonderful, Haskell, absolutely wonderful. Here's a little something to thank you for your effort and encourage you to keep up the bumbling work. Now get him out of my sight." Tubby said and began to laugh.

As the thugs hurried me out of the room and down the hall toward the front door, I could still hear him laughing. The thug guarding the door grinned in a way that suggested he knew how the meeting with Tubby went. As he held the front door open, I noticed the tattoo on his fingers spelling 'EVIL.' I hurried out the door and headed toward the Escalade.

"Hey, douchebag, where in the hell do you think you're going?" the thug who rang my doorbell yelled.

"I thought you—"

"You heard Mr. Gustafson, Don't try to think, Haskell. This way," he said and pointed toward the wrought iron gate.

I headed down the circular drive toward the gate, not sure what was going to happen. When we got to the gate, he input a code on a keypad and the gates swung open.

"Enjoy your walk," one of them said, and they both laughed.

I headed out to the sidewalk, expecting either to be clubbed or shot at any moment. Neither happened, the gates swung closed, and I headed toward my house, only four miles away. Halfway there, I altered direction, and made it down to The Spot in under two hours.

It was after eleven on a weeknight, and there were maybe a half-dozen people scattered throughout the place. Only two people were talking to one another. Louie still sat at the bar.

"Buy you a drink?" I said, coming up behind him.

"Hey, Dev, What are you . . . Where's Morton?"

"He wanted to stay home and watch TV. Got time for another?"

"Always."

I signaled Mike to get Louie another. He delivered a fresh drink and said, "What are you having, Dev?"

I thought back to Tubby and the crystal glasses. "Give me your best bourbon, on the rocks."

"Whoa, big time. Coming right up, sir." When he delivered my drink, I pulled Tubby's envelope from my pocket, opened it, and pulled out a dollar bill. I double-checked the envelope, but that was all that was in there. One lousy dollar.

Mike looked at me and laughed. "Taken advantage of once again, Dev. Tell you what, they're on the house. Drink up."

The End

Thank you for taking the time to read **<u>Guest From Hell</u>**. If you enjoyed the read please consider leaving a review. It really, really helps. Thanks in advance.

Don't miss the sample of **<u>Art Attack</u>** on the next page.

Sneak Peek

Art Attack

Second Edition

MIKE FARICY

Prologue

yles Rossler struck the paint brush on the canvas, creating the exclamation point behind his signature in the lower right-hand corner. He set the brush in the jar of turpentine and stepped back from his easel. This had to be his best work to date, but then, he always thought that. "I think that should just about do it. Another work of genius, if I do say so myself. Come on over and take a look," he said to the naked beauty stretched out on the red velvet couch.

She sat up on the antique couch, smiled, and ran her tongue seductively over her lips. Her tanned skin, juxtaposed to the small patches of white a bikini had covered only served to highlight her attributes. She stood and stretched, diverting his attention from the canvas to her figure. Once she had his full attention, she strutted toward him.

"Oh, Myles," she said, leaning over and nibbling his ear lobe. "It's marvelous. Beautiful! How do you do it?"

"I can't help it. The good Lord blessed me with a marvelous talent."

"As he did me," she said and fluttered her eyes. "Ready for a down payment?"

"Sounds wonderful."

"Why don't you get undressed, and I'll meet you in the sauna. I'll mix up a pitcher of vodka martinis for us and join you for the first of a number of workouts."

She placed one bare foot in front of the other, and strutted into the kitchen as if she was walking down a fashion show runway, aware without looking that she had his undivided attention. She assumed a pose, bending down into the lower cabinet, arching her back, and slowly reaching in to grab the glass pitcher. Before she stood, she looked over her shoulder and said in a tempting tone, "Baby, hurry up and get in there. I want you all to myself."

As Myles hurried out of the kitchen, he tossed his t-shirt on the living room floor. He unbuckled his jeans as he picked up speed and hopped out of them halfway down the hall. His socks and boxers came off just outside the sauna before he stepped inside. It was wonderfully warm, bordering on hot, as he closed the door behind him and climbed up onto the top wooden bench. A pair of pink plastic handcuffs hung from a brass hook on the wall. He stretched out along the bench, centering himself, leaving just enough room for her to position a leg on either side.

She placed the pitcher on the counter, took the bottle of vodka out of the freezer, and arranged the stemmed glasses on the tray just in case he peeked out. She waited a couple of minutes before wrapping the towel around her. She hurried down the hall, quietly slipped the four solid brass deadbolt locks into place, and dialed the thermostat up to the number ten setting, two hundred and forty degrees Fahrenheit. It had been a relatively simple procedure to override the high-limit switch, so she turned the timer all the way to the maximum three-hour mark before she headed into the bathroom to shower.

She heard soft thumping on the six-inch insulated sauna door when she stepped out from her thirty-minute shower. She turned on the hair drier and spent the next half-hour drowning out any sound he might make. She took her time dressing in-between watching a Kardashian special on the cable channel then spent fifteen minutes looking for her car keys. Once she found them, she slung her purse over her shoulder and double-checked herself once more in the mirror before setting out on the forty-minute drive to work.

As she walked past the sauna door, she gave a quick glance at the four deadbolt locks. They appeared undisturbed, and when she placed her ear against the door, she was unable to detect any sound from inside. The timer showed slightly more than twenty minutes remaining. She turned it back to the three-hour mark, just to be sure.

One

I'd just been paid, in cash, and was thinking things couldn't get much better. True, at least for the moment.

"Congratulations again on your successful investigation," Louie said. He laughed and pushed his empty glass across the bar. "I should probably take off, Dev. I'm in court first thing in the morning."

It was our fourth round, not that it mattered. I was feeling no pain, in fact, I was buying. My Golden Retriever, Morton, was at the foot of the barstool, half-asleep after finishing his second bag of pork rinds. An inner voice said something along the lines of *'You idiot, get in the car and go home.'* But why listen? Instead, I said, "Hey, Louie, let me get one more round."

"Well, since you twisted my arm. How can I say no? So, tell me again how this went down."

"It's not all that complicated. My client, the insurance guy, called me and said they had a question on some woman's claim for benefits. Apparently, she went blind from working on her computer all day."

"Working on . . . that sounds like some weird preexisting condition that was either exacerbated by staring at a screen or the computer had absolutely nothing to do with it. Sounds like whatever caused her blindness might have happened anyway."

"Yeah, only not quite. It turns out, she was in a relationship with an eye surgeon, and he filed a series of false reports. Once the insurance checks started coming in, she dumped the guy. After groveling in front of her for a week or two, he contacted my client and came clean."

"But you only investigated for a couple of days."

"Just one day, actually. I parked in front of her place at eight in the morning, and forty-five minutes later, out she comes, hops in her car, and drives to the casino."

"She's driving?"

"Yeah, in her new car, a Nissan. I followed her inside the casino. People who work there are saying, 'Hello Betty. Nice to see you again, Betty. Have a nice day, Betty.' Come to find out, she's a regular. She played the slots for three hours, took a break for lunch, then played until almost four in the afternoon before she headed out to the grocery store. She did a little shopping and went home. I was still parked in front of her place at eight-thirty that night when out she comes, dressed to the nines. She went dancing and brought some guy home around twelve-thirty. Amazingly, the guy is a chiropractor, and she'd been talking to him about filing a back injury claim if only he would help her out."

"Sounds like a pattern," Louie said and took a healthy sip. "She's liable to end up doing some time."

"The eye surgeon has already agreed to testify. Said he couldn't live with himself after falsifying documents. I'd guess he was just pissed off about being taken for a ride. He's retired, so losing his license wasn't that much of a threat. The chiropractor has an attorney, and he's agreed to testify as well. You'd think, under the circumstances, she'd want to keep a low profile, but that thought didn't seem to enter her mind."

The front door to The Spot suddenly flew open, and eight women stepped inside. The noise level went up about a thousand percent, shrieking, laughing, and yelling back and forth, obviously not their first stop. There were only three other people in the place besides Louie and me. A blonde woman, definitely over-served, was wearing a white lace veil. She was surrounded by the others, all laughing and raising the beer cans they'd carried as a toast. She had a sign on her back that said something about it being *'Her last night to misbehave.'* One of the women had beautiful blonde hair and a well-endowed figure. She maybe looked familiar, but I couldn't place her.

"Appreciate the drinks, Dev, but I think this is the warning that tells me it's time to go home," Louie said.

"We're right behind you, Louie. Come on, Morton," I said. We gave Mike, the bartender, a wave and headed out the side door. He waved back and rolled his eyes at the hen party. Although it's not like any of us hadn't done the same thing in our day.

TWO

Morton and I slept in the following morning and headed to the office around 9:30. I pulled behind a black Toyota and parked. As I let Morton out of the backseat, a voice said, "Dev Haskell?"

I turned and gazed at a beautiful, blonde-haired woman wearing tight jeans, a short sleeve blouse, and pink lipstick. She looked somewhat familiar. Morton immediately approached and thrust his nose between her legs.

"Yes?" I said.

"Dev, it's me, Kristi McKenzie. Long time no see."

Her voice sounded as sexy as I remembered, and as she said her name, the slightest hint of a beautiful perfume drifted over me. For a brief second, I was seventeen again. Kristi Mckenzie. High school homecoming queen, princess for the prom, and my senior year sweetheart. Oh, the things we taught one another that summer. Kids. She dumped me for some college art school student the following September, and I went into the Army. I think her first beauty pageant had been when she was five, Miss Kindergarten or something. She won Sandbox

Princess at age eight and went on to become a professional beauty pageant contestant; St. Paul Winter Carnival Princess, Miss Ramsey County, Queen of the Mississippi River Headwaters, Miss Upper Midwest, Princess of the Prairie, the list went on.

"Kristi? Wow. Sorry, I didn't recognize you. I guess I never expected to see you again. I'll say it's been a long time. What was it? September after high school graduation. You, well, you look great. You still competing?"

She shook her head. "Dev, that was another lifetime. I gave all that up. How many times do you have to win a pageant before it just gets boring?"

"I guess I never considered that."

"I thought it was you in The Spot last night," she said. "Long, crazy, night. I was going to talk to you for a minute, but when I turned around, you had already left. I asked the bartender—"

"Mike."

"He never told me his name. I asked him if it was you, and he said it was. Then he told me this is where your office is. I think he was trying to come on to me." She turned and glanced at the building. "He said you're a private investigator. No offense, but I thought you were dead. Otherwise, I would have—"

"Don't believe everything you hear. So, you were with the bride to be last night. The girl with the wedding veil. Isn't that wedding later today?"

"Not until late this afternoon. It's over at Lookout Park."

"Right, on Summit and Ramsey Hill, nice location."

She nodded and said, "I was wondering if we could maybe talk. I'm thinking of hiring someone to find a missing person."

"A missing person? Tell you what, if you have some time, come on up to my office. I'll put some coffee on, we can catch up, and you can tell me what you're thinking. I mean, if you have time."

"Oh, Dev, thanks, so much. I'd love to. Sorry to just show up, but I didn't know how else to get in touch with you."

We headed up to the office. Morton seemed more interested in Kristi than anything else. Louie Laufen, my office mate, had already been in, and the coffee was on. If I remembered correctly, he had a 9:00 court date.

"Grab a chair, Kristi. You take cream or sugar?" I said, hoping she didn't because we were out of both.

"No, black is just fine."

Fortunately, she seemed to be focused on Louie's picnic table desk, which gave me a chance to dump his half-empty mug into the sink and refill it for her.

"Here you go," I said, handing her Louie's refilled mug. It wasn't lost on me that the next two buttons on her blouse were suddenly undone. A large diamond pendant was wedged in her cleavage. "Grab a seat and tell me what you've been up to," I said as I stepped behind my desk and sat down. Kristi looked at the chair with the masking tape over the arms and took the other one. She couldn't have weighed more than a hundred and fifteen pounds, but the chair creaked as she settled in, compliments of ne'er do well crime lord, Tubby Gustafson's occasional visits. "So what are you doing now?" I asked.

"Oh, you know, a little bit of everything. Now, be quiet for a minute and listen Dev. Before we go any further, I just want to say that breaking up with you was probably one of the dumbest things I've ever done. No wait, it was the worst thing I've ever done. Since then, nothing seems to have gone right for me. I literally kick myself every day for being so stupid."

"Oh, I wouldn't be too hard on yourself. I think we were headed in very different directions. You were going off to college and all those beauty pageants, and I was going into the Army."

"When I heard you'd been killed, I was absolutely devastated. By that time, I was in Paris, at the Sorbonne. I was crowned 'Princesse de la Sorbonne'." She paused for a moment to let that sink in. "I couldn't get back home, it was the end of term, and I had papers due, not to mention all my French Princess duties. You know how it goes."

Actually, no, I didn't, but I shot her a smile and nodded all the same. "So, you mentioned you might need help finding someone?"

She set Louie's coffee mug on the edge of the desk and smiled. Another wave of beautiful perfume floated over, and I inhaled deeply. "Yes. It's my husband, actually. Well, former husband, to be more accurate."

"When did you get married?"

"A couple of years ago, common law to be honest. We've been together, more or less for seven or eight years."

"Oh, gee, I'm sorry to hear that."

"What? That I have a husband?"

"No, I meant—"

She laughed and slowly ran her tongue back and forth across her upper lip. "Thanks, but its okay. He was starting to go batty, and then one day, he just up and disappeared."

"You've checked with his family? Friends?"

She nodded and said, "Yep. I even went so far as to place an ad in the paper. He's a painter."

It wasn't lost on me that she used the present tense. "He's a painter? Houses? Offices?"

"An artist," she corrected. "A very good artist, as a matter of fact. The occasional portrait but mostly landscapes. He's a modern impressionist. I even talked with the galleries that handled his work. It's like he just up and vanished into thin air."

I was taking notes as she talked. "What was his name?"

"Chandler Hancock. He's originally from St. Michael, Minnesota. We met in college, went our separate ways for a bit, and then reconnected and suddenly I looked up and we'd been together for a number of years."

I stopped writing for a moment. Chandler Hancock. She met him before college. He was the reason she'd dumped me. I'd wanted to kill him, but instead, I went off to basic training with the idea I would hone my killing skills and pay him a visit down the road. By the time I came back home, I couldn't have cared less. Amazing.

"How long has Chandler been missing?"

"Five or six months?"

"So tell me about it. What happened?"

"Not much to tell, one day he's there, and the next day he's gone."

"Anything like a ransom note, an affair, or maybe mental instability?"

"No nothing," she said and didn't even blink at the suggestion of an affair.

"Did he pack a suitcase? Has there been any online interaction? Tweets he may have posted?"

"No, no, and no. Nothing, Dev. He simply disappeared, not so much as a word or a post."

"Did you contact the police?"

"I guess I never thought of that."

I had to fight to keep my eyes focused on the notes I was taking. Finally, I looked up. "You never contacted the police?"

Three

I watched out the window as Kristi left the building and walked across the street to her car. A couple was walking down the street, the guy was pushing a baby stroller. While he stared at Kristi he ran the stroller into the fire hydrant, and his wife slapped him hard on the arm. I took out my binoculars and waited until she pulled away from the curb so I could get her license plate number. I ran a quick check on her plate. She came up clean.

I phoned my friend in homicide, Aaron LaZelle, and left a message. I Googled Chandler Hancock and came up with as many women as men with the name. There was an image of a landscape entitled 'Season Opener.' A lake scene actually, painted by Chandler Hancock along with a picture of him. I remembered seeing him once or twice but only from a distance, and that was at least fifteen years ago.

His online picture made him look like a clueless young eccentric. He was sitting in a chair in front of a fireplace. He appeared to be wearing a smoking jacket. He had a pipe in his mouth and what looked to be a tweed cap on his head. There was a landscape painting hanging above the fireplace but no indication whether or not he was the artist. The article was almost two years old and said the lake scene painting was on display at the Find Art Gallery down on Fifth Street. I phoned the gallery, but no one answered.

I was about to head out when my phone rang. "Haskell Investigations."

"Dev, Aaron, returning your call."

"Hi, Aaron, thanks for calling back."

Aaron headed up the city's homicide unit. I'd known him since we were kids playing hockey.

"What can I do for you, Dev?"

"I've got a strange deal. A woman stopped by and asked me to help find her missing husband. Common-law marriage, not that it makes any difference. He's been gone for six months, according to her. Strange thing is, she said she never bothered to contact you guys."

"Sounds like she might be happy that he's gone and just wants to play the part of the concerned wife. It's happened before. You suspect foul play?"

"No, I don't think so. At least she doesn't strike me as the type."

"And just what type would that be?"

"Point taken. Can I give you the guy's name and have you check to see if anything turns up on your records?"

"Give it to me. I'll run it right now."

"Chandler Hancock," I said then spelled out the last name. I heard the keyboard clicking in the background.

A moment later, Aaron said, "Nothing coming up on our records. Never reported missing and, according to our records, never involved in anything. Not so much as a parking ticket. No indication of a domestic situation if you were thinking in those terms."

"Okay. Sorry to take up your time."

"Not a problem. Nice to hear your voice. We're overdue for a get-together."

"You usually have more on your plate than I do. Give me a call when you have some time, and we can grab dinner."

"Thanks. Anything pops up with this Hancock thing let me know. Later," he said and hung up.

I phoned the Find Art Gallery again. This time, I got a recording that said they were open from 11:00 until 7:00. It was almost 11:30, so I hung up, filled Morton's water dish, left a note for Louie, and was about to head out the door when Louie stepped into the office.

"You coming or going?" Louie said.

"I'll be gone for maybe an hour. Ignore my note on your desk. Everything go okay in court this morning?" Louie had built quite the reputation in town for the guy to go to if you were charged with a DUI.

"Well enough. I've got another hearing scheduled for three o'clock downtown."

"I should be back long before that. Just on my way to an art gallery."

"Is there a display of coloring books?"

Four

I parked a block away from the Find Art Gallery on Fifth Street. It was located in a red-brick building built in 1885 and just across the street from the Top Hat bar. The front window looked in on an impressive gallery with polished maple floors that were probably original to the structure. I stood on the sidewalk and peered in for a minute or two. There were a number of large paintings hanging on the walls. Abstract Expressionism things, drips and drizzles on canvas, like the stuff Jackson Pollock created. I never got the attraction, and the paintings I could see through the window wasn't going to change my mind.

The door had an image of a clock face hanging on the inside with a sign that said 'OPEN.' The hands on the clock were set for 11:00, almost an hour ago. As I opened the door, I heard a tone sound in the rear. A moment later, an attractive woman stepped out from a back room.

"Good morning," she said. "Can I help you with anything or just looking?"

I glanced at one of the drip and drizzle paintings on the wall. It was entitled 'D'; the painting next to it was entitled 'E.' I didn't want to ask about the titles, so I said, "A while back, you had a painting by Chandler Hancock. I'm interested in his work."

"Oh, really? I believe we've three of his works in the back that I could show you."

"Would you have time?"

"Certainly, if you'll wait just a moment," she said and walked to the front door. She locked the door and adjusted the hands on the hanging clock sign. "Come on back. I'm Diane Turner, by the way," she said, holding out her hand. She had dark hair, brown eyes, and sparkling white teeth that looked even brighter next to her suntan.

"Dev Haskell," I said as we shook hands. "Do you handle a lot of his work?"

"Chandler Hancock, yes, from time to time, we've sold a piece. He's got a bit of a following. We have an exclusive with him, so we're the only local gallery. Now, I know he deals with a gallery in New York. I think Tampa and San Francisco as well. I'm not sure about New Orleans," she said as we made our way toward the door she'd stepped out of only a moment ago.

"Do you sell any of this?" I said, indicating the abstract work on the walls.

"Oh, there's a market," she said but didn't elaborate as she opened the door to the backroom. A cubicle with a countertop, two chairs, a laptop, and a sandwich next to the laptop was positioned in the corner. The ten-foot ceiling in the room was open, exposing solid wooden floor joists that were at least a hundred and thirty years old. Row upon row of eight-foot high shelving filled with plastic covered paintings extended toward a distant back wall. She stepped into the cubicle and flicked three light switches, illuminating all the shelving.

"Let me just check the location. You said, Chandler Hancock?"

"Yes, that's right. The piece I saw on the internet was listed as 'Season Opener,' I think."

"Mmm, a Plein Air. I remember it, a lovely work." She placed a napkin over what was left of the sandwich and slid it behind the laptop then said, "Yes, here we are, beta seven-four," she said and headed for one of the shelving aisles. She stopped maybe halfway down, reached up to a shelf, and pulled out a canvas. There was a small extension attached to the front of the shelf, and she set the canvas on it and carefully removed the bubblewrap covering it. The painting was the same one I'd seen online, although it was a hundred times more attractive.

"Yeah, that's the one. 'Season Opener'."

"He completed it in one day. Most of his work has been done in that manner, following Van Gogh's convention. It is very lovely. Let's view it in the light booth. Shall we?" she asked and, without waiting for my response, slipped the bubblewrap over the canvas and headed back down the aisle.

The light booth was just that, a metal cabinet on legs. The cabinet was maybe six feet wide and four feet high. The interior was white. She uncovered the painting, leaned it against the back wall of the booth, and turned on a switch. The lights in the booth came on immediately.

"The light temperature is five thousand Kelvin."

"Perfect," I said, not knowing what she was talking about.

She shot a quick glance in my direction but didn't comment.

It really was a lovely painting. A narrow beach, small waves, a clear sky. I felt like I could put a worm on a hook and catch a sunfish. I figured the thing probably had a price of close to five hundred dollars. "Just for the sake of discussion, what price do you have on this piece?"

"It's a real steal at fifty-one, five."

"Five thousand, one hundred and fifty dollars?" I couldn't believe it.

She looked at me, shook her head, and then smiled. "No, the price is fifty-one thousand, five hundred dollars."

"What?"

"You're not a collector, are you, Mr. Hassle?"

To be Continued...

A possible rematch with a high school sweetheart? Dev Haskell in the art world? Things are about to get even crazier, better grab your copy of **Art Attack**…

Books by Mike Faricy
Crime Fiction Firsts

A boxset of the first four books in four crime fiction series:

Russian Roulette; Dev Haskell series
Welcome; Jack Dillon Dublin Tales series
Corridor Man; Corridor Man series
Reduced Ransom! Hot Shot series

The following titles comprise the Dev Haskell series:

Russian Roulette: Case 1
Mr. Swirlee: Case 2
Bite Me: Case 3
Bombshell: Case 4
Tutti Frutti: Case 5
Last Shot: Case 6
Ting-A-Ling: Case 7
Crickett: Case 8
Bulldog: Case 9
Double Trouble: Case 10
Yellow Ribbon: Case 11
Dog Gone: Case 12
Scam Man: Case 13
Foiled: Case 14
What Happens in Vegas… Case 15
Art Hound: Case 16
The Office: Case 17

Star Struck: Case 18
International Incident: Case 19
Guest From Hell: Case 20
Art Attack: Case 21
Mystery Man: Case 22
Bow-Wow Rescue: Case 23
Cold Case: Case 24
Cash Up Front: Case 25
Dream House: Case 26
Alley Katz: Case 27
The Big Gamble: Case 28
Bad to the Bone: Case 29
Silencio!: Case 30
Surprise, Surprise: Case 31
Hit & Run: Case 32
Suspect Santa: Case 33
P.I. Apprentice: Case 34
Rebel Without a Clue: Case 35

The following titles are Dev Haskell novellas:
Dollhouse
The Dance
Pixie
Fore!
Twinkle Toes
(*a Dev Haskell short story*)

The following are Dev Haskell Boxsets:
Dev Haskell Boxset 1-3
Dev Haskell Boxset 4-6
Dev Haskell Boxset 7-9
Dev Haskell Boxset 10-12
Dev Haskell Boxset 13-15
Dev Haskell Boxset 16-18
Dev Haskell Boxset 19-21
Dev Haskell Boxset 22-24
Dev Haskell Boxset 25-27
Dev Haskell Boxset 28-30
Dev Haskell Boxset 1-7
Dev Haskell Boxset 8-14
Dev Haskell Boxset 15-19
Dev Haskell Boxset 20-24
Dev Haskell Boxset 25-29

The following titles comprise the Jack Dillon Dublin Tales series:
Welcome
Jack Dillon Dublin Tale 1
Sweet Dreams
Jack Dillon Dublin Tale 2
Mirror Mirror
Jack Dillon Dublin Tale 3
Silver Bullet
Jack Dillon Dublin Tale 4
Fair City Blues
Jack Dillon Dublin Tale 5

Spade Work
Jack Dillon Dublin Tale 6
Madeline Missing
Jack Dillon Dublin Tale 7
Mistaken Identity
Jack Dillon Dublin Tale 8
Picture Perfect
Jack Dillon Dublin Tale 9
Dublin Moon
Jack Dillon Dublin Tale 10
Mystery Woman
Jack Dillon Dublin Tale 11
Second Chance
Jack Dillon Dublin Tale 12
Payback Brother
Jack Dillon Dublin Tale 13
The Heist
Jack Dillon Dublin Tale 14
Jewels To Kill For
Jack Dillon Dublin Tale 15
Retirement Scheme
Jack Dillon Dublin Tale 16
The Collector
Jack Dillon Dublin Tale 17

Jack Dillon Dublin Tales Boxsets:
Jack Dillon Dublin Tales 1-3
Jack Dillon Dublin Tales 4-6
Jack Dillon Dublin Tales 1-5

Jack Dillon Dublin Tales 1-7
Jack Dillon Dublin Tales 6-10

The following titles comprise the Hotshot series;
Reduced Ransom! Second Edition
Finders Keepers! Second Edition
Bankers Hours Second Edition
Chow Down Second Edition
Moonlight Dance Academy Second Edition
Irish Dukes (Fight Card Series)
written under the pseudonym Jack Tunney

The following titles comprise the Corridor Man series:
Corridor Man
Corridor Man 2: Opportunity knocks
Corridor Man 3: The Dungeon
Corridor Man 4: Dead End
Corridor Man 5: Finger
Corridor Man 6: Exit Strategy
Corridor Man 7: Trunk Music
Corridor Man 8: Birthday Boy
Corridor Man 9: Boss Man
Corridor Man 10: Bye Bye Bobby

Corridor Man novellas:
Corridor Man: Valentine
Corridor Man: Auditor
Corridor Man: Howling

Corridor Man: Spa Day

The following are Corridor Man Boxsets:
Corridor Man Boxset 1-3
Corridor Man Boxset 1-5
Corridor Man Boxset 6-9

All books are available on Amazon.com
Thank you!

Contact the author:
- Email: mikefaricyauthor@gmail.com
- Twitter: @Mikefaricybooks
- Facebook: Mike Faricy Author
- Website: http://www.mikefaricybooks.com

Published by

MJF Publishing